CONFESSIONS OF A
TEENAGE CLOSET CASE

Also by
ALEX BLADES
If I Fall

CONFESSIONS OF A
TEENAGE CLOSET CASE

A NOVEL BY

ALEX BLADES

Edited by Eleanor Stamer
Cover art by Cherie Fox
Interior design by Alex Blades

Printed in the United States of America

FIRST EDITION

Hardcover ISBN 978-1-7357839-1-8
Paperback ISBN 978-1-7357839-0-1

Fiction: Young Adult Contemporary
Fiction: Coming-of-Age
Fiction: LGBT/Gay

For the dreamers
Never stop aiming for the stars.

And for those struggling to accept their true selves
You are valid. You are strong. You are loved.

CHAPTER ONE

ELLIOT

Riding tricycles down the toy aisle isn't exactly what I had in mind when I said we should get out of the house for a while.

I stop pedaling and stare up ahead at Aimee. "Do you realize how ridiculous we look right now?"

Here's the thing: I met the beautiful and amazing Aimee Elizabeth Nguyen-Nelson on the first day of the sixth grade when she practically ambushed me during lunch one day and forced me into a friendship, and we've been kind of inseparable ever since. It pretty quickly turned into a full-blown *Grey's Anatomy* "you're my person" situation, which was a nice change from not really having any friends at all.

I truly admired twelve-year-old Aimee's bravery and dedication to adopting a best friend on her first day at a new school. She's never really cared what anyone thinks about her and that's always reflected in her style. Her hair is always livened up by different colored streaks and she's always experimenting with her makeup. I'm not exactly sure what it was about me that drew her in because we really are two sides of the same coin, but I wouldn't take back the last six years for anything. She's always there when I need her the most.

"No one's staring yet, so we don't look ridiculous enough," she says.

"You couldn't think of anything else to do?"

Aimee backs into me with a huff and leans against the handle bars. "You shot down my first idea, so unless you have a better idea —"

"We are *not* egging Tate's house. He's not even worth it."

"Come on, man! You're no fun."

"You say that now, but you wouldn't if I'd let you and you went to jail."

"You know what your problem is? You think way too much. Tate wouldn't send me to jail."

"Your problem is you don't think enough," I say as I readjust my ass on the child-sized bike seat.

"Exactly! Which is why we're friends. You keep me from doing all the stupid shit that will get me killed, and it's my job to make sure you don't die old and alone."

"Hey! I am *not* going to die old and alone."

She looks me up and down, her brown eyes piercing my soul. "Oh, honey. You do *not* want to open up that can of worms right now."

"And what exactly is that supposed to mean? I—I talk to people."

"Chatting with an anonymous guy you met on Whisper just because he's from around here does *not* mean you're talking to someone."

"Hey, he is not anonymous, okay? We happen to know each other pretty well now."

"Oh, so you know each other's names now?"

"Well—I mean we—"

"And you've met in person and actually had a date? You sure didn't tell me about it if you did." She's looking me up and down again, this time her brow is arched like it always is when she's calling me out on my bullshit and knows she's not wrong. "That's what I thought. He could be some sixty-year-old perv lying to you about his age for all you know."

"Okay, so we haven't met, and I don't exactly know his name, but we talk all the time and I feel like I really know him. It's like we have this special bond going."

Aimee catches my gaze and proceeds to wheel away, leaving me sitting in her dust. Her ponytail rocks from side to side as she struggles to push the tiny pedals and disappears around the corner.

There's a slight buzzing against my thigh, and I slide my phone out of my pocket. A notice for a new email pops up on the screen. It's the first one since yesterday afternoon, and suddenly I can't breathe, and I can feel that lump in my throat that all of the romantic novelists are always talking about.

My hands are shaking, and I take in a deep breath before finally forcing myself to open the email and read it.

To: cinderfella0204@gmail.com
From: milojuni1221@gmail.com
Subject: First Day Back
Dear Cinderfella,

I am so, so sorry that I wasn't able to reply till now. My family decided that it would be a fun idea for all of us to drive up to take my sister back to campus together. It was also just kind of an excuse to get away for the weekend and spend some time in Chicago before school starts again tomorrow. It was definitely a pretty crazy weekend. I am so exhausted, but I had a lot of fun which is actually pretty rare when it's with my family.

To answer your earlier question, I don't really know what I want to do after graduation. Actually, that isn't technically true, but if my parents knew that I wanted to pursue art, they would totally flip out on me. I know what's expected of me by my parents, but I just don't know if I can do what they want me to do. I just don't think I can imagine spending the rest of my life being some big shot doctor like they want me to be.

I'm kinda stuck though, so there's really no need in complaining.

Do you have any plans for after graduation? I'm sure you do; you seem like you have your shit together and aren't afraid of anyone else's opinion.

— Milo

There's nothing I hate more than being able to do absolutely nothing for him. All I want to do is grab him and tell him that everything will be okay because it's just him and I against the world. I can't do that without giving up this secret identity though, and I don't think that I'm ready for that. Not just yet anyway.

Aimee's shouting at me. "Earth to Elliot!"

"What?" I ask, my mouth half open. "Were you saying something?"

"I turned around and you just kinda disappeared. What are you doing?"

"Nothing . . . why would you think I was doing anything?"

There's that damn look again; the one that makes me want to reevaluate all of my life choices.

"Okay . . . fine. Just stop looking at me like that. It freaks me out." I tap the lock button on the side of my phone and slide it back into my pocket. "He finally emailed me back."

"Okaaay, and that's a secret because?" she asks.

I just shrug slightly and start playing with the little bell on my handlebar. "I don't know. I guess I just don't want you to feel like I'm rubbing it in your face or anything. Tonight's all about you."

"Because Tate and I broke up?" She lets out a laugh and lifts herself off the bike seat before taking me by the hand and helping me up. "I'm not like bitter or anything, El. Not totally bitter at least, and I'm the one that broke up with him anyway."

"So, it doesn't bother you?"

"Of course not, you big dummy," she says, punching me lightly on the shoulder. "I like seeing you happy, even if I don't approve of you not knowing who this guy really is."

"I know," I say.

"Because for all you know he could be some murderous lunatic that already knows your identity and is just waiting for his perfect moment to—"

I put my hand up to her mouth and shush her. "Alright, dude. I get it. You don't like that I'm talking to a stranger online. It's not like I'm the only other person that does it these days though."

She grabs me by the arm and removes my hand from her face. The look in her eyes just screams dead man. "Boy, shush me again and see where that hand ends up, and it ain't gonna be pretty."

She's probably right. I'll never tell her that, though. The truth of the matter is I don't know who he really is. He could be just about anybody. He may not even be a "he" for all I know. All I do know is how he makes me feel every time I get a new message from him. It's like for just a moment everything else suddenly doesn't even matter anymore. There's no way it's all a lie. There's no way *he's* a lie.

Aimee is walking again before I even realize it and I have to sprint to catch up with her, which isn't easy after subjecting my butt to sitting on that stupid tricycle seat.

"Hey, do you think you could swing by and pick me up tomorrow morning?" she asks.

"What's wrong with your car?"

"Mine's fine, but my mom's taking her car into the shop and has to use mine until it's done."

As much as I love Aimee, I also love the little bit of quiet time I get between leaving home and walking into school. But, if she needs me, I'm there for her. That's just kind of how we roll.

"Yeah, I can give you a lift. It's no biggie."

She weaves her arm around mine and lays her head on my shoulder as we walk. "Thanks, boo! You're the best!"

"I am pretty great, aren't I?" I chuckle.

"Mm, not so much now."

There's another buzz and a ding from my pocket and I can feel my stomach jumping again. What are the chances that could be him again before I've even had the chance to say anything else? No matter how much I talk to him, my brain still manages to overthink literally everything during our conversations.

"Is that lover boy?" Aimee asks.

I try to calm my breathing as I slide my phone back out and take a look at my notifications.

Michael: I need you to go in and help Anna close up tonight.

Fan-freaking-tastic.

"False alarm," I say. "It's Cruella de Shithead wanting me to go in and help close up tonight."

"Just say no. He doesn't own you."

My eyes roll out of sheer habit, which makes me feel like a complete jerk. "I think you're forgetting that he actually kind of does own me until I can get my ass to college."

"Aye, you are no one's property even if he thinks you are. If you need me to help you cover up a murder all you have to do is ask."

The scariest part is I don't think she's kidding either.

"As tempting as that sounds, no one is getting murdered." I let out a sigh and turn my attention back to my phone.

Me: Ok, I'll be there soon.

Michael: I need the kitchen deck scrubbed tonight too.

Me: I've got it.

I slide my phone back into my pocket. "I have to go, but I'll see you tomorrow morning at 7:15 sharp," I say as I'm walking in the direction of the front door. "And please don't be late!"

If there's anything I hate more than Michael, it's being late.

CHAPTER TWO

JUSTIN

To: milojuni1221@gmail.com
From: cinderfella0204@gmail.com
Subject: Re: First Day Back

Dear Milo,

You don't have to apologize for being busy. I'm really glad you enjoyed your weekend. At least one of us did. I wound up having to work all weekend, but then again what's new lol. You'll have to tell me all about your trip some time because I can honestly say I've only been to the city once, but that was several years ago, and I don't really remember much about it.

As far as post-graduation plans, I honestly don't really know what I'm doing, which I know is really bad considering there's only like a month and a half left of high school. While I would much rather get as far away from here as I possibly can, I think it would be much more realistic to expect being at Illinois State for the next four years. New York would most definitely be endgame, I think. It's kind of a pipe dream though so I don't plan on getting my hopes up or anything. As for your post-grad plans, at least you have some sort of direction with how you'd like your life to go, although I'm sorry to hear that your family has other plans for you. I can't imagine how frustrating that must be. My family is . . . different? They don't really have any expectations for me. Hell, they don't really notice I'm there half the time unless they want something from me.

And on that depressing note, I have to go get all of my shit together for our first day back tomorrow. Is it awful that I just need this year to be done already? The senioritis has officially kicked in and I just want to get out already. I'm ready to go out into the world and experience life on my own finally. Maybe then I can finally be free.

— Cinderfella

I'm just sitting here staring at the blank reply page and watching that little line blink on and off. You know the one that flashes so you know where you're typing? Is there even a name for that thing? I don't know, I guess I'll just have to Google it later.

I place my fingers on my keyboard and begin typing out what I'm sure will be a riveting continuation.

To: cinderfella0204@gmail.com
From: milojuni1221@gmail.com
Subject: Re: First Day Back
Dear Cinderfella,

Damn, I'm so not ready to go back tomorrow. I feel like break went by so fast. This entire year has gone by crazy fast come to think of it. Way too fast if you ask me. I'm so not ready to be pushed out into the real world. Not just yet anyway.

Why do you say New York's a pipe dream? It doesn't have to be if that's what you really want, especially since you say your family doesn't really have any expectations for you. The way you describe your fam sounds kinda sad, but it might also be a good thing if you think about it. They aren't sitting there planning out your entire life for you without even asking you what you want. You have the ability to literally shape your entire future to be however you want it. I'd kill to have that kind of freedom. It's never gonna happen for me. I'm just kinda stuck in this ideal future my parents have for me.

I have no doubt that you'd be thriving out there in the world. One of us should at least.

Alright, well I should probably go finish up the rest of the homework that Ms. Tyler assigned. I swear she's just trying to make us miserable. Talk to you later.

— Milo

I hit the "Send Message" button, and now it's hitting me. Oh, shit! Shit! Shit! Shit!

I really hope I didn't just totally out myself by saying whose class I'm in. I mean, I know that Ms. Tyler has a lot of students, but now he can narrow it down a little bit. I'm just overreacting here, right? I have to be overreacting. There's no way he could figure it out from that . . . unless . . . no, there's no way! I'm just freaking myself out now.

There's a light tapping on the door behind me and I about fall out of my chair as I hastily close out of my email account and pull the Stanford admissions webpage back up. I catch my breath for a second before finally managing to utter a soft, "come in." I'm scrolling through the webpage that I've read more times than I can count (I'm pretty sure I could recite it line by line from memory).

"Are you decent?" my mom asks.

"Yeah, everyone's decent here."

The door creaks open and she steps softly across the wooden floorboards and hovers over the geometric black and white rug in the middle of my room. "Do you have everything ready for tomorrow?"

"Yep," I say, still scrolling through the Stanford site.

"All your homework is done and you have everything prepped?"

"Yeah, mom. Everything's done and prepared."

I'm getting a little annoyed and I think she can tell. Her eyes are narrowing, and the gears are starting to rotate in her head a little bit. She grabs the pillow off my bed that has "take more naps" printed on the front and takes a seat at the very edge of the mattress. She knows something's up. She always knows. I twist my head around slightly and now her bright blue eyes are trying to read mine.

I often wonder if people ever think I'm adopted or something when it's just her and I together. There's no way people could ever guess our blood relation with her fair skin, blonde hair, and blue eyes next to my brown eyes, dark brown hair, and what someone once described to me as like an almost honey skin tone (I'm not exactly a fan of comparing myself to food, but whatever). Of course, once you throw my dad into the mix, it's a little more obvious, which honestly kind of sucks. I'm not exactly white enough to totally fit in the "white crowd", but I'm not Mexican enough to fit in with that community either.

I can't even imagine how different people would treat me if they found out I wasn't straight enough to fit in with the straight crowd either. Especially not my family. Especially not my dad.

She's still staring into my eyes and trying to get a read. She tilts her head slightly to the right before finally speaking. "Is everything okay?"

"Everything's fine, why do you ask?"

Why do you ask? Who the hell am I? An English school girl?

"You just seem a little off lately," she says.

"I'm fine. Really."

"You know you can talk to me about anything. I'm all ears."

What the hell am I supposed to say to that?

Hey, mom. Yeah, I'm totally not okay here because I just really, really don't want to be a doctor, and I sure as hell don't want to go to Stanford. I'm gonna do the exact opposite of what you and dad want and go to art school instead. Oh, and I'm gay! I'm sure you and dad and the rest of the family are going to just love that!

I certainly can't say that. Any of it. I just sit here playing with one of the several fidget toys sitting on the desk. "I'm fine, mom. I've just been a little stressed lately. . . that's all."

"Oh, I know, honey. And I know that it might feel like your father and I are only putting on the pressure, but we just want you to have the best life possible. He only wants you to have the opportunities he didn't have."

"I know . . . I think I'm just gonna finish up this homework and then go take a shower before bed."

"Okay, sweetie. Just let me know if you need anything, okay?" She stands up and reaches for the door, stopping one more time to take a second look back. "I love you."

"Love you too." I watch from a distance as she makes her way back out into the hall. "Hey, mom," I say. Is this it? Am I finally going to come clean about everything? It's just three words, how hard could it be to just say that?

"Yeah?" she asks.

Come on, you can do this. It's just three words.

"Mom, can—you shut the door on your way out?"

Damn it! How am I ever supposed to say anything about how I feel when I get that speech every time I start working up the courage? Maybe I will one day. Or maybe I'll just live the rest of my life trying to live up to what everyone else wants me to be.

Maybe things are easier that way.

CHAPTER THREE

ELLIOT

I'm supposed to be on my way to my next class right now, but I can't seem to make my legs move. My feet are planted to the ugly white and red tile flooring and my attention is shooting back and forth between the hordes of people flocking down the hall and the blank email screen in front of my face.

The more we talk, the more I find myself wondering if we're both just wasting our time—or worse—I wonder if *I'm* just wasting *his* time. At the rate of how things are going, the probability of us ever actually meeting is pretty low. The chances of him actually liking me if we ever do meet are even lower. What if he thinks I'm annoying in real life or he thinks I'm a total loser just like everyone else in this hell hole? What if he thinks I'm ugly?

No, Elliot! Do not go down that road! You just have to stay positive for once in your life.

That's easier said than done, though.

To: milojuni1221@gmail.com
From: cinderfella0204@gmail.com
Subject: Re: First Day Back
Dear Milo,

Ugh, first day back from break and Wagner's already busting everyone's ass. Like geez! Can't we have a couple of days before he starts handing out study guides for the next test?

Alright, I'm done complaining now. How's your day been so far? Mine was off to a bit of a slow start—in the sense that I slept

through my alarm twice, had to wait for my friend, who was
supposed to be ready when I picked her up, and then almost missed
my first class. So – yeah – that's been my day.

In reply to last night, I feel kinda bad now about like whining
about my family situation and all that. I guess I do sort of have more
options for how my future is gonna turn out without all the
expectations placed on me by family. I didn't mean to sound rude or
ungrateful or anything.

On that note, I should probably get to class soon. Hope the rest
of your day goes well.

– Cinderfella

My finger's hovering over the Send button when I get a
jolt from behind, and my body just about attempts a swan dive
into the tile. "Holy shit! Don't do that!"

"Geez, why you so jumpy?" Aimee asks, tapping away on
her phone.

"I tend to get jumpy when someone comes up and grabs
me from behind when I'm focused on something," I huff.
Aimee's eyes peer down at my phone screen as I hit Send and
shove it back into my pocket.

"Messaging your mystery guy again?"

I'm trying to organize my books in order of my classes for
the rest of the day. I know she doesn't fully approve of the
entire situation and I'd much rather not talk about it. She just
doesn't know when to give up. "I am, as a matter of fact."

She breathes heavy, and right about now I'm so happy that
I'm not a mind-reader like Professor X or an empath like
Phoebe Halliwell. Having a brutally honest best friend is
actually a double-edged sword. On the bright side, she always

tells me the truth. On the not-so-bright side, she always tells me the truth.

I pull out my theatre textbook and close my locker again. "What now?"

"Wow, attitude check much?" She crosses her arms and a slight smile starts to form on her lips. "Look, all I'm saying is that I think the two of you need to just meet already. It's been how long again?"

"I—I don't know . . . since Christmas break, I—I think."

"El, come on. Just hurry up and meet the guy! I know you want to, and if he's really as great as you say he is, then I'm sure he wants to meet you too."

"I just—I'm not ready for that. It's a big step."

She grabs me by the shoulders and forces direct eye contact with me. "Yeah, I know it's terrifying, but sometimes you just have to take the plunge and go for it."

"I'm not like you, Aimee. I'm not brave like you. I can't just be out and proud like that—especially not while I'm living under you-know-who's roof."

"Voldemort?" She lets out an exasperated gasp and puts her hand to her mouth. A stifled laugh escapes her lips. "Everyone does it at their own pace, I definitely know that. But the two of you have been talking for months and I think you owe it to yourself to meet him and see if it could ever work. What's the worst that could happen?"

"Uh—he could think I'm an ugly ass loser and could want nothing to do with me?"

"And that's a very real possibility, my friend."

And saved by the bell.

Aimee wraps her arm in mine and starts pulling me down the hall for our next class. It's sadly the only class we got together for the entire semester, and we don't even get to sit together. "I'm messing with you. If he doesn't want anything to do with you, then that's his loss, because you're pretty damn fantastic."

"Aw—are you just saying that because I'm your ride home?"

"Hmm . . . you'll never know, will you? Love ya!"

I break my arm free as we walk through the doorway and find my desk in the corner of the room. That's what's so totally ridiculous about senior year. You're still expected to abide by assigned seating. Something about wanting us to socialize with different types of people or some shit like that. Ya'll, it's senior year. If I had wanted to talk to those preppy assholes I would've done it by now. Okay, not that we were never "friends" per se. Some of us used to be close, but then we got to middle school and they all got into sports or cheerleading or whatever else, and I got into literature, music, and writing. We're all in our own worlds now and there's nothing that's going to change that.

My eyes keep darting back to my phone, though I'm not even totally sure what I'm waiting for. I literally just sent it and I can't expect him to be glued to his phone to talk to me like I am to—

HE REPLIED. I REPEAT. HE REPLIED!

To: cinderfella0204@gmail.com
From: milojuni1221@gmail.com
Subject: Re: First Day Back
Dear Cinderfella,

Did you just give me a little bit of a clue to who you are? Wagner only teaches like 4 science courses if I remember correctly lol. I'm just messing with you. There's like 20-25 people per class. I'm terrible at guessing anyway. But I totally agree that he's a little much sometimes. The senioritis is real and he's not making it any easier.

Don't worry about last night. I was just kind of in a bad head space, but everything's fine now. I'm sorry if I went off or made you feel uncomfortable. I didn't mean anything by it.

Moving on. Are you as hungry as I am? I could really go for some pizza right about now. Ooh, or some ice cream! Question: What is your favorite ice cream? And be cautious when you answer because this just might be a critical piece of information. People tell me I'm kinda weird with my ice cream because I really like to put together mint chip and cookies and cream. It's literally the greatest combination ever. Kind of like a mint Oreo, but better.

— Milo

"Good morning, class."

I peer over my screen and see Mr. Jameson plopping his stuff down on his desk. Oh, I mean "Charlie", which we're technically not supposed to call him to any of the other teachers, but he kinda hates it when we call him Mr. Jameson since he's not much older than most of us. I've never really had a teacher that was only like four or five years older than me, so it's kinda weird. It's also kind of nice because he actually understands how much pressure we're all going through since he was in our place not too long ago.

There's still chattering going on around the room and Charlie's just staring at everyone from the front, his arms folded across his chest and his back against the white board. I feel bad for the guy. It's his first year of teaching and all these assholes just walk right over him.

"Guys, as always I'm so glad we can all come together as a class and be social, but how about we get the day started, huh?" The murmurs slow to a stop. Charlie picks up his famous blue and bronze stress ball and plants his feet at the front of the room beside his desk. "So, how was everyone's spring break? Did anyone do anything interesting?"

As per usual, a collection of the "fine", "it was fun", and "we went to Florida" responses ring around the room. Typical midwestern responses. Although I have to say that I'm not really paying very close attention to what's going on right now. It's funny, for the first time it's starting to hit me that right now I'm in the same place as him. Like we're actually in the same building right now. He could be anywhere—what's even scarier—he could be anyone.

He could even be in this room

Looking around, my choices don't really seem all that . . . overwhelming? Don't get me wrong, there are plenty of good-looking guys in here, but I just don't think they're on the level of emotional and mental maturity that Milo is on. There's Shawn Desmond with his glowing sun-kissed skin, naturally light hair, and greyish-blue eyes. He's not—technically speaking—a dick, and he's never actually been rude to me to my face, unlike a lot of other people in this building. He's also not the brightest person in the world. I remember last year we were all grading each other's tests, to make it a little easier on the teacher, and he asked me why his answer of "blue" wasn't right. We were in algebra and that wasn't even one of the multiple-choice options. I'm astonished by how he made it to senior year.

There are also the Jordan twins. They may be extremely hot, but they're also two of the biggest assholes I've ever met in my life. They make season one Nathan Scott look like a walk in the park.

And then there's him. Justin Herrera with his big brown eyes, thick dark hair, and a smile that could light up any room. I can't say how many times this semester I've caught myself staring at him. He was the star of football season and now he's killing it in baseball too. He's like the epitome of human perfection. Even if he wasn't straight and dating the most popular girl in school, I'd never stand a chance. He's so hot and I'm—so not.

I'm startled back to reality by a knock coming from the hallway and look up in enough time to see some mystery girl walk through the doorway. Her curly dark locks fall over her shoulders and her deep brown doe eyes are scanning every crevice of the room. She looks to be about mine and Aimee's age.

"Hi, can I help you?" Charlie asks.

"Uh—yeah—I'm new here and I think I have the right room? I'm Vanessa Berk," she says.

A light goes off in Charlie's head and he starts shuffling through a stack of papers on his desk. "Yes, I do remember getting the email that you'd be joining our class today. It must have slipped my mind." He stands upright again and looks at her. "And I must've forgotten to print out the information I wanted to give you. Do you mind running back here after school? I'm so sorry."

"No worries, I'll be here."

"Fantastic. In the mean time you can go have a seat next to—" His eyes are scrolling across the class looking for an empty seat, which the last one just so happens to be next to me. "—Elliot. Just let me know if you have any questions."

"Will do." She turns and looks right at me, a smile forms on her face as she makes her way to the back corner of the room and takes the seat beside me.

I'm not typically the type of person to reach out and talk to new people, I never have been and that is precisely why the idea of going to college absolutely terrifies me. I don't see myself having an actual life outside the walls of this school, not that a social life exists for me anyway. Where was I going with this? Oh, right... I've never been the best with talking to new people, but I'm pretty sure she's wearing a hoodie from Selena's *Rare* collection, and I'm trying not to totally fangirl right now.

I lean in and try not to disturb Charlie while he's talking about his spring break at home in Colorado. "Hey, is that a *Rare* hoodie?"

"Huh?" Her eyes are puzzled for a moment before she looks down and realizes what she's wearing. "Oh! Yeah it is. Are you a fan?"

"I love her so much. I've always wanted to see her live."

"I saw her *Revival* tour and she's so amazing." She tucks some of her curls behind her ear and extends her hand out. "I'm Vanessa by the way. It's nice to meet you."

"I'm Elliot." My grasp meets hers and I grin. "It's nice to meet you too. When's your lunch period?"

"Uh—let me check—I think it's next but I'm not a hundred percent on that," Vanessa says, digging through her bag. She pulls out a folded-up piece of paper and scans through her schedule for the rest of the day. "Yeah, I have it next."

"Awesome, you should join me and my friend Aimee. You'd love her."

The corners of her mouth curve up into a smile and her eyebrows raise slightly. "That would be great. Thank you."

My eyes are drawn back to the front of the room when I hear Charlie mention warm ups and everyone starts pushing the desks to the outer perimeter of the classroom.

After class, I went with Vanessa to her locker so she could drop off her things and escorted her to the cafeteria to meet Aimee, who had already made a run for it to avoid coming face to face with Becca, Tate's cousin, in the hall. Breakups are efficient when the other person lives an entire town over, but not so much when their family members still go to the same school as you.

Vanessa decided to make a pit stop at the bathroom beforehand, which gave me the opportunity to finally reply to Milo, or whatever his name actually is.

To: milojuni1221@gmail.com
From: cinderfella0204@gmail.com
Subject: Re: First Day Back
Dear Milo,

Maybe I did give you a clue to my identity . . . or maybe I didn't lol. I guess that's just something you'll have to try to figure out. I also second that on the senioritis. I just need it to be over sooner rather than later. And you didn't make me feel uncomfortable, so don't worry about it. I don't think there's really anything you could do that would make me uncomfortable, Milo. In case you haven't noticed by now, you're pretty amazing.

I do have to say that's quite the interesting ice cream combo. I never really thought about that, but I'll totally have to try it out some time soon. I'm getting so hungry and I could definitely go for some pizza right about now. I don't think I can take another damn sloppy joe day in the cafeteria.

— Cinderfella

By the time Vanessa and I make it to the lunch line and sneak ahead to join Aimee, the cafeteria is totally flooded with people. For the school not being all that big, there sure are a hell of a lot of kids. I can't say I'll miss any of it.

"Aimee," I elbow my way through the crowd. "This is insane."

"Yeah, I guess they decided to surprise everyone with an ice cream bar with every lunch today." She looks through me and straight at Vanessa, her interest peaking a bit. She softly pushes me to the side. "And you're the new girl in our theatre class, right?"

"This is Vanessa. Vanessa, I would like you to meet Aimee, my best friend."

"Uh, don't you mean your only friend," Aimee says before taking another swing at my shoulder. Extending her hand out she says, "Hi, Vanessa. It's nice to meet you. Where'd you transfer here from?"

"My mom and I just moved here from San Diego."

The line's moving again, and I tug at Aimee's shirt sleeve.

Walking backward and without batting an eye she says, "Why would you move to Lakeview of all places?"

"Well, my dad's in the Navy and he's gonna be gone for the next like eight to twelve months, so they just decided that it would be best for us to be around family so we weren't all alone in Cali. Quick question though, and not that it matters or anything, but am I about to become this school's like only black spokesperson?"

"I can definitely see where you'd get the idea," I say. "But no. There's Sean Perry, he's actually one of the nicest guys in school if you ask me. There's also Alicia Palmer, but she spends most of her time in the auditorium rehearsing for her next show."

"Oh, and don't forget Bobby Clarkson. He's the school's resident hottie."

"Actually, he doesn't go here anymore, remember? His family moved back to Texas back in January," I reply

"So, that makes me the third then."

"Don't sweat it, dude," Aimee says. "At least you're not the school's only Asian chick . . . and the only person that's openly bisexual. They've got me pulling double duty here, so count yourself lucky."

I'm just now realizing that Aimee still has Vanessa's hand in hers. They haven't even broken eye contact since they started talking. "Well, welcome to LHS," I say, still being ignored. "Line's moving again, guys." My elbow smacks into someone's back and a jolt runs through my body.

The look on Aimee's face is all I need to know that I've severely messed up.

CHAPTER FOUR

JUSTIN

To: cinderfella0204@gmail.com
From: milojuni1221@gmail.com
Subject: Re: First Day Back

Dear Cinderfella,

Pretty amazing, huh? I don't know about that one, Cinder. I feel like if you met me in person, if we haven't already crossed paths because it's not that large of a school, you might not think I was such an amazing human being. But I do appreciate the thought. I happen to think you're pretty amazing as well.

As far as the food goes, I definitely get what you mean about the sloppy joe day. I don't even know how they call any of what they serve actual food. I do have to say that the pizza's pretty decent. It's just about the only thing that seems at least half edible. Although rumor has it that they're giving us all ice cream today, so I guess we can't be totally mad about it.

So, I almost came out last night to my mom. She was just sitting there in my room talking to me and for a split sec I thought I could do it. Like I really thought that was gonna be it. But I chickened out as usual. I don't think it's ever gonna happen. Part of me feels like I should just officially get a girlfriend just to appease everyone in my life if I'm gonna have to marry and start a family someday. Ooh! Or maybe I can run away and join a monastery and become a monk or whatever. They can't do anything with either gender, right? I think life might be a little less complicated that way.

— Milo

Sometimes I wonder if I'm just wasting both of our time, but mostly his.

I mean, at this point these emails are mostly just a way for me to get shit off my chest and talk to someone that can at least partially understand where I'm coming from. There's no way that we could ever be together, even if he is literally the sweetest person I've ever talked to. There's no hope of me ever having a future that I actually want. He seems to have a chance to get out of here and find freedom.

This entire situation has me seriously messed up.

I cram my books back into my locker and make a beeline to the cafeteria for lunch. Danny's already sitting at our table with a major spread. Must be nice to have a chef for a mom while the rest of us suffer with whatever the hell the school thinks they can pass off as food.

Makes me think about all of the sleepovers we had growing up. We'd stay up all night playing video games and eating all the desserts his mom made for us until his dad would figure out we were still awake at like three in the morning and then make us go to bed. Man, those times were so much simpler. Makes me wonder if he would think different of me if he knew. He's cracked gay jokes in the past, but I don't know how serious any of that really was.

There's no need in dwelling on that though. I'll probably never get the chance to figure out whether or not he'd be cool with it.

I'm just about sit down when Tommy freakin' Jenkins pops up out of nowhere with a chair and plops down. I seriously hate that guy so much. Okay, so maybe "hate" is a relatively strong word here. I'm just not really his biggest fan. He rubs me the wrong way with his weirdly elevated attitude, like he's so much better than everyone else. I've never seen anyone with such an inflated ego before, even if he is kinda cute with those big blue eyes and bright white smile.

No, Justin! His beautifully polished exterior does not make up for his rotten personality and is no excuse to treat people like complete garbage.

"J-man!" Tommy shouts, making my skin crawl. "How's it going, man?"

I suppress the urge to vomit. "Just fine, T-man."

"That's awesome. How's Steph? She still fine as hell?" Tommy asks.

"Dude! That's my sister you're talking about, so watch your mouth."

How could I forget that Tommy had like this total obsession with Stephanie when we were kids? He was practically drooling every time we would pick him up for our little league games. Watching him stutter and make a total fool out of himself was kind of entertaining, but it was also really weird.

"Okay, dude. We get it. Stephanie's hot, so just cool it," Danny finally chimes in.

I step back from the table and start heading in the direction of the food. "Whatever. I'm gonna go get in line now. Be right back."

"Aye, wait for me," Tommy yells as he runs to catch up.

Of course, Tommy. Why wouldn't I wait for you? I just have to smile and wave for the next two and a half months, and then I'm out of this hell hole. I can do this . . . I think.

Just up ahead, Gabbi's waiting in line. Her nose is stuck in her phone as usual and she's probably spreading more gossip on her Finsta, not that she'd ever actually admit to running the

Lakeview Hell High account. That's where all of her power lies.

"Dude, I think I'm gonna ask Gabbi out, "Tommy says.

"Dude, do whatever you want."

The guy seriously talks like he's trapped inside of a 2000s rom-com.

"Damn, I love when she gets fired up like that. She's so hot."

I glance ahead again, and she has her evil look on. The one with the narrowed eyebrows, pursed lips and icy cold glare. Thankfully I've never been on the other side of that look, but I can't imagine it would be pleasant. I can't read her lips, but I'm pretty sure she's bitching someone out mercilessly. "Tommy, isn't that your brother she's freaking out on right now? Elliot, or something?"

"Step-brother," he corrects. "Don't get us confused as blood-relation, okay? Either way though, he probably deserves it. Dude's a lame ass fairy."

"A fairy?"

"Yeah—a damn faggot."

Oh, someone kill him before I do, even though he for sure deserves a fate much worse than death.

"And he's said that he's a—that he's gay?" I ask.

"Well, not exactly in those words. But just look at him. I don't know who he thinks he's fooling. Hey, do me a favor and hold my spot. I've gotta go take a piss."

It takes every fiber of my being not to punch him square in the back of the head as he struts off. I mean, who the hell seriously uses the F word anymore? I guess I've just not had to deal with any of that firsthand before. Do I even have a right to be upset over it if I don't even have enough guts to be open? I really don't know.

My eyes are drawn forward again and glued to Gabbi's face. Watching her explode like that is like watching a bad accident. You just can't look away, but you also can't help but feel like you should be doing something about it. Should I do something about it? Will that make me look suspicious? Could I live with myself if I don't do something about it?

Damn it. I'm going in.

Every fiber of my being is screaming at me to not do anything ridiculous as I start pushing passed the people in line. My head is spinning, and I can't feel my hands as I reach for Gabbi. "Gabs, how's it going?"

She tucks her dark locks behind her ear and her brown eyes zone in on mine. She bites her bottom lip and says, "Justin, what a surprise. How was your break?"

"It was good. How was Miami?"

"Oh, it was so amazing. I needed that so bad with prom and everything coming up. It's gonna be so damn stressful." She steps closer, her hand reaching for the collar of my shirt. "Maybe you could help me out with a little . . . destressing some time."

"Uh . . . totally." My hand reaches up and grabs hers without even thinking about it and pulls it away from my chest. "Hey, I think I heard Kelsey's looking for you to talk about last minute prom queen campaigning stuff. You should go find her. Might be important."

"Ugh, a queen's work is never done, am I right? Do me a favor and save me a seat?"

"Definitely."

She does that weird finger-wiggling wave thing and flips her hair as she struts off and disappears down the hall. Her and Tommy might actually make a really good couple after all.

"Sorry about her," I say, centering in on Elliot. "She's been kinda stressed out lately . . . makes her a little bitchy sometimes." He's just staring at me with big beautiful blue eyes. "It's Elliot, right?"

"Yeah," he says in barely a whisper.

I feel kind of bad for the guy having to grow up with step-siblings like Tommy and Hailey. Not to mention I heard his step-dad is a total dick.

How have I never noticed that he's actually pretty cute? He's got beautiful dark brown hair with the perfect amount of wave to it. I'd be lying if I said I didn't want to just run my fingers through it. He looks like he could use a little sun, but it's actually kind of a nice change from all the guys trying to be tall, dark, and handsome. And the little freckles painted gingerly on the bridge of his nose and sporadically around his cheeks aren't half bad either.

Oh shit. Have I been staring too long? I have, haven't I? This is totally getting weird now.

"Uh . . . well, you guys have a good one. I'm just gonna go find my seat now. Bye."

I don't get it. Just yesterday I was freezing my ass off in a light jacket, and now I swear this freak heat-wave is cooking every ounce of blood in my body. One thing I won't miss about this area when I get shipped off to the West Coast is the bipolar weather.

Danny hasn't shut up the entirety of practice about beating Brettwood High in a few weeks after they totally wiped the floor with us last season. He apparently has this long-time feud going with the captain of their baseball team over who stole whose girl in seventh grade or whatever. Kind of ridiculous, but at least Danny's persistent. I'll give him that much.

Coach has us running bleachers, which I honestly used to despise, but lately it's been kind of an escape. I'm so busy dying during the workout that I can't think, and then by the time we're done, I'm too exhausted to care or think about anything else. Like the fact that my entire future was literally mapped out for me before I even had a chance to take my first breath. I don't even know why I'm complaining. It's not like I haven't known what's expected of me my entire life.

The whistle blows in the distance and my body's ready to hit the ground as all of us struggle to make it down the stairs without toppling over. The adrenaline rush is starting to die down and now I'm remembering just why I was never a huge fan of bleacher runs—or running in general—that shit sucks big time. Who the hell invented cardio in the first place?

"Alright, guys, gather 'round," Coach White says in his drill sergeant voice. "We're off to a good start this season, but we're not outta the woods yet. This Thursday we have our game against Maroa-Forsyth, and I have no doubt in my mind that you're gonna wipe the floor with each and every one of them." His beady eyes are unavoidable. "And then after that we'll be facing the likes of Eisenhower, Central A&M, Pana, and Shelbyville. Use these as practices, because our day of reckoning is coming."

Coach White's all-in-all a pretty decent guy, but damn he's intense. Not that it isn't exactly warranted though. I heard that he had a promising future in the major leagues before his older brother died in service and he decided to enlist in honor of him, where he actually did wind up becoming a drill sergeant. He's been coaching the Lakeview baseball team since he left like fifteen years ago.

"Our game against Brettwood has been officially set for the end of May. After our loss last year, I know you guys are going to work your hardest to make them pay for kicking us out of the running for the championships. Let's kick some ass and take some names!"

There's a collective roar that shakes the bleachers. I'm also pretty sure one of my fillings is about to pop out from the vibrations.

"Now everyone hit the showers and do your homework!"

My legs are jelly as I make my way down the remainder of the bleacher stairs and down the track.

"I'm totally fucking psyched for that game, dude!"

I peer over my shoulder and spot Danny. His gorgeous auburn hair is pushed back from his face and damp with sweat. He's still at least ten feet away, but I can still see those gorgeous eyes from here. They're this really pretty golden brown with specs of green. He has a bit of a habit of using the bottom of his tanks to wipe the sweat from his face, flashing his beautifully sculpted torso in the process. If we weren't practically family by this point, I'd probably be pining from afar like every other stereotypical closet case.

"Oh really? I never would've guessed," I say.

He's shaking his head, but the edges of his mouth are curving up into a slight grin. "Oh, shut up."

We trek across the high school's parking lot and Coach lets us through the back doors of the building and we all funnel back into the gym. The cold air felt good for a moment, and now it's cold as hell. My wet clothes stick to my skin, making me feel like I could go into shock.

I trail behind Danny and the rest of the guys into the locker room, and a shiver travels up my spine. Wish I could say it was only from being cold though. I've been involved in sports since sixth grade, all ranging from track, football, basketball, and baseball, although I can't really even say why I've been doing sports for so long. Initially it was fine and just kind of something to do, but as time went on and I started becoming more and more aware of the fact that I was — different — and it got a little weird. Not in the *oh shit, I hope nothing pops up and outs me kind of way,* but rather the *I feel creepy about accidentally seeing something and being attracted to a few of these guys* kind of way.

Should I feel creepy about being secretly attracted to some of these guys? We've all been such a close-knit group for so long. What if they feel like betrayed or something if they find out somehow? Especially Danny. I don't know what I'd do if I ever lost him as a friend after all these years.

"J, where's your head at?" Danny asks. He's standing there in nothing but a towel now and his body wash is wafting through the air. I'm trying not to stare, but it isn't easy with the water glistening over every curve of his body.

"Hmm?" I ask, avoiding looking anywhere below the neck.

"What's on your mind?"

I can't exactly tell him, so it just kind of comes out in a stutter. "I—I'm just thinking about . . . college. We're supposed to be getting acceptance letters in the next week or two and I'm just kinda nervous."

Danny grins at me and squeezes my shoulder as I lace up my Adidas. He makes it so difficult not look at him when his eyes light up like that. "Don't worry about it, man. You're a smart dude and any one of them would be lucky to have you." He slips a black tee on over his head and pulls his towel off, no thought about it, before slipping into his briefs. "Hey, some of us are gonna go grab some food after this. You wanna come?"

"Oh, that sounds really great, but I'm gonna have to pass this time. I have to do some . . . family stuff. I can't really get out of it. Can I take a rain check on that?"

"Definitely. Just shoot me a Snap if your night frees up."

"For sure."

It's pouring and there's a group of like six college kids, all wearing something with the name Illinois State on it, running for cover. There's a strange mixture of pizza and coffee scents snaking its way around the first floor of the building, the Bone Student Center they call it, and the last thing I want to be doing right now is focusing on Advanced Bio.

If Danny knew where I really was right now, he'd probably have a field day with it.

"Alright, Justin, next question," Brooke says, her eyes flicking back and forth between me and the booklet in front of her. "What are the chemical substances located between connective tissue cells?"

My eyes can't help but wander back to the entrance as another couple of students pile in and head straight for the dying Starbucks line. This time it's two guys . . . and they're actually holding hands. The best part is that they don't even seem to give two shits who sees it. Is it totally wrong for me to be somewhat annoyed right now? Like how dare they, or anyone else, have the guts to showcase who they really are while I'm completely miserable.

It's not fair. Any of it.

"It's extracellular matrix," I finally say. I never said I'm not good at biology. I just don't particularly care for it.

"Awesome. Now, what are the four basic types of tissue?"

It's like she's not even trying at this point.

"The four basic types are gonna be epithelial, connective, nervous, and muscular tissues. Are we almost done here, Brooke?" It comes out a little shorter than I intend it to.

She runs a hand through her shoulder-length blonde hair and stares at me. "We've barely been working thirty minutes. You've got this."

"Exactly, I have this. So why do I have to keep going over it over and over again? Can we at least take a break or something?"

Brooke lays her pen down beside her notebook. "Fine. We can take five minutes, but after that we need to get back to work, okay? I'll be right back. I'm going to the ladies' room." She throws her bag over her shoulders and heads for the restroom down from McAlister's Deli.

I think it's time for coffee.

The line is kind of intense, or rather, the people in line are kind of intense. The couple of girls behind me are currently chatting about some dude named Jackson that girl number one had a date with over the weekend. Apparently, Jackson decided it would be fun to have a few drinks and wound up getting so drunk that he passed out in the middle of making out, so she just put his trashcan next to his bed and did the walk of shame across campus. Except it was his shame, and not hers. Poor guy. College girls can be total savages. This guy Jackson shall forever serve as the textbook definition on how not to behave in college.

I take a step forward in line and start to feel a set of eyes on me from up ahead. Or at least I think he's looking at me. Nope, he is most definitely staring at me. He locks eyes with me for just a moment and nibbles a little bit on his bottom lip. That lip bite has me feeling some type of way, and I only pray that there's no physical evidence of it. It somehow feels wrong—almost dirty—to even be checked out by other guys. Like I haven't earned that right yet. Like I'll never earn that right.

Once the line finally starts moving again, I try my best to avoid eye contact with the guy in front of me as I order a grande vanilla sweet cream cold brew from Wyatt, the cute barista behind the counter. It's probably the most basic of the hipster drinks at Starbucks, but do as the college kids do when you're on campus, right?

I dig my phone from the pocket of my jeans and start reading the email I got from Cinderfella again. I need to remember to figure out if there's another name I can call him, because "Cinderfella" is getting to be a bit of a mouthful.

Also a little strange.

He told me not to worry about not being able to come out to my mom last night because it's something that'll have to come in its own time. Pretty wise for someone that hasn't even come out himself. He also went on about how brave I am for even considering coming out. I definitely wouldn't say I was brave. More like totally insane for even having the thought pop into my head. He found my plans to join a monastery hilarious, but I don't think he realizes that wasn't one hundred percent a joke. I might actually have to someday.

"Hey, have we met before," the guy checking me out earlier asks.

I peer up at him from behind my screen. "Uh . . . I don't think so. Sorry."

"You just look so familiar. What's your major?"

"Actually, I'm not a student here. I'm just here with my — my friend," I mutter

"Oh, are you from around here at all?"

I slip my phone back into my pocket and inhale the scent of the coffee. "I live like thirty minutes away, but yeah."

"That's really cool. Do you think maybe if you're ever in town you might want to grab a bite to eat some time?"

How the hell am I supposed to reply to that? "Uh — listen — you seem like a really nice guy. You really do. But I'm not . . ."

"Oh shit, I'm sorry, I totally didn't mean — I didn't mean to assume anything."

I can't help but let a subtle smile tug at the corners of my mouth. "No, it's totally fine. Really. I'm honestly flattered though."

The light is casting a golden ray over his deep brown eyes and my attention is drawn to his gorgeous lips.

Holy shit, Justin! Stop staring at his damn lips! No matter how full and gorgeous and kissable and — damn it!

"Cold brew for Justin," another barista behind the counter finally yells out.

"That would be me," I say. The barista slides my cup across the counter and tells me to enjoy my night. I turn back to him and say, "And on that note, I should really get back to my friend. But it was nice meeting you —"

"It's Kevin. Maybe I'll see you around?"

I'm smiling again. "Maybe."

I take a sip from my cup and float back to mine and Brooke's table. She's already back by the time I get there.

"What are you smiling about?" she asks.

"Nothing." I cover my face with my other free hand. "Shall we get back to work now?"

CHAPTER FIVE

ELLIOT

It's a quarter to four and I'm starting to regret telling Aimee that I'd give her a ride home after her club meeting. She for sure made a name for herself by petitioning to start the school's first fashion design club. Who knew that so many people would be interested in that?

This heat's finally starting to hit me. The air conditioning in my 1995 Ford Escort can't keep up with the temperature outside anymore, so the sweat is pouring down my face at this point. A kiddie pool could be filled with the amount of sweat that's been soaked up by my white ISU t-shirt.

The only thing still distracting me from the heat is Selena Gomez's *Rare* album that's currently blasting from my speakers. I've had the need to play it since Vanessa walked into class this morning. I probably look like a complete idiot, but at this point I don't really give a shit. It can't be any worse than what we went through with Gabbi earlier.

Mostly everyone's cleared out now anyway, aside from a couple of the stoner kids that I'm like 98% sure are currently getting high at the other end of the parking lot, and Sam Green, Lakeview High School's very own out and proud gay kid. Not that he's been the first or anything like that, but he's the only one in the school right now that's felt brave enough to come out and just say it. He gets a lot of flak for it, especially from my dick of a step-brother, Tommy, but he doesn't seem to let it bother him that much.

I'm not sure if I could do that.

The entirety of the baseball team is out on the football field doing a bunch of workouts. They kind of look like a bunch of little ants from my vantage point, but it's still a pretty good view if you ask me. Occasionally they'll get close enough that I can make out who is who, but there's honestly only a few that I actually care to look at.

I can just barely make out Justin Herrera in the distance. His dark wavy locks are blowing in the wind and the sun is reflecting off his glistening skin, highlighting every curve of his biceps, which are bulging from beneath his maroon and gold LHS baseball shirt. Up until last spring, he was kind of little. Not like scrawny or anything, but he was never that big. When we came back for school in August, he had beefed up a little bit and he was *fine*! Not that he wasn't cute before, though.

I have to say I was a little surprised when he stepped in at lunch to save me, Aimee, and Vanessa. We've never actually talked in the twelve or so years we've gone to school together, unless you count riveting group discussions as conversations. I did appreciate it though.

The beautiful Cooper Thomas is just barely in my view. I must have a type because he's almost a copy of Justin, except I'm pretty sure his tanned complexion is more so the result of time spent out in the sun than just naturally being a bit darker. Other than that, their hair and eyes are pretty much an exact match.

Fortunately, or unfortunately depending on the way you look at it, I've been lucky enough to get to know Cooper at the grocery store a little better after he got hired last fall. We haven't talked a whole lot since then, but he seems like an overall nice dude. He's basically one of the only "popular kids" that's never given me any grief. Except for Justin of course.

There's a thud on my passenger side window and I jump. A shriek escapes my lips as Aimee pulls the door open, sending her into a laughing fit. "Th—thank you for making literally the rest of my week." The words barely come out between her gasps for air.

I reach for the volume knob and turn it way down. "Don't do that shit! You nearly gave me a damn heart attack *again*!"

"Dude, I can hear that music from all the way across the parking lot."

"It soothes me," I answer.

Aimee peers over the dashboard in the direction of the field where all the guys are practicing. She raises her brow. "I don't think Selena is what's soothing you right now, dude."

"I don't know what you're talking about." I've never been good at lying. Especially not to Aimee. "I'm just—admiring their athletic physiques. You know, so I can see what I might want to look like someday maybe."

Technically speaking that wasn't exactly a lie. It would be nice to look like some of those guys one day. I've worked really hard this last year and a half to lose some of my excess weight, but I'm definitely not where I want to be yet.

She knows me better than that though.

"Admiring their athletic physiques? You are totally ridiculous." She laughs and slips her seat belt over her torso and clicks it into place. "If you're never going to meet this guy—whatever his name is—then maybe you should just go meet someone else. They have dating apps for a reason."

"There's only one major issue with that suggestion. I can't just be out and open like that. I'm not brave like you are."

She rolls her eyes and suppresses a grin. "*Brave*? Not by a long shot, El. I was just so tired of hiding part of who I am. I was tired of trying to please everyone all the time and worrying about what they think of me. That wasn't a life worth living anymore."

I grip the steering wheel tighter, avoiding her know-it-all glances.

"Look, I know it's terrifying on literally every level, but don't you think you owe it to yourself to finally be happy?"

Stop making sense, Aimee.

I wonder if anyone else actually dreads walking into their own home. Actually, I shouldn't really say that. It's not my home, or at least it hasn't been for a long time. Not since Mom was around.

Walking through the front door is just a painful reminder of what was and will never be again, especially since it barely even looks like the same house anymore. Over the years, Mom's things started disappearing from every room. Different couch, new flat screen, fresh paint. Everything's just different now. It was all so subtle that I didn't really even notice it until it was too late. The only evidence that she ever lived here are some old family pictures hanging up on the walls, but even those are dwindling down to practically nothing.

Feet come shuffling down the stairs and stop dead at the bottom. "What the hell are you doing, freak?" a voice asks. Hailey, the Wicked Bitch of the Midwest—I mean my step-sister—is giving me the evil eye. "You know what . . . I don't want to know, so don't even answer that."

Only I could've been so lucky as to inherit Hailey Jenkins as a step-sister. I'd like to say that we got along at one point or another, but I'd be lying. Even as kids we could never seem to get along in class. We were always clashing about something. Wanting to be classroom helper, spelling bees, and even trying to see who could out-sell the other in classroom fundraisers. But things got worse right before the end of fifth grade when my mom and her dad announced that they had been seeing each other for a few months and we'd all be moving in together to be one big, happy family.

They got the big part right. The ball was kind of dropped on the happy family part.

"My dad on his way home?" She's not even looking at me when she asks. She's standing in front of the mirror reapplying lip gloss.

"How am I supposed to know? I literally just got here."

"Ooh, touchy today, aren't we?"

"What? I—just never mind." I slide my bag off my shoulder and set it down by the staircase before heading into the kitchen. I was so thrown off by everything with Gabbi that I barely ate lunch and I am *starving*.

Hailey's sandals come clacking into the room and I'm greeted by another icy cold glare.

"May I help you?" I ask.

"Actually, yeah." She's twirling a strand of her long blonde hair around her finger tip. "You don't have a life, right?"

"Uh, I mean I wouldn't say—"

"Oh, of course you don't, what am I saying?" A giggle escapes from between her pink stained lips and she smiles. "I'm gonna need you to do me just the teensiest favor and finish up my American Government homework for me tonight."

I toss the bread I'm holding on to a plate. "And is there a reason you're not doing your own homework?"

"Of course, silly. The girls and I are going prom shopping tonight. We found this super cute little boutique and we have to get there before all the good ones are taken. I just don't think I'll be making it back in enough time tonight to finish it for tomorrow. You understand, right?"

"Hailey, come on, I already have enough shit on my plate right now. You're just gonna have to do it this weekend or something."

The grin slowly vanishes and is replaced by pursed lips and a hand on the hip. Do all high school girls work together to perfect that look? "Well, I was trying to be nice before, but I wasn't really asking."

"I don't really care. I'm not doing it. I already have enough to do as it is."

Hailey nudges forward a bit, her expression going blank. She rolls her eyes and runs her hand over the countertop. "Fine. I guess I'll have to do it myself then since you won't help me out. I just hope that my dad doesn't somehow find out that you were the one that put that scratch on the side of his car."

"What? I didn't do that, and you know I didn't, Hailey."

"Oh, do I though? I mean, who is he going to believe? His precious little angel that's his own flesh and blood, or you?" The grin's back, this time a bit more mischievous than before. "What's it gonna be?"

I don't say anything. How am I supposed to? I just stand there like a damn deer in headlights.

"That's what I thought. Nothing less than an A. I have my GPA to maintain." She swipes her keys off the counter and looks at me again. "Think you can handle that? Good." She flips her hair and skips out, slamming the front door behind her.

Did that really just happen? I'm actually being blackmailed for something that I didn't even do now. I'd say my day can't get any worse, but that never seems to be true. At least I'm finally alone.

The front door creaks open and shuts again.

Footsteps against the wood floors echo through the house and stop at the doorway to the kitchen. Just the person I wanted to see.

"Good, you're here," Michael says

The quiet was nice while it lasted. I should really just stop talking.

"Yeah," I reply, taking a bite out of my sandwich.

"Well, don't get too cozy. I need you to go down to the store and help Anna close up tonight."

"But this is literally my only day off until next week and I'm drowning in homework right now. Can't you get like Ian or something to do it?"

"That's exactly the reason I need you to go in. Ian just quit."

If there's one thing I've learned in recent years, it's that there's no arguing with Michael about anything. I suppose that comes from having your evil step-father also be the general manager at your place of employment. Unfortunately, there aren't many job options in Lakeview, otherwise I would've left long ago.

"I wasn't asking, Elliot."

I set my plate in the sink behind me and lean over the counter. "Like father, like daughter," I whisper.

"What was that?" he asks with a dead stare.

"N—nothing," I stutter. "I'll head that way in a few."

Would it have been too much to ask for him to have dropped me off at an orphanage?

I check the clock on the wall by the sinks. It's outdated just like every other thing in this building, so I have to recollect all of my knowledge of reading busted old analog clocks. It's 8:07, but the last time I checked, that thing is like ten minutes fast, so I still have just over an hour left in this hell hole, that is, until tomorrow right after class. And that's assuming we get out on time, which only happens on rare occasion.

My manager Anna has me wrapping up all the stuff in the cold cases while she does inventory of everything that needs to be replaced for tomorrow, which she has been informed is a really bad choice because plastic wrap and I don't get along majority of the time. Her response every time is that practice makes perfect. At least I'm not the one that has to pay to replace all the wasted plastic.

To be honest, Anna is the only reason I haven't quit this job yet. Well, that and the fact that I need money to pay Michael every month for rent, which is so messed up if you ask me. So much for "family", right?

Anna and my mom were like sisters growing up. I don't really have a lot of memories about my childhood, but Anna's in 99% of the ones I do have. Pool trips during summer vacation, sledding down Turner Hill after a blizzard, late night drives for ice cream. Those were some of the best moments of my life. She tried her best to keep the good times going after Mom passed, but it was never really the same. I did appreciate the effort though. I probably would've asked her if I could stay with her instead of continuing to live with Michael had it not been for her raising two little ones of her own.

Anna shouts over the sound of the sink hose. "Can you guys take out the trash really quick? The one by the fryers and the one over there by the sink? I'll take out the other trash before I leave."

"Sure," I holler back.

The hose stops and Cooper shouts over his shoulder. "Yeah. Just give me a sec to dry off my hands."

I always get a little tingle of excitement when Anna puts us together for a job. Even if it is just to take out the trash. A little time is better than no time at all, I suppose. Even when Cooper's drenched in water and has some flour stuck in his hair, he's still totally gorgeous. I can't be certain whether that really is just because he's really cute, or if it's because he's one of the only few guys at school that hasn't treated me like some piece of trash thanks to Tommy and the rest of the douchebags from the football team starting rumors about me. Sure, the rumors about my sexuality are true, but there's no way I'm admitting to that.

I finish wrapping the thing of macaroni salad in my hands and set it back into the case before tying up the trash bag by the fryers. I wheel it to the front of the deli and through the side doors. Cooper follows me with the other can.

An intense wave of odor floods my face as I swing the back door open, triggering an immediate eye-watering response. "Holy shit."

"Looks like someone missed the dumpster earlier," Cooper says, pointing to the busted gallon of milk on the side of the loading dock. "Must've baked in the sun. That's totally rank"

I put the inside of my elbow to my face to block out some of the smell. "Let's just throw this out and get back inside." I tug on the bag and slip it out of the can while suppressing the urge to vomit and toss it into the dumpster. Cooper and I practically kick drop the garbage cans back inside before slamming the door shut again. "That was disgusting."

A small chuckle escapes from Cooper's gorgeous lips, eventually turning into a full-on laugh fest back and forth between the two of us. I never noticed how adorable his laugh is until now. It probably sounds really weird, but it almost takes me back to my trips to the beach with Mom and Anna before every part of my life changed. It's just comforting in a time where nothing is certain anymore.

I wouldn't be upset if Milo turned out to be Cooper.

"Do you think we should tell someone?" he asks.

"Probably, yeah."

"You're not going to, are you?"

I puff my cheeks and raise an eyebrow. "Hmm . . . probably not."

That gets another laugh out of him, which I am more than happy to hear any time of the day. We start heading back in the direction of the deli.

"So what's it like working for your step-dad and having to live with him?"

"Trust me, you'd rather not know the answer to that one."

We stop at the sink and start soaping up our hands.

"That bad, huh?" he asks.

"You don't even know the half of it. Just picture being grounded at home, and then your punishment spilling over into the work you have to do at your job. He once made me scrape all the gum off the table in the break room because I fell asleep and didn't do the dishes one night."

"That's messed up." He cranks the handle of the paper towel holder and starts drying off his hands before getting one for me. "On the bright side though, you got paid while you did your punishment."

"You got me there, I guess." My fingertips lightly brush the palm of his hand as I reach for the paper towel, which sends miniscule shockwaves over every inch of my skin. My eyes can't help but explore every visible inch of his body, taking a pit stop at those deep golden-brown eyes. I pull myself back to reality and head back in to finish wrapping the case.

Cooper pushes the door open again. "Hey, did you catch when Miss Wilson said the test would be for the book?"

"I think it's Friday. Don't quote me on that though."

"I trust you, thanks." He smiles and his eyes light up. "I'm actually gonna run to the bathroom really quick. I'll be right back."

I can't help but watch as he walks away, and now I wish I hadn't.

"El, you bad boy. I totally saw that."

Aimee's standing there with her arms folded and a giant grin plastered across her face. No, I take that back. It's more of a smirk than a grin.

"I don't know what you're talking about."

"Oh really? I could roast a marshmallow over the heat between the two of you just now. Not a bad choice either." She giggles and rests her elbows on the other side of the glass casings.

"W—what? No, that's ridiculous. He's . . . and I'm . . ."

"You're awesome, that's what you are. Also a little weird, but you're cute, so it's fine."

"Oh, shut up." I whack her arm with the rag hanging from a hook below me. "What are you doing here anyway?"

"Well, I was going to ask you if you wanted to go see that new Anna Kendrick movie with me after your shift. Looks like I might be losing you to ole' lover boy, wherever he went."

"First of all, he's not "lover boy", okay? I'm like 99% sure he's straight. Even then, I have Milo. I can't just quit on him like that. Second, I can't. I have so much homework to do tonight. I don't even see myself sleeping tonight."

She's got that familiar look in her eye. The one that just screams disappointment. And I have a feeling I know why.

"El, come on."

"I know, I know. You've told me more than once."

"It's just not healthy for you to keep holding onto the fantasy of this entire anonymous email thing. You need something real, not the idea of who you hope this person might be."

"Yeah, I get it. I should probably get back to work. Talk later though?"

"Totally." She pats my arm and starts walking backward. "Love you, Bitch."

I roll my eyes and say, "Love you too, Bitch."

I pull the last of the potato salad out of the case and set it down on the table. From the corner of my eye I see the doors swing open again and Cooper walks through with his nose stuck in his phone. I'm captivated by his smile until my phone starts vibrating in my pocket.

My heart skips a beat when I catch a glimpse of my notifications.

To: cinderfella0204@gmail.com
From: milojuni1221@gmail.com
Subject: First Crushes
Dear Cinderfella,

Awe, thank you for that. But I most definitely would not call myself brave. You were the one that posted first about living in a world where you're forced to hide this insane secret. I'd say you're the brave one.

Can I ask you a question?

When did you know? That you were gay, I mean. I don't really have any other gay friends to talk about this kind of stuff with (or is the more inclusive term to say LGBT friends? I don't really know). Don't laugh at me when I tell you this. I finally figured it out back in like sixth grade when I saw Mr. Hart, that really hot P.E. teacher, washing his car shirtless in his driveway one day. Obviously, there were signs before then, like my crush on Kal from Halloweentown 2, also Kevin Jonas who is severely underrated to this day, but Mr. Hart was definitely when I realized I wasn't like everyone else.

Also, where exactly did you get your pseudonym? I decided to take "Cinderfella" to Google and some old movie from like the 1960s popped up. I take it you're a serious movie buff.

— Milo

Interesting.

To: milojuni1221@gmail.com

From: cinderfella0204@gmail.com

Subject: Re: First Crushes

Dear Milo,

Wow. Sounds like you like the bad boys with that Kal confession. Let's hope I can add up. As far as your 12-year-old obsession with Mr. Hart, I definitely get it. What I wouldn't have given to see that with you that day. I was a pretty awkward and shy twelve-year-old though, and I still am to this day, so who knows how I would've reacted to that.

As for me, my first crush was Ricky Ullman from Phil of the Future. Every time he smiled, I just melted inside a little bit. And those EYES! Ugh, I'm a total sucker for brown eyes! What are the chances of yours being brown? I could totally imagine it now. Lying in bed watching movies on a rainy day while I stare into those gorgeous eyes, whatever color they may be. For real sounds like a perfect day.

But I should probably get back to work. I have so much homework that I need to finish up tonight.

— Cinderfella

p.s.

I actually am kind of a movie buff, but I'll confess I didn't even know about that movie. It was originally supposed to be a cute attempt at playing with the title of that movie A Cinderella Story, the one with Hilary Duff and Chad Michael Murray, which continues to be one of my favorite movies to this day. I know it's super cheesy, but I really like the super cheesy and predictable movies. I always have and I'm not really sure why. I guess it could have something to do with it also being my mom's favorite and we used to watch them together all the time. I really do have to get back to work, but I'll talk to you later. Bye!

CHAPTER SIX

JUSTIN

Wednesday, March 25

I don't think I've ever been so relieved for a game to be over. I'm not sure what it is, but I just haven't been too into playing this season. It could just be the stress of graduation coming up. Everyone's obsession with being on their game so we're prepared to beat Brettwood all the way at the end of May isn't helping anything either.

It's the end of the seventh inning and the entire team is on their feet and applauding Jason, who scored the last run, giving us a win by one point. Danny seems pretty annoyed that it's only by a single run, but I'm just happy for it to be over.

We all get herded like cattle back across the parking lot and into the gym. A bunch of the guys are jumping up and down and hollering like mad men in celebration of our third consecutive win of the season, despite the fact that it's still super early and we have a lot of ground to cover before making it to Brettwood. My stomach lurches a bit when a few of them start stripping off their shirts as they run across the gym and disappear through the locker room doors. I started playing baseball so that Danny and I would have something to bond over, but I most certainly stayed for the cute guys in baseball pants that hug every beautiful curve.

As usual, I'm one of the last couple of stragglers to reach my locker on the far back wall of the locker room, which is thankfully out of sight of most of the other guys, apart from Danny at least. It makes it easier to prevent any unwanted visitors. Not that I'm saying Danny isn't totally hot, because he really is, but we've been friends so long that he's more like family than anything else. I'd never tell him this even if I was out because I don't want to ruin our friendship, but he was one of my first crushes before I even knew it was a crush.

"Good game, man," Danny utters from behind me.

I glance back, and there he is standing butt ass naked with a towel in his hand. Sometimes he makes it really difficult to not see him as anything more than a best friend or like part of the family. "Thanks, but I didn't really do a whole lot today."

"Don't be so modest. You got us the first run. That's not nothing."

"I guess so." It comes out before my brain can even register the situation and tell itself to shut the hell up.

He throws the towel around his waist, most likely realizing that his crotch staring me in the face doesn't make for a very comfortable potential heart to heart situation. "You okay?"

Danny knows me better than I know myself sometimes, so he can usually see right through me when I'm lying. "Everything's fine."

The other good thing about him is that he never blatantly pushes to get anything out of me. It's never stopped him from trying to hint around the subject though. "You're really sure? You've just seemed kind of off lately."

I avoid eye contact of any kind. "Yeah, I promise everything's fine." I'm such a terrible liar that not even I believe what's coming out of my own mouth.

"Alright then," he huffs. "I know it probably sounds totally gay, but I've got your back if you ever need anything. You're my brother from another mother." The corners of his mouth curve up into a grin and he playfully swings at my shoulder. "Now hurry up and shower. We're all going out for shakes after this, and before you try to come up with some excuse, you're going too, no excuses this time."

"Okay, let me just text my dad and let him know real quick."

The waitress at Steak n' Shake crammed Danny, Cooper, Gabbi, Melissa, and me into a table in the back corner of the restaurant over by the window. As soon as we sat down, Gabbi started complaining about the air conditioning vent above her head and convinced Coop to switch spots with her just by batting her eyelids. I wish I could get whatever I wanted like that. She was still under the vent, but at least now she gets to sit next to me.

Ain't it grand?

"Dude, Coop, did you see the way Justin just slid into home like that at the last minute at the end of the first inning? The look on their coach's face was fucking priceless," Danny says in between gulps of his mint cookies and cream shake.

"I try," I say. I just kind of wish he'd shut up about it already.

Gabbi lightly rests her hand on my shoulder while tucking her hair behind her ear with the other. "Well, you certainly succeeded."

I can feel my face getting hot and I'm just hoping it's not reflecting on my cheeks. "Thanks, Gabs," I say, trying to avoid her gaze. I almost feel bad about it until she starts rubbing up and down my leg with the edge of her foot. In all honesty though, trying to deflect her all the time feels really shitty because she's really not a bad person, even though she may not always be the nicest person in the world. It's just really difficult when I have no idea who I really am or what I actually want. It wouldn't be fair to her.

Kind of like how it would be unfair for me to reveal myself to Cinder right now.

"Hey, Melissa," Gabbi says, pushing herself away from the table. "Do you think you could come help me out in the bathroom for a sec?"

The girls get up and disappear into the bathroom, leaving me to be stared down by Danny and Coop. "What?" I ask.

"You and Gabbi," Danny says.

"What about it?"

This time Cooper chimes in. "Is there something you're not telling us?"

I stifle a laugh and resist the urge to roll my eyes. The response is becoming a habit with these guys. "Guys, there is absolutely nothing going on between the two of us. We're just friends."

Danny takes another gulp of his shake. "Justin, she is shooting off signs left and right. You can't tell me that you're not picking up on that."

"Well, I am, but—"

"Nope, there are not "buts" here. You two are practically meant for each other. You need to hurry up and seal the deal. She's not gonna wait around forever, man."

If I keep turning down Gabbi in front of Danny and Coop then I might as well tattoo "Teenage Closet Case" on my forehead and dig my own grave. No straight guy in their right mind would turn down a girl like Gabbi. Head cheerleader, future prom queen, and not to mention drop-dead gorgeous.

I just hate that all of these lies keep building up. I'm never gonna get out of this one.

"Look, I get what you guys are saying. You just have to be patient. It'll happen when the time's right." Here's to hoping the time is never right. Or at least not until I've been moved halfway across the country to Stanford and it's too late to do anything about it.

The girls' return is marked by their fit of uncontrollable laughter as they make a beeline back to the table.

"What's so funny?" Danny asks.

"Oh, wouldn't you like to know." Melissa shoots a wink at Danny from across the table.

"I most certainly would. Maybe you can tell it to me later." He winks back and all I want to do is tell them to go get a room. Or the backseat of a car. Just as long as they're not doing that here I'm fine. "Oh, by the way, I just found out my parents are going out of town this weekend for their anniversary, so party at my place. No excuses not to go, and I'm talking to you, Justin."

He really does know me well.

It's 3:03 a.m. and I haven't even slept yet. I just can't get the conversation with Danny earlier out of my head. Everything's just so messed up and I don't know if I'll ever be able to make any sense of it on my own.

To: cinderfella0204@gmail.com
From: milojuni1221@gmail.com
Subject: one big disappointment
Dear Cinderfella,

Do you ever just lay awake at night wondering if life would be so much simpler if you could just pack a bag with only the necessities and run off somewhere far, far away to start a whole new life? One where there's no expectations of where you're going based on where you've been or what everyone else wants out of you. I'm just so tired of giving every part of me to everyone. The messed up part is that I complain about it, yet I continue to do it because the thought of disappointing anyone in my life is too much to handle. I don't think I even know how to take anything for myself.

I have these things that I know I'm supposed to do. I need to get the best grades possible, get into the school that my parents want for me and earn my medical degree. Then I need to come back home and become a family doctor while I raise a family with the girl that literally everyone wants me to be with right now. I just don't know how much more of this I can take before I finally snap. I feel like I'm being suffocated by my own life and I don't know what to do anymore.

Let's do it. Let's just run away together and never look back. We can start a new life somewhere else and both just be free for once in our lives.

— Milo

I scan over what I've written and hit send. Why do I keep doing this to myself? Life would just be so much easier if I would just get my head out of my own ass, stop being scared, and just tell them. Everything. That I'm gay and that the idea of going to med school makes me die a little more inside every time I think about it. I'd probably leave out the part about emailing back and forth with some random guy I met online though. Well, not "random" per se, but there is like a one percent chance that he's not who he says he is, and they would have a trip about that one.

CHAPTER SEVEN

ELLIOT

Thursday, March 26

To: milojuni1221@gmail.com
From: cinderfella0204@gmail.com
Subject: Re: one big disappointment

Dear Milo,

I relate to that on a spiritual level. Half the time I'm so stressed out with everything that's going on that I'm lucky if I get more than like three hours of sleep at night. It's crazy how everyone spends so much time babying us, just to throw us out on our asses as soon as we turn eighteen.

Am I even making sense anymore here? I honestly don't know.

If it's any sort of consolation, I don't want you to be with this mystery girl that everyone else wants you to be with. But I definitely do get where you're coming from in a way. I don't have the kind of expectations placed on me like you seem to, but I definitely get just being tired of pretending to be someone you're not. It's exhausting. The funny part is that I probably could just come out and be myself once I'm, unfortunately so, at ISU in the fall. The more I think about it, the scarier it all gets.

Running away and just starting over does sound really nice. No expectations, no assumptions about us based on who we are or where we come from. That would be the perfect life.

— Cinderfella

I toss my phone into the passenger seat after hitting send and pull away from the curb.

Getting the chance to meet Milo face to face would be nice, but it's terrifying at the same time. I'm not exactly well liked around school, so what would make things any different with him? He may say all these super sweet things, but when it comes down to it, I don't think he'd really be all that interested in me. Why would he be? It's not like I'm anything special and he could do so much better than me. It's better just to keep the image of who he thinks I could be alive in his head.

I don't know if I could take any more disappointment in life.

It's 7:45 by the time I pull into the school parking lot and manage to find a spot at the outer edge. I knew I should've skipped the McDonald's drive-thru, but lately my body hasn't been able to run without its daily caffeine drip in the form of vanilla iced coffee. Figured I better not risk it.

I speed past the sea of other kids shuffling through the parking lot on my way inside, no doubt looking like some sort of spaz. It hits me again as I make my way through the senior hallway that any one of these people could be Milo. Well, any of the guys. At least I certainly hope he's actually a dude. It would make things really awkward if he isn't. I've grown up with so many of these guys and I just can't figure out how any one of these guys could be hiding a secret like that. They all just seem so . . . straight.

Up until last September I could've pictured Milo being Pete Harper. I mean, he's been in theatre since freshman year, he's played either the lead or major supporting role, GBF type characters included, and he isn't exactly the most masculine guy in school. He kind of squashed those rumors as soon as he started dating his latest love interest Sarah Ashmore. Although I'm not totally convinced that it's not a beard.

Maybe I should get a beard. It definitely couldn't damage my reputation any more than it already is.

"Hey, Elliot." Cooper's waving at me from a few lockers down, a smile plastered on his face as usual. "You working tonight?"

"Yup, four to nine tonight," I reply.

"Sweet." He pulls a couple of textbooks out of his locker and shuts the door. "I get in at five tonight. See you in class, man." He waves again before walking off in the other direction.

There is a part of me that kind of hopes Cooper would turn out to be my mystery guy by some damn miracle. He's sweet and smart and athletic, not to mention totally gorgeous. I could look at those golden-brown eyes every day. I know I'm probably just grasping at straws here, but I think there could be a chance that he really is Milo. I got an email the other night at work, right after he disappeared into the bathroom and came back smiling at his phone. That can't be a coincidence, right?

A guy can dream.

I slide my bag off my shoulder and stuff it into my locker before pulling my copy of *The Help* from the top shelf and piling it on top of the notebooks for my next three classes. We were supposed to read like the last 150 pages over break, but that never happened. I'm pretty sure Miss Wilson knew that probably wouldn't happen. Shmoop and Cliffnotes were my best friend the entire break.

Since Miss Wilson started working here a couple years ago, her class has always been the most comforting of all. She's got this little corner of the room dedicated as like a chill zone or whatever. There's this cute little black futon set up with some throw pillows and two little tables on either side. The corner's even been completed with a couple sets of those white string lights, a salt lamp, and a cozy blue shag rug. I'm not sure how she convinced Principal Hollace to let her bring in a futon, but we're all fortunate that she did. I've come here a few times during study hall to relax and just get away from it all.

I honestly don't know where I'd be without Miss Wilson and Charlie, the only two gay icons I have that aren't Lady Gaga or Neil Patrick Harris. Not that I've ever told them about my sexuality. It's just nice knowing that they're there should I ever get the guts to do it.

I'm trying to figure out if I should try to sit by Cooper, or if that would just look totally weird. I mean, we're coworkers, but does that really constitute us as friends that can have conversations in school that aren't work or academic related?

I'll just play it safe and sit adjacent from him. Seems fair enough.

I slide my phone out of my pocket again and see the notification for a new email from just a few minutes ago lighting up the screen. I wasn't expecting a reply so fast.

To: cinderfella0204@gmail.com
From: milojuni1221@gmail.com
Subject: Tired of waiting
Dear Cinderfella,

I went back and read the email I set you last night. I was kind of out of it, so I apologize for the melodrama. I was all up in my feels.

It did get me thinking though. Why do I keep doing this to myself? Why am I continuously putting my own needs on the backburner when I could be living my own life for once? Everything would be so much easier if I just come clean. I'm gonna do it, Cinder.

I'm gonna tell them. About everything. My gayness, that I don't want to be a doctor, that I want to pursue my own thing for once in my life. I deserve to be free.

I'm telling them. Tonight.

— Milo

Holy shit.

English went a lot better than I thought it would. I managed to get away with relatively limited knowledge of the more minute details of the book and Miss Wilson handed out an additional study guide on top of everything she'd already given us for extra help before the test tomorrow. I'm just looking forward to finishing the test because we'll be starting the movie on Monday, and she's set aside two and a half days to watch it. She knows just as much as the rest of us that we're totally over senior year, so the less work toward the end the better.

What I couldn't stop thinking about all class though was Milo's last email. He's actually going to come out. Does that mean he's going to want to meet finally? I don't really know if we're ready for that. I don't know if *I'm* ready for that.

Aimee's standing in front of my locker chatting it up with Vanessa. I love Aimee, but I swear that girl jumps from person-to-person faster than a young Lex Luthor. The version from Smallville, not the classic comic version, which I honestly can't say I know too much about.

She tells me that *I'm* an obvious flirt.

"Get a room, you guys," I almost blurt out as I'm opening up my locker. I can tell I just embarrassed the hell out of Vanessa by the panicked look in her eyes. "That was a joke."

"Oh, you'd like that, wouldn't you?" Aimee laughs. "Hurry up or we're gonna be late for Charlie's class."

"Charlie?" Vanessa asks with this adorably puzzled expression.

Aimee's resisting a smile. "Mr. Jameson. He prefers that we all call him Charlie, but if the principal ever asks, we call him nothing but Mr. Jameson. I think it's a theatre teacher thing."

I yank my book for theatre out from under the books for geo and government and slam the locker shut with my leg. "It's most definitely a theatre teacher thing."

We push through a group of kids talking about their weekend plans on the way to class. Yet another Danny Peters party that we will not be getting an invite to. Not that it really bothers me anymore. I accepted the ways of the high school hierarchies a very long time ago. It just sucks to be leaving high school without any sort of experience at a real party. I've heard they're almost never worth it, but it would still be nice to learn that firsthand.

Aimee finds her seat on the other side of the room and Vanessa and I plop down into ours. "Hey, I'm sorry if I made you uncomfortable or anything about the "get a room" comment," I finally say.

"No, you're all good."

"Are you sure?" I'm trying to gauge whether or not she's just trying to make me feel less awkward. "I don't want to make it weird or anything. It's just kind of a thing that her and I do. We've been friends for so long that I sometimes forget that other people might think our relationship is a little weird."

"It's really fine, I promise. It's kind of nice being in on the jokes." She's running her finger over the carving of a stick figure in her desk. "It's never exactly been easy being the army brat of the school. I've never been in one location for more than a few months at a time."

"You said you're gonna be here for like the next year, right?" I ask.

"That's what it's looking like."

Vanessa's lips tremble as if she's fighting a smile, but I can see the happiness radiating from her deep brown eyes. It has to be mine and Aimee's mission to make the rest of this year and her senior year the best it can be. Even if it kills us. She deserves that much.

The door squeaks open and Charlie walks in holding his Best Dog Dad mug in one hand and some books in the other. Would it be alright to buy *him* a present for *my* graduation in the form of a bigger shoulder bag that he can fit all of his stuff in? I hate watching him struggle all the time.

"Good morning, class," he says, setting his things down on the desk. "I certainly hope you've all been enjoying the first week back from break."

There's a collective groan.

"That's what I figured, which is why today I'm giving you all the chance to socialize with one another. Before you get excited though, there is a bit of a catch. For the next three weeks, we will be working on a project that will give each and every one of you the chance to start creating."

Just looking around the room, there's a few people that aren't all too thrilled about the concept of having a project in theatre when they just kind of assumed it would be an easy blow off course. I'm actually kind of excited about it. I don't have a lot of experience with theatre, but I've always wanted to be a director or writer for film and television, so this could be fun.

"I know some of you thought this was going to be a class you could just skate by in, and I'm talking to some of you seniors, but let's try to make this fun, okay?" He slips a sheet of paper from between the pages of one of the books he brought in with him. "Now for the part I know most of you are going to hate me for. I have chosen your partners for you because I know if I let you choose your friends, nothing will get done. When I call your names, I want you to go sit next to your partner and I'll be passing around the assignment sheet shortly."

There goes the prospect of working with Aimee. He's seen us together enough times to know that the odds of us getting work done together are pretty slim to none.

I've never been all that huge into religion, although we do go to church on Easter and all that just to kind of keep up appearances, but I'm praying that I don't get stuck with Robbie Martins. He's not exactly a bad person, but the guy doesn't know when to shut the hell up. All he talks about is Pokémon cards. Third grade was not an enjoyable time when Mrs. Johnson sat us next to each other.

"There are fifteen of you in here, so there will be six groups of two and a group of three. And before you ask, there will be no switching. Most of you in here are seniors, and you're going to have to learn to work with people that you don't like whether you move on to college or go out into the work force."

How many times are we going to get that speech this year?

"Okay, groups are going to be Garret and Tiffany, Oliver and Gavin, Madison and Shane, Aimee and Justin, Nathan and Jamie, Elliot and Vanessa, and the group of three is going to be Bethany, Robbie, and Taylor."

Oh, happy days! If people didn't already think I was some sort of freak, I'd be doing a happy dance right now. Not too sure if it could really hurt me a whole lot at this point, but I kind of prefer to not take any chances with it.

"Alright so what I'm handing out to you now is the assignment sheet. What I want you to do for this project is create a short play that makes a statement of some kind, big or small. Just like the invisible theatre performance we were able to see. It doesn't have to be quite so large scale, but it needs to get people talking. It needs to be able to start a conversation for change. Use the pieces on moment work that I sent you all a few weeks back to help if you get stuck, and as usual feel free to come to me if you have any questions. Get creating, everyone!"

The classroom is roaring from everyone getting up or scooching their desks across the floor if they're too lazy to just get up and move to their partner. If I couldn't get Aimee as a partner, then I'm certainly happy that it was Vanessa.

Aimee makes eyes at me from the front of the room, like she's not all that satisfied with her partner. Justin doesn't seem like a bad choice for a partner though. Sure, he's one of the school's poster boy jocks, but last time I checked, he's been a straight-A student for forever. On top of that he seems like a nice enough guy and he's definitely not bad to look at.

Not counting today, I have two more days until I can finally get a couple days off from work, making that seven days in a row that I've been forced to work. There's got to be some sort of labor laws against that, but when did that ever stop Michael before?

There's only twenty minutes left until closing, so Anna's in the back finishing dishes and sweeping up. We got absolutely hammered from 7:30 to like 8:20 thanks to the store's new discount on family sized buckets of fried chicken every Thursday, so now Cooper's upstairs taking his break.

"Any big plans this weekend?" Anna asks, patting her hands dry on her apron.

"Oh, the biggest," I say. "We're gonna start off by renting a party bus, and then we're going on a bar crawl around Bloomington where we're going to get as messed up as humanly possible before buying some coke on the corner, which we're doing in the presidential suite we have all lined up for a huge party. We even got Marshmallow to DJ for us."

Anna's mouth is gaping open and her laugh lines are starting to show, no matter how much she tries to hide her amusement. "That sounds like a blast." And she's lost it. "But seriously, please tell me you're at least doing something this weekend."

"You realize you're talking to the guy with the evil step-father, right? I don't get weekend fun. I get weekend *work*."

"Really? Evil step-father? Are we stuck in a gender-bend Disney movie right now? He's really not all that bad if you'd just get to know him. Your mom wasn't a bad judge of character."

I think I really am stuck in some gender-bending version of a Disney movie. The whole being forced to serve food and sweep thing isn't helping much with the imagery.

"What about prom? Are you planning on going to that?"

"Maybe — I don't know — do I really want to be that loser that shows up without a date?"

"You could go with Aimee. You two have always seemed super close and I can't help but wonder if . . ."

I cut her off. "Oh, no. Aimee and I are just — we're close friends and that's it. She's practically family."

Sometimes I forget that I'm not out to Anna. It's not that I don't want to be honest with her about who I really am, but it's more terrifying to come out to her than it would be to anyone else. She's been kind of like a second mom to me my entire life. Especially in the last five years when it really counted.

"Okay, well you can still go as friends. The point is I want you to enjoy the last bit of your senior year. It only comes around once, so you need to make sure you do it right. That includes graduation. You have to be ready to get out of here."

I stop sweeping and lean my chin against the handle of the broom. "If by "get out of here" you mean go to ISU for four years while continuing to work here for the duration of the time, then yes. I will be ready to get out of here."

"That is not what I meant, and you know it, Elliot. You need to get out of here. Out of Lakeview. Out of Illinois, period. Your mom didn't want this life for you."

"She may not have wanted it for me, but it's the life I'm going to get. I can't escape this place. I'll never escape it."

As much as I wish I could say I'm just being overly dramatic about the entire thing, I know it's the truth.

I'm stuck.

CHAPTER EIGHT

JUSTIN

Thursday, March 26

Predictably, I take the long way home. Any extra time I can get to muster up the courage to tell Mom and Dad is much appreciated. I don't think they'll like kick me out or anything — at least I hope not — but I can't help but feel like after I do this, everything's going to be different. What am I saying? It definitely will be different.

I remember when my cousin Hector came out to his parents a few years ago. They tried to force him into therapy and just kept repeating over and over again that he was "sick". Fortunately, he was over the age of eighteen, so he just refused and moved out instead, but that didn't stop the family from disowning him. Granted, most of Dad's side of the family actually lives in Mexico, but either way it swings, sexuality isn't really something that gets talked about a whole lot in Mexican culture.

I don't know how this is going to turn out for me. I can only hope Mom will be a bit more understanding than Dad will.

My hands are trembling as I pull my Mirage into the driveway and put it into park. It's 4:02, which means that both of them should be home now. Dad's probably showering and washing all the dirt and grime off from today's construction work, and Mom's probably in the kitchen getting dinner started. I'll do it in that little time frame between Dad's T.V. time and dinner. That's usually when they're at their happiest and might be less likely to freak out on me.

I take a few deep breaths in and exhale as I reach for the front door, which helps to settle the trembling a bit, but only enough that it isn't totally noticeable that I'm on the verge of a panic attack. I'm still suppressing the urge to drive out into one of the cornfields surrounding the town and just scream for a few hours.

I walk in expecting to be greeted by the familiarity of the sound of the abnormally loud shower and the scent of whatever Mom's whipping up in the kitchen for that night. All I get is silence and whatever wax mom has in her burner right now.

The sound of the door latching behind me bounces off the hardwood flooring and echoes through the rest of the house. Not a moment later, there's footsteps racing down the creaking staircase. Mom and Dad practically hurl themselves down the last few steps and into me.

"Holy—" The F word almost flies out of my mouth before I catch myself. My sexuality would be the last of my worries if my mom heard that one. "What's going on?"

Neither of them is speaking. They just have these huge, giddy smiles plastered across their faces that are making me kind of uncomfortable. It's a little earlier in the evening than I was expecting, but they seem to be in a pretty good mood. This might be a good time to tell them.

"Hey, I—there's something that I want—or need—to tell you," I stutter. If my heart beats any faster, I'm sure they'll be able to hear it. I've put it off long enough.

Mom touches her palm to my cheek. She's smiling, but there's a buildup of tears in her eyes. "Okay, but first . . ." She whips her other hand out from behind her back, revealing a large envelope clutched between her fingers.

My eyes scan over the lettering on the front. "Is—that's from Stanford?" I don't mean for it to come out like a question, but it does.

"Just open it," she says, practically throwing it at me.

I take my time ripping open the seal and glance up at Mom and Dad again, their eyes longing for a definitive yes from the school they've dreamed about for one of their kids for so long. From their perspective, I probably look nervous that it's going to be some sort of rejection or an announcement that I've been put on a waitlist or something.

I'm scared that it says I got in. Why else would they send such a hefty package that weighs like two damn pounds?

I wipe the sweat from my palms on my shorts before picking off the last of the seal and take one more deep breath as I slide out the contents of the envelope and sweep my eyes across the letter on top. "I—" My throat's on fire as I continue reading. The words don't want to come out right. "I got in." It's barely a whisper, but both of them seem to understand what I said.

Mom shrieks and before I know it, her arms are wrapped around me and her lips are planted to the top of my head. "That's so great, sweetie! I'm so proud of you!"

I peer over Mom's shoulder and catch Dad's gaze. I swear I see him wipe away a tear, something I've never seen in my eighteen years on this earth. Mom lets go of her grip on me and Dad comes in for a hug.

"Congratulations, Mijo," he says. "I knew you could do it."

I force a grin and just hope it's convincing enough. "Thanks, Apá." My eyes trail back down to the pile of papers and the booklet in my hands.

Why today of all days?

Mom's still grinning from ear to ear. "Are you in shock, honey?"

"I guess you could say that."

Mom cups my face with her hands and locks in on my eyes. "Well, believe it, sweetheart. You did this! You really did it! You should be so proud of yourself right now. And to celebrate, the three of us are going out for dinner tonight, wherever you want."

Awesome. My last meal before the death of my old life is finalized and the new one where I'm totally fucking miserable twenty-four hours a day begins. Better make it a good one.

"Before that though, your dad and I have some errands to run, so keep an eye out for Brooke. She's coming by to help you study up for that calculus test since she'll be out of town this weekend."

"Will do," I mutter.

Mom lifts her purse off the hook by the door and swipes her keys off one of the end tables. "Oh, and you said that you had something to tell us?"

I can't do it now. Can I? After all of that? After they told me how proud they were of me and that I finally did it? I'm finally becoming a picturesque version of what they've always wanted me to be. Maybe the only choice I have now is to finally give into the cookie-cutter image that everyone has of me.

"Uh," I stammer, trying to come up with something else to say. "Yeah, Danny's having a party tomorrow and I just wanted to let you know that I told him I'd go, if that's alright."

Dad playfully punches my shoulder and smiles. I force a weak grin and try to fight back the stinging in my eyes.

"Of course," he says. "You deserve to have a little bit of fun, Mijo. Go celebrate with your friends."

They both give me one last hug before disappearing outside. I stand at the window and watch as they get into Mom's Camry and start pulling out of the driveway. I'm still clutching the envelope from Stanford against my chest when they vanish behind a cloud of dust from gravel that's spilled out onto the road.

It's like someone's broken the flood gates when I finally know they're really gone. I fumble for the nearest wall for support and drop my acceptance letter onto the floor. I'm suffocating. It feels like someone threw me into a coffin and buried it six feet deep and left me to die. I can't find a single point of focus as my back slides down the wall and my body hits the floor with a thud. The living room is spinning and I'm hugging myself for dear life.

I'd give anything for this to be a dream right now.

Brooke got here about fifteen minutes after my parents left and I finished up with my meltdown. As I suspected, Mom sent her a text and told her that I got in to Stanford before she even got here, which meant I was greeted by even more support that I had to be "happy" about.

Hiding part of me for all these years has turned me into a pretty convincing liar, I guess.

It didn't take long to dive right into the calculus studying. It's pretty much the only reason I really need tutoring. I've never gotten along with the class, but I've somehow managed to secure an A all semester thanks to Brooke.

I glance over my notebook and watch Brooke as she's grading a stack of papers for the class that she TAs for. "Thank you," I say.

"For what?" she asks, never looking up.

"For helping me as much as you do. I know you probably have better things to do than teach some high school kid."

Brooke sets her pen down on the stack of papers she's finished looking through and glances up at me. "Well, it is my job, but you're welcome, I guess. But you're also a good guy and I enjoy helping you. And you don't need to thank me. Finding out you got into Stanford was reward enough and I'm proud of you."

If only she knew how tired I am of hearing that already, and it's barely been two hours.

"Thanks. So, my mom says you're going out of town for the weekend. Somewhere fun, I hope."

"Actually, yeah. My mom and I leave for LA tonight to go visit my brother for a few days."

"Oh, that's awesome. What does he do over there? I'm going to assume he's a struggling actor or something that works as a Starbucks barista during the day."

That gets a bit of a laugh out of her. At least one of us is able to do that right now.

"Am I getting warm?" I ask.

"That's a pretty fair guess, but he's actually a not-so-struggling writer." She fumbles through her bag on the table and pulls out a bound stack of pages. The title on the front's been marked off by a black maker, but it's followed by the name Noah Carlisle.

"His name sounds so familiar," I say, trying to place it. "Wait, wasn't he in the Lakeview Journal a few weeks ago or something like that?"

"Yeah, his book got picked up by Hale Publishing after working there for like a year as an assistant. They loved it so much they somehow got it picked up by Fox for a movie, and it's not even supposed to be published until fall."

That is exactly what I want. Not the book publishing part, because I could barely even read *The Help* for my English class, let alone write a book of my own. But just seeing someone from this shit hole town that was able to make it doing what he wanted is inspiring. I need the chance to do my own thing.

"Can I look through it?" I ask.

"Eh, I don't know. They don't really want it getting out."

"Just a quick peek? I promise I won't say anything."

Her nose is scrunched, and her eyebrows arch as her fingers tap along the front cover. "If you've finished the problem correctly, then yes."

"Uh . . . about that," I mumble. My lips purse and my eyes narrow.

Brooke lets out a loud sigh and rolls her eyes before yanking my notebook out of my hands. "What have you done n—" she trails off. The look of annoyance has been replaced by something else. Shock maybe? No, that's not it. Embarrassment? "Justin, is this—is this me?" She flips the page back around in my direction to show off the sketched portrait I've spent the last hour working on."

"Sorry," I say. "If it's creepy I can just rip it up and throw it out."

"What? It's not creepy, Justin. This is actually really good. Have you ever considered doing anything with art?"

"Oh, no. It—it's just a hobby. It's something fun to pass the time."

"Well, either way, it's really good. You should definitely keep working on that skill, but in the mean time you really need to focus on studying for this test if you want to keep your place at Stanford. You can't afford to let your GPA slip."

I should just blurt it out. There's no going back now anyway. *I don't want to keep my place at Stanford. I don't want to be a doctor. I don't want to keep pretending that I'm someone other than who I really am.*

I just want to be free.

"I—uh—" I can't get the right words to come out. If I just say it, then maybe I'll feel better. Maybe I won't just be this big ball of anger, hatred, and pain anymore. "I will."

I'm such a little bitch.

"Good. You keep working on that problem, and I'm going to run and grab a drink. Do you want anything?"

"No, I'm good," I say.

I don't know why it's so hard for me to say it. I don't want to go to Stanford. I want to go to art school and pursue what I really want—I want the chance to be with Cinder, even if I don't know who he really is.

The screen of my phone lights up, followed by the usual new email sound, which brings the first bit of happiness I've felt since I got home. Just the person I wanted to talk to right about now.

Except it's not.

The screen unlocks with my finger print and I tap on the Google Mail app.

Dear Justin Herrera:

Congratulations! On behalf of the Admissions Committee, I am delighted to offer you a place in the Class of 2024 NYU Steinhardt undergraduate Studio Art program. We look forward to meeting you this upcoming fall.

Whoever's running my life up there must have a majorly screwed up sense of humor because I'm sure as hell not laughing at this one.

CHAPTER NINE

ELLIOT

Friday, March 27

Aimee sent me a text around sixth period telling me that her parents said she could have me and Vanessa over for a pizza and movie night. I'm pretty sure she was more interested in it only being Vanessa so she could put the moves on to test the waters, but there's no way her parents would allow that. I've usually been the buffer for her and whomever she's interested in at the time, which still beats being stuck at the house with Tommy and his douchebag friends from the basketball team. Last time I was around them all as a group they spent the evening trying to come up with new "creative" ways to insult me. It must've taken some serious brain power between the four of them to come up with "Faggiot".

Really the greatest minds of our generation. Bravo.

By the looks of it, I'm the first to get home, which means I'll be able to get ready for work and get out without having to deal with Hailey and her fascination with blackmailing me. She's strangely good at it, and it's sort of scary.

I wait another moment before cutting off the engine to let the rest of Ben Platt's "RAIN" play out. That man can sing me to sleep any time of the day. I mean damn! I'd come out for him if he asked me to.

I sit in silence for just another second and watch as little rain droplets race down the windshield. It takes me back to the days of my childhood. On rainy days, Mom and I would stand at the window and we'd both pick out a rain droplet and see whose would get to the bottom of the window first. Back then it was just us against the world. That was all we really needed. Or at least I thought so.

I about slip and fall face first into the soaked wooden steps on my way up to the front porch. I'm so done with this day already.

First, I was late to first period because my locker was freaking jammed, so I had to run all the way back to the front office and wait for a janitor, so I had to come back to class during my study hall to finish my test over *The Help*. Then at lunch I became that doofus that dropped his tray in the middle of the cafeteria, so everyone—and I do mean everyone—started staring and clapping. I could've crawled into a hole and died.

I'd say this day couldn't get any worse, but I know my life, so I know better.

As I'm unlocking the door, I see a huge envelope sticking out of the of the mailbox. If I'm lucky maybe it's something telling me I have some secretly rich relative on the other side of the country that wants me to scoop me away from Michael's hell house and give me a whole new life.

I push the door open and pull everything out of the mailbox before disappearing inside.

"Bill . . . bill . . . bill," I murmur, flipping through all of the ordinary crap sent for Michael. I set everything down on the key table next to the front door and flip over the bigger envelope to see ISU's logo plastered over the front along with the name "Elliot Cole Brown".

"Well, there you have it, Mom." I rip open the seal and pull out the acceptance letter and all of the information packets. "Dear Elliot, congratulations, you have been admitted to Illinois State University." I let the envelope and all its contents hang by my side as I trek up the stairs to my bedroom. "Shocker."

I know I should be happy about getting in somewhere at least. There's a lot of people that don't get the opportunity to go to college at all. An English Education degree isn't exactly my first choice, but I guess I'll take it.

Whatever gets me out of here the fastest.

It's a little after 9:30 when I finally pull up in front of Aimee's house. We had a new lady named Debby start today, and I got stuck showing her how to do all the closing duties while Anna finished up a bunch of inventory paperwork. She caught on a lot faster than I was initially expecting her to, but it still wasn't how I would've liked to spend my Friday evening. I just wish that Cooper would've been at work tonight, but he gets the day off every time he has a game.

The only really good thing to happen the entire night was an email that came through from Milo. I didn't want to pry, but I'd been going crazy since he told he was going to come out and tell his parents everything. He didn't give any details, but apparently he chickened out at the last minute, which I can't really blame him for. I've chickened out of going public more times in the last two or three years than I can count on both hands.

As much as I act like it would be, coming out wouldn't really be all that big of a deal for me. I mean, I'm already scrutinized over everything I do. How much of a difference would this one detail really make for me? Everyone already thinks I'm gay anyway.

From what Milo's told me though, this would be a total make or break situation for him. Obviously I know that there are a lot of details about his life that he keeps private from me, and vice versa, but we're generally a pretty open book when we talk. This is a huge deal for him.

It majorly freaking sucks. All of it.

Aimee's adorable husky Aspen is the first to greet me at the door with a bunch of kisses. She's probably my favorite thing about coming over to Aimee's house, which I will deny if Aimee ever asks. It's the closest to having a pet I'm ever going to get as long as I live under Michael's roof. He says he's allergic, yet he's never had a problem anytime I come back with dog hair all over me. He's just a jerk that won't let me have a dog.

Apart from Aspen though, I really love coming over because it gives me the chance to be around a family that genuinely seems to care about each other. And they listen to each other.

Aimee's mom is in the kitchen icing up some chocolate and vanilla cupcakes with the help of CJ, Aimee's little brother. Though I use the term "helping" loosely. I think he's wearing more flour than was used to make the cupcakes and he's got his finger in what little bit's left of the icing bowl.

This is exactly what I needed after how today's gone.

"Elliot!" CJ shouts at the top of his little lungs. "Mommy, can I stay up and watch the movie with Elliot and Aimee?"

"It's already way past your bed time, little man," she says, wiping the excess icing off his fingers with a dish towel. "Go say goodnight, and then head upstairs. I'll be up in a minute to help you into your jammies."

CJ hops off the chair and jumps up into my arms. "Elliot! I lost another tooth!" He opens his mouth wide and points at a tiny open space at the front of his gums.

"Oh, that's awesome! You better get that tooth under your pillow before you go to sleep. You don't want the Tooth Fairy to miss it."

His little brown eyes pop before he wraps his arms around my neck and jumps down in a frenzy to get up the stairs. He's so adorable. Makes me wish I'd had a younger sibling. Or at least a sibling that didn't look at me like they wanted to kill me every second of the day just for existing.

I catch a whiff of the famous cream cheese icing that Mrs. Nelson makes from scratch and it's like heaven. What I wouldn't give to live in a house that smells like baked goods almost twenty-four hours a day. "Those smell really good, Mrs. Nelson."

"Thank you, Elliot. But how many times do I have to tell you to call me Diana. You're part of the family."

"Uh—sorry—just kind of a habit, I guess."

A fun fact about Aimee's mom is that she was actually the Foods teacher at school before Aimee's dad got this huge promotion at work after our freshman year. She decided it would be a good time to follow her dream of opening up her own coffee shop-bakery hybrid in town, and she was supported by her husband every step of the way. They're kind of the perfect example of the kind of relationship I want some day.

There's a stampede coming from the staircase leading from the basement into the kitchen and Aimee and Vanessa pop out from the doorway.

"Well it took you long enough," Aimee huffs.

"Sorry, I got stuck training the new girl. It's a whole thing."

"Alright, well everything's set up downstairs. There's pizza, soda, popcorn, and some Twizzlers because I know you like those."

Diana jumps into the conversation. "And the cupcakes are finished if someone wants to take them down too."

"Awe, Mom. You're the best," Aimee says as she wraps her arm around her mother's waist and leans her head against her shoulder.

I never noticed until now just how much they look alike. They always said that when she was a kid, she looked a lot like her biological father, who left before she was born, but now they're practically carbon copies of each other.

I think part of the reason that Aimee and I clicked as well as we did is that we bonded over both having step-fathers, except that she actually likes her step-father and has been raised by him since she was about two. Not all of us can be so lucky.

Aimee scoops up the plate of cupcakes from the countertop and pushes me and Vanessa out of the kitchen and down the stairs into the basement.

The first time Aimee invited me over to her house back in the eighth grade and dragged me downstairs to the basement, I hadn't really known what to expect. Basements had always creeped me the hell out, and they still do for the most part, so I wasn't about to let her drag me down into one. I've seen way too many paranormal films in my life.

I can smell the garlicy aroma of the pizza the moment I hit the bottom step, which triggers immediate drooling. If there's one thing that's certain, it's that Aimee definitely knows how to put on a grade-A movie night.

Aimee drops the cupcakes down between the two large pizzas and the bowl of chips. "Alright, so what are we in the mood to watch tonight? Something scary?"

"No," I almost blurt out.

She knows that I don't handle scary well, especially not if I don't get to watch a comedy afterward.

"Oh, don't be a wuss puss," she giggles. "How about a rom-com. I know you love those."

"I'm not sure if I'm really in the mood for one of those."

It's becoming clear, now more than ever, that things with Milo probably aren't going anywhere. Even if by some miracle we meet and he decides that he likes me, which honestly isn't even all that likely because—well—I'm just me, who's to say that it would actually even work out? I'm stuck going to Illinois State, and if his parents have any say in the matter, he definitely won't be sticking around the area much longer.

We'd be doomed before we even begin.

"Okay, fine. How about that Gina Rodriguez movie, *Someone Great*? It seems pretty fitting in our current situation."

"Huh?" Vanessa asks, biting into a slice of pepperoni and sausage.

Before I can even make some sort of sarcastic remark about her most recent breakup, which Aimee would either laugh along with or smack me for, she's shoving a piece of paper into my face.

"What's this?"

"Just read it, El!"

My eyes move from the freakishly giddy smile on Aimee's face to the letter now gripped between both my thumbs and index fingers. "Dear Miss Nguyen-Nelson, Congratulations! On behalf of the Fashion Institute of Technology's Admissions

Committee, it is my great pleasure to offer you a place in the Fall 2020 class for the Fashion Design Two-Year AAS program . . ." I trail off and keep reading it over and over again, hoping it's some sort of joke.

It's a little early for an April Fools prank though.

I glance over the top of the page and Aimee's beaming. I don't think I've ever seen her this excited about anything in her entire life. Vanessa slips the letter from my fingertips and reads over it.

"Isn't it exciting?" Aimee asks. Her voice is almost melodic right now.

"Wow — this is . . ." I can't get the words out that I really want to use without sounding like some sort of masochistic asshole. "This is really great, Aimee. I'm so proud of you."

"So, when you get your degree and start your own fashion line, I get to try out your clothes, right? Like wear them out on the street and help with publicity and all that in exchange for free pieces?" Vanessa asks.

I feel bad that I'm not more excited for Aimee, but it's a little difficult when literally my only damn option is Illinois State University. There's no chance in hell I'm ever getting into the film department at NYU. Last time I took my question about the chances of getting through the door to Google, the acceptance rate was like less than 30%.

"Now we can go to New York together! Ooh, and we can go a little bit earlier than what it would be for move-in and stay with my aunt Tess. It's going to be so much fun!" Aimee's got her arms wrapped around my torso and she's jumping up and down. "Why aren't you jumping? You should be jumping."

I grab her by the shoulders and pull her back down to earth.

Don't you cry, Elliot. Don't you dare fucking cry right now.

"I didn't get an acceptance letter." The words fight to come out and are razor sharp as they do. "I'm not going to New York."

"Just because you haven't gotten your letter yet, doesn't mean you're not going to. There's still time. You just have to stay positive!"

"I appreciate the sentiment, Aimee. I really do, but I don't think I'm getting in. There are way better candidates out there than me."

She pulls me in again, this time for a hug. I've always loved her hugs. They're warm and inviting and usually make me feel like everything's going to be okay, but it's just not cutting it this time. I really don't know if everything's going to be okay anymore now that she'll be leaving me.

"If you don't go, then I'm not going," Aimee states firmly.

If I don't light a fire under her ass, then she really won't go, which wouldn't be the absolute worst for me. But I know that if she doesn't go, then she'll resent me one day for being the reason she stayed, and that's what I'm scared of the most. I'd rather lose her for a few semesters than for the rest of my life.

"No. You have to promise me that even if I don't go, then you'll still go." My words are barely audible again.

"I—I don't want..." she stutters.

I wipe my cheeks dry with the palms of my hands. "You have to promise me that you'll go. Even if I don't get to. You've dreamed about this way too long to ruin it all just because of me."

Aimee's lips are pursed are her arms are crossed. Typical.

"You are so stubborn," I laugh as I wipe away more tears. I outstretch my arms for both Aimee and Vanessa. "Bring it in guys. And that's an order." Aimee buries her head in my neck and Vanessa's head is against both of ours. "You worked your ass off for this, and you got it! I'm so proud of you."

"I'm proud of you too," Vanessa says, trying to match Aimee's earlier energy.

"There's a reason they have FaceTime and these new things called airplanes that come in handy for seeing your loved ones that are halfway across the country. Not sure if you've heard of them or not."

It's subtle, but Aimee's muffled laugh escapes from the crevice of my neck. She wipes her face dry with the sleeve of her sweater. "I don't know how I'm gonna get through freshman year without you by my side."

"You're going to do it like the total bad ass you are. If anyone can do it, you can," I say.

"That just means you're gonna have to come visit me in the city," Aimee says. Her eyes dart from me to Vanessa. "And that means the both of you."

"Nothing short of the world ending could keep me away," I say. "I would also just like to announce that you're not allowed to replace me. I will cut a bitch."

"No one could replace you. You're kind of one in a million."

"I'm not really sure how to take that, so I'll just say thank you."

Aimee runs her fingers through her hair and puffs out her chest. She grabs a slice of pizza from the box and shoves a bite into her mouth. "Now both of you grab more pizza, something to drink, and let's get this party started!"

I knew we might be separated a little bit for college. I just didn't think we'd have over a thousand miles between us.

CHAPTER TEN

JUSTIN

Saturday, March 28

There was no getting out of this party. Not even my parents were going to let me miss it, although they made me promise that I wasn't going to drink.

I'm kind of stuck between a rock and a hard place with the whole drinking thing. On one hand, with the way life's been going the last week or two, just getting drunk and forgetting about everything for the entire night sounds pretty fantastic. On the other hand, with the way the last week or two has been going, I don't know if I can promise myself that I won't out myself in front of Danny and the rest of the guys. I'm not exactly known for my subtlety when there's a few drinks in my system. I can count my blessings that I haven't done it yet.

Danny lives out in the middle of nowhere, so it's kind of the perfect place to have a party when you don't want anyone calling the cops on you, which actually happened at a party my buddy Jake threw last Halloween. I dodged the cops by running through the back door and cutting through the Winklers' backyard. They still don't know that I'm the one who broke Mrs. Winkler's garden gnome, and I'll take that to my grave.

I'm one of the first few people to arrive. Danny's in the backyard with Cooper, a few of the other guys from the team, and Tommy Jenkins. That dude's there every time I turn around. I didn't even know that he and Danny were friends. They're two completely different people and just do not mesh well as friends. Danny's always been such a headstrong, kind guy and Tommy's kind of an arrogant dick that only cares about himself. Give it like ten years and he'll probably be that guy with a beer gut, three kids, and stuck in an unhappy marriage wishing he'd left his hometown and explored all that life had to offer.

Danny's throwing more wood onto the fire when he sees me walk through the backdoor. "Aye! You actually made it. I thought you'd come up with some sort of excuse."

That makes two of us.

"Guess I kinda had that one coming," I say.

"Maybe a little." He throws the last piece of wood in his hands onto the fire. "Come in here and help with the keg."

I still don't really understand how Danny talked his older brother into buying us a keg. Back when Taylor was a senior and we were freshman, he was such a little goodie two shoes. Straight-A honor roll, class president, honors society. Hell, he was even prom king. He was the definition of Mr. Perfect. The kind of image I've always tried to live up to. I figured that if I did that, who'd think to care about whether or not I was dating a bunch of girls?

Within an hour and a half, the entire property was bursting at the seams with high school kids that just wanted to let off some end of the year steam. There's even been a few guys here that graduated last year, no doubt looking for a good time and an excuse to remember what it was like before the stress of college and adult life punched them in the gut.

There's a line of like a dozen kids that look no older than fifteen standing around for the keg. I know that since we're not twenty-one, we're not technically supplying alcohol to minors, but it still feels creepy as hell to watch a bunch of fetuses getting drunk off their asses.

Danny's over at the beer pong table in a fight to the death with Tommy, and by the look on Tommy's face and the fact that he can't stand without using Natalie Quinn as a support beam, Danny's grinding his ass into a pulp.

It's the best thing I've seen all week.

"Aye, Jenkins. You sure you don't want to bow out now?" Danny laughs, sinking yet another ball on Tommy's side of the table.

"Wh — no, man! Keep it — keep it going. I can't still win this thing. I mean I can still." Tommy's speech is slurred, and I'm surprised he's been standing for this long. It's oddly satisfying to watch.

"Alright, dude. But it looks like you've only got one glass left and I have four. Your odds aren't looking too great."

Tommy picks up another ping pong ball and drunkenly starts trying to aim at one of Danny's remaining cups.

I'm starting to realize that I barely recognize majority of the people here, and that's saying something because it's not a very big school. Yeah, a lot of them are people I've seen around the halls or had in class, though I'm pretty sure the other half are from schools in the surrounding area, but it just goes to show how much hiding part of who I am has put a serious strain on my social life.

It's nights like tonight that I just wish I was like everybody else. No secrets to hide and in control of my own future. A part of me wonders if I never should've sent that message to Cinder. At least before I opened up to him, it was just my own dirty little secret and mine alone. Before I opened up to him, I didn't catch myself wondering if every face I pass in the hall or every car I see in the parking lot belongs to him.

I'd give anything to hear his voice. Just once. Pandora's Box has been opened and I can't get the lid back on.

Tommy's still wobbling in place and trying to aim at one of Danny's spare cups. He finally decides to go for it and misses by a long shot. It's not very clear where he was aiming, but it definitely wasn't one of the cups.

"Ooh, too bad!" Danny shouts over the sound of Doja Cat blasting from the bluetooth speaker. He grabs his last ping pong ball, and almost without even trying, he takes aim, shoots, and scores. His fists are in the air and he's making some sort of obnoxious animalistic sound. "I. Am. The. Champion! What sucker wants to go up against me next?"

"I'll take that challenge," some rando guy and his goons say.

Some guy is standing in front of the fire pit with a couple of his buddies as backup.

"Well if it isn't Cameron Davis. I don't remember inviting you," Danny says. His jawline is tensing up and there's a fire in his eyes I've never seen before.

It's actually kind of hot.

"I'm gonna need you to leave," Danny says, still fired up. "And you can either go voluntarily or I can force you to go. I would be totally fine with either—though I think I'd almost prefer the latter."

"Ah, come on," Cameron says. "Just one game, and then we'll go."

Danny lets out a forced laugh. "What's the matter? Is us destroying you in a few weeks not gonna be enough for you? Or do you just like embarrassing the hell out of yourself?"

There's a manicured hand on my shoulder and a whisper in my ear. "How's it going, sexy?"

"Hey, Gabbi." I can't take my eyes off what's going on between Danny and Cameron.

"What's going on?" she asks.

"Just a bunch of middle school drama bubbling to the surface again."

"I'm not gonna ask you again," Danny says. His fists are trembling at his sides and I don't think I've ever seen him this pissed. "Leave or be forced out."

Cameron steps closer and the lights from the side of the house illuminate his light bluish-grey eyes. His dirty blonde curls are purposely disheveled on the top of his head, and he's got this grin painted on his face that would be kind of sexy if it didn't have a touch of evil to it.

"Why don't you make me leave, pretty boy."

Oh crap.

No, "crap" doesn't even describe it.

Oh *shit*.

Yeah, that seems like the right word, as in *holy shit, this guy just stuck his foot in his mouth.*

As far as I know, Danny's only been in one fight his entire life, but that was more than enough for me to realize that he can be pretty brutal when someone's made him angry enough. Not that Danny has anger issues that would ever warrant like anger management or something, but he's got a pretty short fuse. His parents enrolled him in taekwondo when he was a kid so he'd have something to channel the energy into, but all it really did was give him the skills to beat the shit out of someone if he needed to, which is pretty rare.

"Hey, Danny. Maybe—" I start to say.

"Stay out of it, Justin." His voice is cold and flat. "You need to leave, Davis."

"I thought you said you wouldn't ask again," he laughs.

Before anyone even knows what's happening, Danny swings his fist into Davis' face, and now there's blood spewing from his nose. A lot of it. My body stiffens from the sound of Danny's knuckles hitting his face again.

A few of the girls from the squad are backing up and look like they're about vomit. This is exactly what I was afraid of. All I see is Davis charge headfirst into Danny and they both fall to the ground punching and screaming.

"Yo! Cam, get off him. You've made your point!" One of the guys with Davis yells as he's sinking his fists into Danny's face.

If no one else is going to do anything, I guess I know what I have to do.

For a moment, I struggle to open my eyes or find the will to move. A twinge of pain scatters from the bottom of my jaw and up the left side of my face and radiates against my cheekbone. My vision is out of focus and I can barely make out a figure standing over me. They press something up against my eyebrow. It's cold at first, but it's quickly replaced by a stinging sensation that sends a yelp echoing through the room.

"Oh, I'm so sorry," Gabbi says. "I should've warned you it might sting a little bit."

I push myself up and lean my back up against the headboard of Danny's bed. "What happened?"

"Well, long story short, you tried to stop the fight and then you got an elbow to the face and went out cold. It was kind of scary, actually."

"One hit, and I was out like that? That's so embarrassing."

She winces and tries to cover it with a grin. "But on the bright side, Davis was so scared after he knocked you out that he ran away. So, in a way you sort of did stop the fight."

"That's me, Lakeview's own hometown hero. Maybe I should get a secret identity."

If only she knew how ironic that statement is.

She puts a bandage over my brow and looks into my eyes. "Well, you're *my* hero."

Gabbi may be kind of bitchy sometimes, but she can be cool when it really counts. Her fingers trace over the side of my face where Davis' elbow made the impact. I resist the urge to wince as they trail down to the palm of my hand.

"Well thank you. At least someone thinks so," I say.

The feel of her fingers brushing against my skin sends a chill through my body and suddenly it's difficult to breathe. Her eyes dart from our intertwined fingers up to mine. The corner of her mouth is twitching, and her hand finds its way to the back of my head.

"Gabbi, I—"

She leans in closer and her breathe is warm against my face.

There's a huge part of me that wants to tell her to stop. I know that I'm not exactly with Cinder—hell, I don't even know anything other than his secret identity and the fact that his family sucks ass—but it almost feels like I'm cheating or something.

But there's another part of me, however small that part may be, that wants this to happen. A small part of me just wants to get this moment in my life over with already. Maybe this is what I need to just be like everyone else.

Her hands reach up and cup my face, sending my heart racing like a jackhammer. For what feels like an hour, she just sits there staring at me, and suddenly I'm aware of how intense her brown eyes are. She lingers another moment and starts leaning in again.

"This okay?" Gabbi whispers into my ear.

What the hell am I supposed to say? No? Then they'll definitely know something's up. "Yeah," I mumble breathlessly, fully aware of where this could wind up going.

Gabbi props herself up and wraps her legs around my waist. She's staring down at me and her fingers lace around the back of my neck before she leans down again and kisses me. First, it's soft, and then she starts getting a little more into it. Her lips are smooth and taste a little like peppermint from her lip balm. Her hands travel up and gently grasp the hair on the back of my head. My hands are on her waist and I hold on for dear life.

My heart's beating mercilessly inside my chest, and she can no doubt feel it against her own chest as she sinks further into me and pushes me back onto the pillow. A subtle grunt escapes from between my lips as my head crashes into the bed, which she apparently takes as something sexual instead of just general discomfort because she moves her lips from mine down to the edge of my jaw, finally finding a resting spot at my neck.

Maybe it's easiest this way. Maybe this is the way it's supposed to be. Everyone expects us to be together anyway, so wouldn't it just be easier to just get it over with? But what if this isn't the way it's supposed to be? What if I'm making the biggest mistake of my life by leading her on and making her think that I'm even in the right state of mind to start anything with anyone at all?

The truth of the matter is that I'm not even sure I know who I am anymore.

"Gabbi," I mutter under by breath.

Her hands slip under my shirt and slide up my torso and her fingers lightly brush up against my chest.

"I c—" I'm out of breath and I'm not sure how much longer I can go before we've reached the point of no return. "I can't, Gabbi."

She sits up again and looks into my eyes. There's this longing on her face that's getting difficult to resist. "You can't what?"

"This. I can't do this right now."

"You can't, or you won't?"

"No, I want to—I really do—but there's just so much going on, and we've both been drinking and I just—"

She peels herself off the bed and pulls her hair back. "Don't even worry about it." She readjusts her shirt before walking back out into the hall and slamming the door behind her.

That went about as well as expected.

The ceiling fan is almost hypnotic right about now. I'm watching it spin around and around, and after everything that went down with Gabbi earlier, there's really only one person on my mind.

To: cinderfella0204@gmail.com
From: milojuni1221@gmail.com
Subject: Why am I still awake?

Dear Cinderfella,

I don't even know why I'm messaging you right now. It's like 3 in the morning, so the odds of you even being awake right now are pretty shitty. I guess I just kind of wanted someone to talk to.

I'll be honest though. I was at a party tonight, so I might be just a tad tipsy right now. I personally wouldn't want to talk to me right now.

— Milo

Apparently I'm not the only insomniac around tonight.

To: milojuni1221@gmail.com
From: cinderfella0204@gmail.com
Subject: Re: Why am I still awake?
Dear Milo,

Actually, I am awake. I don't really sleep a whole lot these days. So, I'm just here in bed staring at the ceiling, kind of wishing I had someone to snuggle.

I think I heard a few people talking about a party in the hallway the other day. I imagine it's probably the same one.

Other than being a little tipsy, what are you up to?

— Cinderfella

To: cinderfella0204@gmail.com
From: milojuni1221@gmail.com
Subject: Re: Why am I still awake?
Dear Cinderfella,

It would be really amazing to be able to snuggle with someone right now. That's been the mood for a while now actually. Everything's just been so messed up lately and it's got me feeling kinda lonely. Is it weird that I occasionally find myself just trying to put a face to the name, or rather the lack of a name, on nights like this? Not that I'm implying that I do anything with that imagery, but I guess I'm also not, not saying that too . . .

Moving on now, because I feel like I'm totally pushing the limits of what we've got going here.

And yeah, it's probably the same party you heard about, but trust me when I say you didn't really miss a whole lot. I'm kind of over the whole party scene these days.

Do you mind if I ask you like a really personal question? You don't have to answer it if you don't want to though. I don't want to like make you feel uncomfortable or anything.

— Milo

To: milojuni1221@gmail.com
From: cinderfella0204@gmail.com
Subject: Re: Why am I still awake?
Milo,

It's good to know about the party. I might've stayed up all night worrying that I was missing something important. Thanks so much for clearing that up for me and making me feel validated for not being invited lol.

And I don't think you're pushing the limits with anything. I'll be honest and say that I've had similar thoughts lately, and I'm kind of enjoying the fact that you're having those thoughts too.

— Cinderfella

To: cinderfella0204@gmail.com
From: milojuni1221@gmail.com
Subject: Re: Why am I still awake?
Cinderfella,
Ooh, we got a feisty one, don't we?

I also enjoy that you've been having those thoughts too. It makes me feel like I'm not so alone around here after all. I just wish that there was something I could do about it.

I do have a legit question to ask, and it's kind of personal, so you are not at all inclined to answer. Have you ever like been with anyone before? Like either gender?

— *Milo*

To: milojuni1221@gmail.com
From: cinderfella0204@gmail.com
Subject: Re: Why am I still awake?
Milo,

I'm just going to assume that when you say "been with", you're not asking if I've ever dated someone. Am I right?

If you do just mean dating, then I guess so? I've had "girlfriends" if you want to call it that, but really it was more of a situation where someone told me they liked me and I asked them out because I thought that, that was what I was supposed to do. It always ended super quick though because I think a part of me always knew that I was gay.

If you're talking about what I think you're talking about then the answer is most definitely no. We've already established that my "relationships" with girls never lasted that long. They never even lasted to the kissing stage. As far as guys go, you're actually the closest I've ever come to being with one. It's sad, right?

What about you? Have you ever been with anyone before? Sexually or in any other way?

— *Cinderfella*

To: cinderfella0204@gmail.com
From: milojuni1221@gmail.com

Subject: Re: Why am I still awake?

I won't lie. I've dated girls, and we've kissed, but I've never gone anywhere passed that with a girl. Another guy either. I will say though that I have kissed a guy before.

— Milo

To: milojuni1221@gmail.com
From: cinderfella0204@gmail.com
Subject: Re: Why am I still awake?

Excuse me . . . you can't just skate passed that statement like that like you never said it. I'm gonna need details.

Was the guy cute? Where did you meet him? Was it enjoyable? How old were you?

— Cinderfella

To: cinderfella0204@gmail.com
From: milojuni1221@gmail.com
Subject: Re: Why am I still awake?

I guess I kinda had that one coming lol.

It was the summer before freshman year. I was at summer camp and my cabin mate was really cute. Of course, I didn't really understand it at the time. One night we were up super late playing video games and we started fighting over something really stupid — I'm not really sure what — and then before I knew it he had pinned me on the floor with my arms above my head. And then he kissed me.

We both didn't talk for the rest of the night and then the next day camp was over, and I never spoke to him again. I know it totally sounds like something out of a cheesy coming of age gay movie, but that's legit how it happened. I've been pretty confused about my sexuality ever since.

Anyway, it's super late, so I should probably get to sleep.

I'll talk to you later.
— Milo

CHAPTER ELEVEN

Elliot

Does the world just have some sort of grudge against me these days?

First, I don't even get a letter from my dream school telling me whether I've been accepted or rejected, then I find out that my best friend in the entire world is going halfway across the country to start a new life without me, and then my day just started out like complete garbage with *another* locker jam. I guess I didn't realize last Friday that I shut the sleeve of the sweater I keep in the door. I was already running behind thanks to a tiny little mishap with the blender this morning, so my locker was just icing on top of the damn cake.

It took ten minutes to get a maintenance worker to come open my locker, which means that now I'm late for English, and showing up to class late gives me anxiety.

I'm standing outside the door of room 146, and the opening scene of the movie, where Emma Stone's character is interviewing Viola Davis' character about her life as a maid. Exactly what I needed. Now everyone's going to be staring at me.

I hate all the attention being on me. Always have and always will.

I take in a deep breath and prepare for all the staring as I grasp the door handle and pull the door open. As expected, all eyes shift toward me as I trail along the edge of the room to Miss Wilson's desk in the back corner. "Sorry I'm late," I whisper, handing her my excused tardy slip from the office. "I was having a locker issue."

She smiles and takes the late slip from my hand. "Thanks for letting me know. The movie's just starting, so find a seat anywhere."

I face the front of the room again and scan all of the desks, finally finding an available seat in the back corner at the other side of the room. Jen Baker decides to stretch just as I'm passing by behind her and whacks me right in the stomach.

"Oh shit. Sorry about that," she says.

"You're good," I say as I continue pushing past.

That's definitely gonna leave a bruise.

I avoid any further contact with anyone at all as I slide into the last available seat and try to disappear into the darkness.

"Looks like your trip over here was a real *hit*," someone says.

I crane my neck around and there's Cooper leaning back in his desk and eyeing me with a huge grin.

"You think you're so funny, don't you?"

"Maybe a little bit," he laughs. "You're late. That's not like you."

So, he notices when I get here? Interesting.

"Um, yeah, I had some locker trouble."

"Oof, that's always rough. The maintenance guys always take forever to come fix it too."

"That's what I'm saying."

Cooper grins again and turns his attention back to the movie playing on the overhead.

Ugh, he's so cute I almost can't stand it. That smile and those eyes just send me into a frenzy. I almost feel like I'm in one of those scenes from *Jane the Virgin* where you can just see her heart glowing every time Rafael or Michael do something incredibly cute, which I know is totally cheesy, but I guess I'm a bit of a sucker for romance.

Watching it on the screen or seeing it unfold within the pages of a book are just about the only ways I even feel comfortable with romance or love. It would be nice to have, but when it comes down to it, I think I'm just as scared of it as everyone else.

Aimee made me watch that Netflix movie *To All The Boys I Loved Before* with her when it came out a couple of years ago (she's not usually one for ridiculously sappy content like I am, but I think she was excited to finally get a film starring a Vietnamese actress with two first names like her), and Lara Jean said it best during her explanation as to why love and dating scare her so much. She said, "the more people you let into your life, the more they can just walk right out". It hit a nerve and I haven't been able to shake those words since.

Cooper's eyeing me again. "So, did you have a good weekend?"

"Yeah, I guess so. I had to work most of it, so it was pretty uneventful. How about you?"

"Mine was decent. Wound up going to a party, but after a fight broke out, it kinda just died."

So, he was at the same party that Milo was at. Not that I'm discrediting the fact that they really could be two different people. Things just seem to be adding up too well to only be a coincidence.

"Oh, that sucks. I hope everyone was alright."

"I think so. Although things didn't look too good for my buddy Justin. He kinda got knocked out with an elbow to the head."

"Maybe it's a good thing I don't get invited to these parties then. Not really a fan of blood."

"You're probably right then," he says. "But you totally need to come to one before graduation. You should experience at least one party before college."

Me? At a party? Does he know who he's talking to? I wouldn't be invited to one of the famous LHS parties if I was the last person on earth. I'm like a whole other species compared to some of the people here.

"I don't know. I'd probably never even be able to get through the door."

Cooper's smiling again. "You could if you were my guest. Just think about it."

"Uh, yeah. I'll think about it."

Halfway through the movie, Miss Wilson wound up busting our asses for talking, which the both of us found funny for some weird reason. I guess that's what happens when the senioritis has finally started taking over.

Cooper wasn't kidding when he said that Justin Herrera took an elbow to the face. He came to theatre wearing a bandage over his eyebrow and his eye was a violent purple. Just looking at it made my stomach queasy. I avoided that side of the room the entire period.

It's 3:42 pm when I pull up outside Vanessa's house to work on our theatre project, and it's honestly really nice seeing a house that doesn't look like every other one in town. Not to be bashing on Aimee's house or anything because it really is beautiful, but sometimes beautiful is just kind of boring.

I pull out my phone and let the rest of "High" by Sir Sly blast through the speakers of my car while I read through the email that Milo sent me this morning.

He apologized for not messaging me back yesterday and said that after church his parents wound up making plans for them all to go spend the day with his grandma, so he didn't really get a whole lot of time to talk.

I was in a bit of a mushy mood yesterday after work, which resulted in me watching all of the 2000s romantic comedies I could find on Netflix. It made me realize that we've never talked about our favorite types of movies before. He said that he was never really all that into romantic movies, but that he'd be willing to watch them with me if I ever wanted to.

I don't know if it's just the fact that I think Milo and Cooper could be the same person, but there's part of me that's sort of wanting to just come out and say who I really am. He *has* been really friendly lately, so maybe if I could somehow get it out of him that he's really Milo, we can laugh about it together and build something real.

To: milojuni1221@gmail.com
From: cinderfella0204@gmail.com
Subject: Re: hopeless romantic
Dear Milo,

I understand family stuff so there's no need to apologize for that. At least one of us has that kind of system lol.

Okay, that was kind of dark. Sorry.

It means a lot that you'd watch a gushy movie with me. I'd never force you to though. Of course, that would involve us finally meeting, which I know is something that's completely terrifying to think about. I get those nervous butterflies just thinking about it. Don't you think we've been doing the anonymous thing for far too long, though? Wouldn't it just be easier at this point if we finally revealed our true identities and stopped hiding from who we truly are?

   — Cinderfella

The last note of the song plays, and I slip the key out of the ignition.

Me: Hey, just pulled up

I've never been totally sure about what the correct etiquette is for arriving at someone's house for the first time. Are you supposed to send them a text to let them know, or is just knocking good enough?

Vanessa: Awesome, I'll be there in a sec.

I grab my bag out of the passenger seat and make my way up the sidewalk and to the front door, where Vanessa is already waiting for me.

"Have any trouble finding the place?" she asks.

"Nope. I've lived in town most of my life, so I pretty much know every part like the back of my hand."

Her eyes meet mine. She doesn't even need to say anything. I never feel fortunate to have grown up in a single town around familiar people until it hits me that a lot of others don't get that experience.

"Come on in and make yourself at home." Vanessa ushers me off the enclosed front porch and through the front door into the living room.

The scent of fresh baked chocolate chip cookies is the first thing I notice when I walk in. The whole place just wraps you up in a warm hug. It's nothing immaculate, but that's what's so great about it.

"I know it's definitely not Aimee's house," Vanessa starts.

"It's perfect," I say. "I really like it."

She smiles faintly and starts moving again.

I know that smile. I had that smile several times before when it was just me and Mom. It comes with the feeling that you don't have as nice of things as everyone else around you. It's embarrassing to see someone else's gorgeous and expensive home and then realize exactly what you don't have. It almost makes you feel like maybe you're not enough, and it's a pretty terrible feeling.

Vanessa leads me into the dining room, where she has a little workstation set up for us, complete with her laptop, a few notebooks for scratch paper, and a couple bottles of water. A woman, probably early 40s, comes in toting a big plate of chocolate chip cookies and sets them down on the table.

"Mom, this is Elliot. Elliot, this is my mom."

"Mrs. Berk, it's so nice to meet you," I say.

"Please, call me Lauren," she replies with a smile. "It's so nice to meet you, Elliot. Vanessa has told me so much about you. And I would just like to thank you for being so kind on her first day at a new school. With us moving around so much, I know it's been hard for her to make new friends."

"Okay, Mom. Thank you. I think we're all good here."

"Fine. I can take a hint. I have to run to the grocery store, and I'll be back in a little while, but let me know if you need me to pick anything up while I'm out."

"Okay, Mom. Will do. Bye!"

She looks at me one more time before leaving. "It was really great to meet you, Elliot."

"You too, Mrs. B—I mean—Lauren." Vanessa and I situate ourselves and I pull my laptop from my bag and set it up on the table.

"Alright, so the assignment sheet says that we have to create a play that will spark some sort of important conversation on a social issue. Do you have any ideas?" Vanessa asks before taking a bite into one of the cookies.

"I've been rattling my brain all weekend trying to think of something and my idea sheet is totally blank. What about you?"

"Okay, so I know it's probably a little morbid, but I kind of feel like maybe we should do something focusing on teen suicide. At my old school, we lost one of our seniors because of it and the entire situation was just kind of a mess. No one expected it. He was one of the most popular guys in school."

"Actually, that's not a bad idea," I say. "I mean, it does suck to even have to think about that kind of thing, but it really is an issue that not enough people put a lot of thought into."

My phone vibrates against the table. Aimee's out prom dress shopping with her mom before she has to meet up with Justin Herrera to work on their project. She says that as her GBF, I'm obligated to give her my brutally honest opinion on dresses. There's about a million things wrong with that ideal, but I can't get mad at the irony of it all.

She sent a snap from the dressing room wearing a skintight black sequined dress with a revealing V-neck and a slit up the thigh. The picture's captioned with the words *Does this dress scream "slut"?*

I laugh and tilt my screen into Vanessa's view, whose reaction definitely isn't what I expected. I guess I half expected a chuckle or something, but all I got from her was a partially dropped jaw and eyes about to pop out of her head.

"You okay over there?" I ask.

She's quiet for another moment before finally making eye contact with me instead of the photo. "What? Yeah, I'm great. Why do you ask?"

"You look like you just saw a—you know what—it's not important. Should we start working?"

That's another face that I know all too well, and I won't be the person that pries the answer out of her.

She's staring at the table top as I slip a pencil out of my bag and lay down a fresh sheet of paper to start taking some notes for the assignment.

"So, do you think this should be like a one-act play sort of thing where it's just one thing after another? Or do we want to have a couple different settings and scenes?"

"Uh . . . I think if we were to do like a few different scenes we'd be able to possibly tell a little bit more to the story and the events leading up to it." She's still staring down and avoiding eye contact.

"Okay. Yeah, that sounds good" I reply.

"Elliot." Her dark brown eyes are looking up at me again and she's picking at her nails. "Can I tell you something and it stay just between us?"

I set my pencil down. "Of course. You can tell me anything."

"I don't even know why I'm making a big deal out of this. My entire family knows and pretty much everyone back in San Diego knew. It's just different here. Being in a small town is something new for me." She relaxes her shoulders and places her hands flat on the table. "I'm gay."

"Okay, that's cool," I say. "No biggie."

"And it's not that I'm ashamed of it or anything, because I'm not. I've actually found a sense of empowerment and pride myself on being a strong, black lesbian woman. It's just this town where everyone knows everyone and their business is just—you know—it's a lot."

"Vanessa, you don't have to explain anything to me. I get it and your secret is safe with me. I really admire your confidence with it though. I remember when I told Aimee I was gay I couldn't stop—"

"Wait, you're gay?"

"Yeah, did you really not know that?"

Her eyes wander blankly around the room. "Honestly no. I mean, I knew that Aimee was bi just from conversations, but you being gay has never come up. How did I seriously not know?"

"Wow, and here I thought I was obviously gay." I laugh and use my arm as a support beam for my head. "You like Aimee, don't you?"

It's not noticeable, but there's a really good chance that she's actually blushing right now. "What? Don't be ridiculous."

"Girl, I saw the way your eyes were popping out of your head when I showed you that Snapchat. It was like watching an episode of *Looney Tunes*."

Vanessa rolls her eyes. "Okay . . . fine. Maybe she is kind of attractive."

"Kind of?"

A stifled laugh escapes from her mouth. "You know what I'm saying. Don't be so weird about it. Besides, it doesn't even matter. It's not that I stand a chance anyway."

"Where the hell did you get *that* idea?"

"She's amazing and beautiful and sexy and sweet and I— I'm not. She'd never be interested in a girl like me. I mean, just look at me," she says as she runs her hands across her body.

I outstretch my arms and grab her by the shoulders. "And you are all of those things too, Vanessa. You don't have to be a size two to be confident in your own beauty. It's taken me a long time to understand that. She hasn't said anything to me but trust me when I say that she's definitely got a thing for you."

Vanessa throws her arms around me. "Thank you," she whispers into my ear before pulling away. "I still can't believe I didn't know you were gay."

"Well then hopefully that means I'm doing a decent job of trying to hide it," I laugh.

"Does anyone know? Besides Aimee, I mean."

"Yeah, you know now too."

Her eyebrow twitches a little. "Seriously? That's it? Not even your family knows?"

"You haven't been around my family before, have you? They're not exactly the most accepting bunch of people. Not to say that they'd necessarily have a problem with the gay thing itself, but they're not really the biggest fans of me as a whole."

"Well, those bitches don't know what they're missing." She grasps my hands in hers and looks into my eyes again. "From this moment on you have a new family. Right here."

I swear it's this girl's goal to make me cry right now.

"Okay, that's enough mushy stuff for one day. We need to get some more work done."

CHAPTER TWELVE

JUSTIN

Monday, March 30

"Dude, what the actual hell? I had him! I totally had him!"

I've never understood Danny's obsession with Overwatch. To be honest, I've never actually understood the game at all. Like, is it played in teams or is it a single player thing? And is each character supposed to have their own special abilities? Not that I'll ever say anything to him about it. I've watched him play this long, and I'm sure he already thinks I'm enough of a spaz as it is.

"You're gonna wind up giving yourself a stroke over this game," I laugh.

"Well, if it kills me, then at least I went out doing something I love."

"You are a sad, strange man."

He rolls his eyes and looks back at the game. "Come on, dude. You can't tell me you wouldn't want to die doing something you love."

I never really thought of it that way. If I could die someday doing what I love, preferably from old age and not some weird disease or something, I think I'd be okay with that.

I can't help but wonder what Cinder would want to do during his last days on Earth.

My phone rumbles against my thigh. I slide it from the pocket of my sweatpants and a smile tugs at my lips. As my eyes peer over the illuminated screen at Danny, my fingers start moving.

To: cinderfella0204@gmail.com
From: milojuni1221@gmail.com
Subject: Re: hopeless romantic

Dear Cinderfella,

We can all go to a kind of dark place from time to time, so no need to apologize for that. You're good and I don't scare very easily. I can't really say that I know what it's like to not have a support system, so I'm really sorry that your family isn't supportive of you. I certainly hope that you at least have some sort of support system set up.

As for the meeting thing, you're definitely right when you say that it's completely terrifying to think about. I hope that this doesn't make you think any differently of me, or affect this thing that we've been building, but I just don't think I'm ready for that. Not yet anyway. I know it probably sounds kinda selfish, but I really like what we have going and I'm not ready to give that up. Once we meet, everything's going to change and neither one of us can promise that it'll be for the better. I just need something in my life to stay the same right now with everything that's coming up for all of us.

I really hope that you don't totally hate me right now. I really do enjoy our conversations, and I don't know what I'd do if I didn't have you to talk to.

— Milo

My thumb hovers over the send button for a solid thirty seconds before I finally get the nerve to tap it and send the message off into the void.

I know he only means well when he says that he wants to meet, and there's a part of me that finally wants to know the face behind the messages. I just can't do it, and I pray that he doesn't one day decide to stop talking to me because of it.

"You pumped about tomorrow?" Danny asks as he starts searching through the Netflix catalog.

"What?"

"For our game against BHS. Are you as pumped as I am to totally destroy them?"

I toss my phone down beside me. "Oh . . . I'm totally stoked."

"Stoked, huh?"

"Yeah," I mumble. "It'll be pretty great."

The sarcasm intertwined within the already brass tone of his voice makes it obvious just how little he believes anything I'm saying. Hell, I don't even believe it.

It's difficult to focus so heavily on the rest of the season, a season that I didn't even want to play I might add, when there are so many other things that I can—and should—be focusing on.

"Yeah," Danny echoes. He sets down his controller and strolls into the hall, returning moments later before tossing a large white envelope into my lap.

"What's this?"

"Just got it in the mail this morning. I got accepted into the Architectural program at U of I."

The thing about Danny is that even though he's feeling the pressure from his family about college, he's actually excited for it. His dad owns a huge architecture firm that he runs with his brother. Danny's been looking forward to joining them after college for as long as I can remember. I envy him for that, but I'm happy that he's found something that makes him happy about the future.

"Oh, man. That's really awesome. I knew you could do it."

"Thanks, man." He's leaning against his dresser now and staring out at the road through his window. "I'm just looking forward to getting out there and experiencing the real world, you know?"

If you count living in an expensive apartment that's being paid for by your parents as living in and experiencing the real world, then sure. Danny has always been like family to me, but he'll never understand what it's like to struggle. He'll never truly understand what it's like to have to go out and create opportunities for yourself.

"Yeah," I say. "I know what you mean."

Even if I'm forced to head off to Stanford in the fall, at least I know that I'll be away from here and have some freedom to figure everything out before I have to come back here and start a family.

"Have you heard anything from any of the places you've applied?" Danny asks.

"Actually yeah . . . I got my acceptance from Stanford a few days ago."

And to my dream program at NYU.

"What?" His brows arch and he catches my eye. "You got accepted into Stanford of all places, and you're just now telling me about it?"

"I guess it just kind of slipped my mind." I shrug my shoulders and sink further into the couch cushions.

Danny steps over my legs and slumps down onto the couch next to me. He's got that look. The one where I know good and well that he's thinking deep about something and trying to put puzzles pieces together. It's actually kind of charming in a way when he gets like that. On the surface, he really does just seem like another hot shot high school jock that doesn't really care about anything other than winning the next game. Deep down though, he's a natural-born analytic. He's got this way of knowing when something seems even subtly off, and I've been lucky enough over the years to be able to see that side of him. Not a lot of people usually get that chance.

He cocks his head. "Anything you want to talk about?"

"Nope," I mutter.

"I've known you long enough to know when something's up. You've been distant and just really quiet. What's going on?"

Where the hell do I even start? That I've been questioning my sexuality since I was twelve? That I can never come out because of my family's expectations and religious viewpoints? That I don't want to even finish off the baseball season because I actually really hate it? That the idea of having to spend my life with a medical degree instead of pursuing Studio Art in New York slowly kills me a little bit each day? That I don't even know who I am?

I don't know how to say any of this without sounding like some whiny little brat.

The worst part is that I don't even know how he'd react to me telling him that I'm into dudes. I can't afford to lose his friendship at a time like this. If I don't have him, then I don't have anyone.

"Dude, I'm telling you everything is fine. It's just the end of senior year and everything that's coming up. It's stressful. And it doesn't help that I got a black eye because you couldn't control your temper with Cameron."

"Yeah, I'm really sorry about that. I should've just left it alone."

"It's fine, man," I say.

"Are you sure that's all it is?"

"Yeah, that's it. Just give me a few weeks and everything will be back to normal." I dig my phone from between the couch cushions and check the time before slipping it back into my pocket. "I have to go meet with my partner for this project I'm working on, but I'll see you tomorrow."

CHAPTER THIRTEEN

ELLIOT

"You cannot seriously think that *Lover* is better than *Reputation*," Aimee shouts over the music blasting from my speakers.

My hands loosen their grip on the steering wheel as I get back over into the right lane. "I never said it was better. All I mean is that it just feels like a much more mature album overall. It's not as angsty."

"But the angst is the best part!" She twists her body around and looks back at Vanessa. "You're gonna have to be the deciding vote here, V. Which one is better?"

"Uh, I'm actually not a big Taylor fan," she says.

I can feel the bruised ego from here.

"Y—you what?"

"Yeah, I just never really got into her music. I'm sorry to disappoint," Vanessa says.

"I can't even believe this right now. You've hurt me, Vanessa. You've really hurt me."

Vanessa laughs and pats the back side of Aimee's hand. "You're such a drama queen."

"I second that," I say.

Aimee twirls back around in her seat and faces the highway coming at us at 67 miles an hour. She rolls her eyes and lets out a small huff. "Mm . . . you're not exactly wrong about that one, but you know you love me anyway."

Vanessa reaches between the two of us and snatches my phone from the middle console and starts shuffling through my Spotify playlist. My cheeks feel hot as she goes through my less than desirable song choices.

"Do you seriously not have any Weeknd on here?"

"I'm sure I do in there somewhere"

"I'm just gonna plug the aux into my phone instead so we can really get this party started. You guys don't mind, do you?"

"Be my guest." Bloomington comes into view and my foot instinctively taps the brake pedal. "Just please no country."

"You do realize that I lived in Texas for a lot of my life, right? They practically breathe country music down there. So just for that, I'm gonna play country for the rest of the drive."

"You're killing me!"

"Do it," Aimee says.

"Hey! I thought you were on my side here!"

"I'm Switzerland," Aimee replies with a half-toothed grin. "But maybe I would've fought a little bit harder if it weren't for you agreeing with her on the drama queen thing. So you really only have yourself to blame here."

Some weird ass banjo-driven tune starts blasting from the speakers of my car. Definitely should've seen that one coming.

Once I merged onto Veteran's Parkway, Vanessa decided to take pity on me and threw on some old school Gaga instead, which I can most definitely deal with. By the time we finally pulled up in front of Eastland Mall, we'd already jammed out to "Just Dance", "Poker Face", "Paparazzi", "Born This Way", and "Bad Romance" thanks to my apparent talent for getting stopped at literally every red light in town.

Being stuck in five o'clock traffic is still better than being trapped at home with Hailey, where I would have ultimately been forced into being her only audience while she rehearses for the spring musical in a couple weeks.

"I have to hit up Ulta first since we're right here," Aimee says, slipping off her seatbelt.

"Ooh, yes! I need to pick up a new blending sponge anyway, so that's perfect!" Vanessa shouts from the back.

"Oh, come on," I reply.

Aimee pushes the passenger side door open and steps out. "Don't give me that. I go with you all the time to shop for stuff. I just have to grab some more eyeliner and then we can go."

"Fine."

Vanessa and I hop out of the car and trail behind Aimee's unbelievably fast, yet short, legs into the front entrance of Ulta Beauty, probably one of my least favorite places in the world. I'm not saying that I'm embarrassed to be in there or anything, because I've gotten used to being dragged along to all of the makeup places by now. I just know that when Aimee says she's going to be like five minutes, she usually means five minutes plus about thirty more on top of it.

I'm so spaced out as I follow behind the girls that I don't even realize that Aimee's completely disappeared and I'm practically walking on the back of Vanessa's heels.

"Watch it, buddy!"

"Sorry. Where'd Aimee go?"

"I think she went down the eyeliner rabbit hole. Now help me look for a blender sponge."

"Uh . . . they kind of all look the same," I say, eyeing the products lining the shelves.

Vanessa's eyes roll and she bends down to deliberate between a few sponges. "You may be gay, but you're definitely a guy."

"Thank you? I think?" Seriously though, what does that even mean? "So, are you gonna ask Aimee out or what?"

"Geesh, you want to say that little louder? I'm not sure she heard you at the other side of the store."

"Oh — sorry — but for real, are you going to ask her out or what?" I ask.

Vanessa grabs a package off the rack and stands up again. "I don't know. I mean, I like her — like a lot — but I don't want to wind up making anything awkward or ruining the friendship, you know? Plus, she got accepted to the Fashion Institute and I'm just not sure if I really believe in long distance stuff."

Can't say I really thought about that. It would make any relationship difficult, not to mention a new and budding relationship. I can't blame her for being reluctant about it.

"But that doesn't mean something couldn't still work out between the two of you."

"I don't know," she says.

"You know . . . I don't think she has a date for prom yet. So that's always a possibility."

Her eyes light up and her teeth sink into her lower lip. "You think she'd actually say yes?"

"How is it that I understand girls better than you do?" I laugh. "Let's go find Aimee so we can get out of here and I can get some caffeine pumping through my veins. I fully intend to enjoy every bit of this day that I can."

Vanessa wraps her arm around my waist and we step together out of the aisle and venture to the other side of the store, where Aimee is standing with an entire collection of makeup in her arms.

"Okay, so I know that I said I just needed to get some eyeliner, but then I remembered that my eyeshadow palette is on its last leg, so I found this super cute palette that's gonna go great with my prom dress. But then I realized that I don't really have any lip colors that go all that well with the dress, so I had to get a new one of those."

"So then are we done here?" I ask.

"Well, I can't have matching eye makeup and lipstick and then not have my nails match the whole ensemble too." Aimee's eyes dart from me to Vanessa. "If I have to go alone, then I might as well look great doing it."

She did *not* just do that.

"Oh boy." It slips out before my brain can even filter it.

"I totally get where you're coming from," Vanessa says. "You only get one senior prom, so why not go all out for it, right? I know this is the last place you want to be right now, Elliot, so I'll help Aimee pick out a shade to match and you can go get yourself some coffee."

"Are you sure?"

"Yes, please go get some coffee," Aimee says. "Sleepy Elliot stresses me the hell out. We'll join you in a few."

The girls turn their backs to me and start foraging the shelves again, completely ignoring the fact that I'm still here.

I've been sitting and people watching for the last fifteen minutes, and still no sighting of Aimee or Vanessa. Not that I should be at all surprised. Aimee once had to be asked to leave because the store was closing, and she ignored their ten-minute warning call. It was pretty entertaining though.

My caramel iced coffee is already half empty, and it's taking everything I have not to go get a refill. I spend enough of my nights staring up at the ceiling as it is though.

Not ten feet away, there's a girl and a guy sitting at another table just talking and laughing and having a merry time. They can't be any older than fifteen or sixteen, and it brings me back to just a couple of years ago, back to when things were so much simpler and this point in life seemed to be so far away. What I wouldn't give to just go back to that point in life for just a day and enjoy not having to worry about where I'd wind up in the next five years of life.

What I wouldn't give to be able to go back in time and be brave enough to just come out and be honest about who I am to the world. Not that I can't still come out, but I've gone this long, and I think at this point it might be best to try to cling on to as much "normalcy" as humanly possible while I still can.

Maybe I'm just making this all so much more difficult than it needs to be.

A hand grazes my shoulder. "Hey, I didn't expect to see you here."

"Cooper. I didn't expect to see you here either. I thought you had to work tonight."

He slides into the empty seat across me from. "Originally yeah, but I overheard Gina from day shift saying that her kid's birthday is coming up and she needed to make some extra cash, so I figured it was kind of a win-win for the both of us."

"Well aren't you just the hero of the day."

Cooper lets out a faint laugh, and holy shit it's so cute. Everything he does is pretty cute if you ask me.

He takes a sip from the cup in his hand. "Yeah, I guess you can say that."

"You had a game yesterday, right? How'd that go?"

"We won actually. Danny Peters got us yet another home run of the season."

"That's really awesome," I say. "Congrats."

"Thanks! I actually didn't think you were all that interested in baseball. Or even interested in sports at all for that matter."

"You caught me," I laugh. "That was always Tommy's thing. I'm definitely not coordinated enough for any of that.

"It's not for everyone, I really only got into sports because it was a way for me and my dad to bond when I was little. Don't tell anyone, but I kinda wanted to get into theatre when I was younger."

His devilish smirk sends my mind racing. My heart thumps wildly against its confines.

"So—in other words—you're the Troy Bolton of the baseball world?" I mumble.

"Hey, you said it. But if you tell anyone that, I might have to kill you."

He's laughing again and, despite the not so serious threat, I just want to jump over the table and squeeze him and ask him whether or not he's the one that's been sending me secret emails for the past few months.

"So, what brings you to BloNo," he asks.

"Oh, just hanging out with Aimee and Vanessa, who both ditched me for makeup."

"That's rough, man." The smile fades from his lips, the glow behind his eyes that I've grown so accustomed to going with it. "So, are you and Aimee like a thing?"

"Me and Aimee? No, we're most definitely not a thing. She's beautiful and amazingly kind and everything, but I—I just don't really see her in that way. She's more like a sister to me than anything else."

"Hey, that's cool. I was just curious. You two seem to be together all the time, so I wasn't sure."

"El, you will never believe how much this chick saved me on all of this—" Aimee starts shouting from like six feet away. "Oh, sorry. I didn't know you had company."

"Hey, Aimee," Cooper says.

"Hey, Coop."

"I don't think we've officially been introduced," he says, his eyes shifting to Vanessa. "I'm Cooper."

"I'm Vanessa. It's nice to meet you."

"You too. Well, I should probably let you three get back to your day. My work shoes finally gave out, so I need to go find myself a decent pair."

Aimee catches my eye. The arch of her brow and signature lip pout turned smirk are all I need to know that the gears in her head are spinning. "Hey, here's a wacky idea. Why doesn't sweet Elliot here give you a hand with trying to find a new pair of work shoes." She drapes her arm over my shoulder. "I'm sure that by now he knows the place like the back of his hand considering how much I've dragged him around it."

"I'm sure that Cooper is more than capable of finding his own shoes."

"Nonsense," Vanessa chimes in. "All of us can use an extra set of eyes sometimes. And we were just talking about making a run to Victoria's Secret, and I doubt you'd like to spend your afternoon in there with us."

These girls are going to be my death, I swear.

"Actually, I wouldn't mind a little help," Cooper says. "If you don't mind helping, I mean."

"See, there ya go!" Aimee says, pushing me in his direction. "We're gonna go grab some stuff and we'll meet back here in like a half hour so we can go grab some dinner."

The two of us stand there and watch as Aimee and Vanessa lock arms and skip off around the corner.

"Sorry about them. They can be a little weird."

"It's cool. I appreciate as much help as I can get. Lord knows you seem to have a better grasp at style than I do."

"I don't think that's all that true, but thanks." I twist my body in the other direction and start walking.

We wound up at Shoe Department Encore down from Old Navy, which is, in my opinion, the only decent place around here to get an alright pair of shoes that aren't going to fall apart a month after you buy them or cause blood blisters on your foot after a week of wearing them. It only took us a solid ten minutes to find a new pair of work shoes for him, but then we spent another ten minutes looking for a pair of running shoes that he could come back and buy later.

Apparently, he runs like five miles a day, and I just can't fathom why some people would put themselves through that any day of the week. When Fat Amy told the Bellas to not put her down for cardio, I felt that on a spiritual level.

"So, have you heard back from any colleges yet?" Cooper asks.

"Unfortunately, yeah. I just got my acceptance letter to ISU."

"Why unfortunately?"

"I mean, I know that I should be totally grateful that I even get the opportunity to go to college—and I totally am—but at the same time, I just sort of wanted to get the hell out of this area after graduation and start a new life somewhere else."

He chuckles and swaps his bag from one hand to the other. "Yeah, I definitely get where you're coming from there. I just got my acceptance to ISU too actually, but I don't even know if I really want to go to college. I just feel like there's something so much bigger out there for me. But, of course, my parents want me to go to school and become a big shot something so I can make a decent living when I'm older and not have to worry about my finances like they did for so many years."

Too many things are adding up for it to be only a coincidence. Milo's parents want him to go off to school and become successful. Cooper's parents want the same thing. Both Milo and Cooper want a life other than what their parents have planned for him.

"I get it. It's tough when you have certain expectations placed on you."

"Ain't that the truth," he says. "I'm just so tired of having to live up to this perfect image."

"I can only imagine." My eye catches his. "Hey, I'm not sure if you're doing anything for the rest of the day, but would you maybe want to come and grab dinner with us at Red Robin? And then we're gonna see a movie later tonight."

"I'd love—"

"Well if it isn't little Cinderelliot."

The sound is like nails scraping down a blackboard.

Does this chick have me lojacked or something?

"Hailey . . . what a surprise," I say.

She's joined at the hip by her loyal followers, both of which are practically copies of her, bottle-blonde and all. "I wish I could say the feeling was mutual." She reapplies her lip gloss before tossing it into her bag. "Crazy seeing you here with Coop."

"Yeah, I was just here trying to find a new pair of shoes for work and I ran into Elliot, who was nice enough to point me in the right direction for where to get a pair."

"Oh, well wasn't that sweet. Elliot here just has a massive—*heart*—for cute coworkers in distress, don't you, Elliot?"

Every fight or flight signal in my head is currently screaming at me to just make a run for it and not stop until I've reached Canada and started a new life with a new name and face. She never ceases to outdo herself.

"Anyway, now that you've gotten what you need, why don't you and I go grab some dinner?" she asks.

"What about us," one of the girls interjects. "You were our ride."

"Well then find another one."

"You know what, I really appreciate the invite, but I forgot that we're all going over to my grandma's for dinner tonight, so I should probably really get going," Cooper says.

"Oh, okay. Maybe we could grab some dinner another time then."

"Yeah, that sounds great. It was great seeing you, Hailey. And thank you again for helping me, Elliot. I'll see you tomorrow at work."

Cooper takes off and disappears around the corner, leaving me alone with Hailey and her sad excuse for a posse. It would feel so good to lay into her right about now, but something tells me that would only stir the pot more than I already do just by existing.

Her hand is on her hip and she's scrolling through Instagram. Without looking up she says, "Back off Cooper."

"Excuse me?"

"You heard me. It's all part of my plan to finally get him to ask me out, and I don't need you getting in my way. Not that I'm worried or anything because why would he be interested in you? For obvious reasons of course. But still . . . stop drooling over my man."

"Not sure why you can't get it through the pea sized brain of yours, but I'm not interested. Not in him or any other *guy*, for *obvious reasons.*"

She's looking me up and down. "That's the story you're gonna continue going with? Okay then, whatever keeps away the bad dreams at night." Hailey slips her phone into her back pocket. "You're gonna have to take a look over my paper tonight for me, by the way. So don't stay out too late."

What the hell is new? At this point it's just easier to agree than try to figure out what new thing she can pin on me this week that isn't even my fault.

"Fine. Whatever," I mutter.

"That's a good boy. Now have fun with your little friends because you have a lot of work to do tonight. See ya!"

Hailey and her little band of bitches wave as they stroll off toward Bath and Body Works.

CHAPTER FOURTEEN

JUSTIN

The thing is just sitting there staring at me, like it knows just how much it ruined my life. It's been a week since I found out that I got accepted to Stanford, a pit stop on the road to medical school so Mom and Dad will finally be happy, and to the Studio Art program at NYU, the one thing that will finally make *me* happy.

> To: cinderfella0204@gmail.com
> From: milojuni1221@gmail.com
> Subject: yay for college
> *Dear Cinderfella,*
>
> *Hey, sorry that it's been a few days. Things have been pretty crazy lately with all this end of the year stuff going on. Not to mention I finally got the answer my family's been waiting for pretty much since the day that I was born. I was accepted into the school of my parents' dreams and into the program of their dreams.*
>
> *Woohoo.*
>
> *Not to mention I was accepted into an art program at a school that I've wanted to go to for as long as I can remember like an hour or two later. So, there's that little tidbit.*
>
> *But anyway, I hope that you're having a decent week and I really am sorry that we haven't been talking as much. Things are just starting to get really busy with the senior trip and prom and finals and graduation and all that coming up all at once. I'll try to talk when I can.*
>
> *— Milo*

I click send before I decide to give away any type of info that could out my true identity and sink down into my desk chair. My eyes find the Stanford acceptance letter and the acceptance email to NYU for the fall that's pulled up on my MacBook.

I wish I could say that I'm surprised in the slightest that life is totally messing with me again.

My phone starts rumbling against the top of the desk. Another FaceTime request from Steph. I'm sure it's pretty obvious by now that I've been avoiding her. Regardless, I slide it off the desk and tap the answer button. I'll have to talk about it eventually.

"Hey, sis," I say as her smiling face pops up on the screen.

"Hey! I feel like it's been forever! Things have been so busy here with exams and stuff coming up in a few weeks."

"Eh, don't worry about it. I know you're busy and nothing too exciting has been happening around here anyway. Everything's pretty much the same these days."

She repositions herself and leans the back of her head against the wall. "You're totally lying to me right now."

"What?"

"I know your secret, Justin. I can't believe you didn't tell me yourself and that I had to hear it through the grapevine. I thought we were closer than that."

Holy shit. She knows. She totally knows. How does she know? Do I just deny it, or do I come clean once and for all about all of it?

"Steph, I'm sorry. I wanted to tell you, I just—everything just got so crazy and one thing led to another and I just—I'm sorry."

"I can't believe you weren't gonna tell me you got accepted to Stanford yourself. That's so amazing and I'm so proud of you!"

The word "Stanford" about knocks the pent-up air from my lungs and it takes all I have not to just fall out of my chair and face first into the floor. I can't believe I did that. I almost totally just folded inwards. And for what?

Holy shit. Is it hot in here?

"Thanks," I mutter.

"I knew you could do it. You worked your ass off to get to where you are and it's finally paying off. You have such a bright future ahead of you and I couldn't be prouder of the man that you're becoming."

You wouldn't be saying that if you knew that I was lying to everyone I knew about who I really am and what I actually want out of life.

Is that the kind of man I'm becoming? The kind that just lies about everything.

"Well thank you. I appreciate it. Are you still coming down next weekend?"

"Of course, and don't think you're getting out of a little brother-sister bonding either. Your accomplishments deserve to be celebrated."

I feel a grin forming. "I wouldn't expect anything less."

"Are Mom and Dad home right now?" she asks. The upbeat energy she had is slowly disappearing.

"No, I think they went out grocery shopping. Everything cool?"

"Well, I guess that just kind of depends." Something off camera grabs her attention and she avoids looking at her screen as she talks. "I was going to wait until I got back home to say anything, but I just really need to tell you first. I can't handle all three of you freaking out at once."

"What is it? Did you get your first C or something?"

"What? No, this is serious. And I need for you to just not say anything to anyone, okay? Do you promise?"

"Of course. I promise I won't say anything." I bring the phone closer to my face, as if Mom and Dad are somehow going to overhear our conversation all the way from the store.

"Okay . . . um . . ." she mutters as she starts running her fingers through the waves in her highlighted hair. "So, you remember that guy I told you about from class that I was seeing for a couple of weeks?"

"I think so. You found out he had been talking to another girl on the side like a month or two ago, right?"

"That's the one," Steph says. She's nibbling at her bottom lip and avoiding my gaze again. "I didn't exactly tell you the entire story."

There's radio silence from both our ends for what feels like an eternity. I've never seen Stephanie look so scared in my life, and I'm afraid to know what the rest of the story is.

"He didn't hurt you, did he? I'm not a violent person, but I'll make him pay for that if he did. And I know Danny will help."

"No, Justin. He never hurt me. He wasn't like that." Her dark eyes find the screen again, and her expression is completely blank now. "Before I found out that I wasn't the only one he'd been seeing, we had this really romantic date night at his place and one thing led to another and then we — you know — and then I started feeling really crummy like a week ago and I realized that I was late."

"Late? What's that supposed to—" It finally hits what she's referring to. "Oh."

"Yeah. I got a friend of mine to get a test for me earlier, and lo and behold, looks like the Herrera family is about to get just a little bit bigger."

"Wow, that's—wow. What are you gonna do?" I ask.

She uses her free hand to cover her face and her eyes wander off again. "I don't know. I really don't know. I just don't know how they're going to react. I'm so scared to tell them, Justin. What if I can't do it?"

I wish I could tell her that I understand where she's coming from. That I know what it feels like to know that there are all these expectations for how our lives are supposed to turn out and to be scared to tell them about anything that would derail the plans they've had for us since the day we were born.

It's comforting to know that I'm not the only one scared of what they might think.

"Look, I can't say that I can really relate to what you're going through, but I get that you're scared and that this came out of nowhere. Just know that no matter what they think, the one thing that won't change is how much I love you and look up to you. You're my big sister and I'll never abandon you."

"Thank you."

"It's what any brother would do," I reply.

"But really . . . thank you so much for being there for me. Most importantly though, I want to thank you so much for making this whole thing so much easier by actually believing everything that just came out of my mouth."

"Come again?"

"April Fools!" She's rolling around on top of her black and white bed spread and trying to dampen the sound of the cackling coming from her mouth with a pillow.

"So, you're not having a baby?"

"Oh hell no! You think I don't take every precaution I can? I can't believe I got you! For once I actually got you instead of you getting me!"

"You're such a little brat, you know that?"

"Yeah, but you love me." She tones down the satisfied grin and positions herself upright again. "But seriously, thank you for offering to stick by me through whatever. It really meant a lot."

"Yeah yeah, let's not get carried away by that or anything, mkay?" My eyes instinctively roll and I fight a smile. "I think they're back, so I should probably go help them carry in the groceries. I'll see you next weekend though, okay?

"Sounds good. Love you, dork," she says as she blows a kiss into the camera.

"Love you too, weirdo."

CHAPTER FIFTEEN

ELLIOT

Thursday, April 2

I know people are just trying to be helpful today, but I can feel myself getting annoyed by every little thing.

It was the one day I was actually unbelievably happy to not have very many classes with Aimee, because that meant I didn't have someone asking me every five minutes if I was okay or if I needed anything or telling me that they were here to talk if I needed to. Anna even offered to convince Michael to let me have the day off so I could spend it with my friends instead, but I'd much rather keep myself too busy to think.

I for sure appreciate the fact that people seem to actually care, but I handle things best when I can just keep myself busy and not talk about it every second of the day. How else am I supposed to handle the crushing truth of my reality? The reality where I've been without a mom for five years officially today. The reality where she never got to see me start high school or get my driver's license. She won't even get to see me graduate high school and get out of this place like she always wanted me to. How is a person supposed to handle that sort of thing, if they ever actually do at all?

It may not be the healthiest way to handle things, but I've always dealt with trauma by just ignoring the fact that it's even there, which is how I fully intend to handle the rest of today. It's 8:23 pm, and we haven't had a customer back here in I'd say close to an hour, which ordinarily I'd be super happy about, but it's not really an ordinary day.

Anna had to take the day shift so she'd be able to go to this parent teacher conference at her son's school, so I'm closing up for the night with Cooper and Jeff, the day shift manager that Anna swapped with.

Since we've been so dead, I've taken the liberty of starting on the dishes tonight to at least get some of it out of the way so we're not all stuck here after close while we finish up. Only God knows how long we'll be stuck here tonight if I don't take some initiative and actually start getting some actual work done around here. Not that I'm saying Jeff is terrible at his job or anything, but he obviously hasn't had to close in a very long time, and I'm not about to sit here worrying about the learning curve when I have more work to do at home.

I wish I could just disappear and never look back at this shit hole.

"Hey, Elliot. I think you have some visitors," Cooper says in the midst of his sweeping duties.

I stop the sprayer and turn my attention toward the front counter where Aimee and Vanessa are busy trying to catch my eye. I let out a sigh and roll my eyes before I can even tell my brain not to do it. I slide the massive water proof apron off and grab a dish towel to wipe my hands dry as I make my way up to the deli counter. "Yes?" The word comes out a little more forceful than I'd intended it to.

"We just wanted to come by and see how you're doing," Aimee says.

"Pretty much the same as I was when you texted me an hour ago asking the same exact thing. I'm fine."

"And we wanted to check and see if you wanted to hang out for a little while after you get off. Maybe go grab some food or something," Vanessa says.

"Look, I really appreciate what you're trying to do, but it's a school night and I have a ton of homework to do when I get home, so I'm gonna have to pass. And unless you're here to get something from the deli, I really need to go get these dishes done."

"Yeah, we get it," Aimee murmurs. "We'll let you get back to work and we'll just see you tomorrow in class. We love you."

"Love you too."

A little bit after Aimee and Vanessa left, we wound up getting slammed right up until a few minutes before close. I was definitely thanking myself for getting a head start on some of the clean-up, but we still didn't get the last of it done until about 9:15, which I guess isn't all that bad considering there have been nights when we didn't get out until almost 10 o'clock.

"Alright, Jeff," I say. "The dishes are all done, the case is wrapped, and the trash is out. Anything else you want us to do?"

"Were the floors swept?" he asks.

"Yeah, I got everything swept and mopped too," Cooper replies.

"Then you guys can go. I'm just gonna get a few things finished up here, but it won't take too long. Have a good night, guys."

"You too," we both say on the way out to our lockers.

I twist in my lock combo and pull the door open. My fingers pick at my name tag and pull it off my polo before throwing it into the back of my locker and I slide my keys off the top shelf. I habitually pull my phone from my pocket and start scrolling through some of the notifications, most of which are just message alerts from my group chat with Aimee, Vanessa, and a couple other people we share our lunch table with, yet never seem to actually hang out with any other time. I stop at a new text from Anna that's time stamped at 9:02 pm.

Anna: How'd today go? Still holding up okay?

Without even thinking, I let a tiny groan escape from between my lips, and Cooper's body lurches in response. It's pretty depressing that not even his cute scare response is enough to make me not pissed at everything and everyone. The worst part is that I know I'm starting to hurt people's feelings with my snappy responses, but I can't help it.

I think I broke the sarcastic asshole filter.

"Sorry. Didn't mean to scare you."

"No, it's cool." Cooper grabs his keys from the inside of his locker and latches it shut again. His watchful brown eyes narrow and he falls silent for a moment. "Everything cool today?"

There's that look again. The same look people gave me after Mom died. The soft eyes, furrowed brow, and thinned lips. The look of pity.

"Everything's fine. Why wouldn't it be?"

"I don't know. You just don't really seem like yourself today."

My locker latches and I lean against it, avoiding his gaze. "So everyone else is allowed to have an off day, but I'm not?"

"What? That's not what I'm saying at all. I'm just saying I'm worried."

"You're worried?" I ask, turning my head toward him.

"Well—yeah—I'd like to consider us as friends, and I don't like seeing my friends have a bad day if I think there's something I might be able to do about it."

I fold my arms against my chest. My eyes follow along a huge scrape in the metallic produce cooler door.

He thinks of us as friends. And he's worried, which means there's some part of him that cares about me and my well-being. He may be Milo, or he may not be. I don't really know much of anything at this point.

The one thing I do know is that if I'm wrong about this, I don't think I want to be right.

"Are you doing anything right now?" Cooper asks.

"I mean, other than going home and working on homework?"

"Okay, so we're not going to be lame for one night. You can do homework this weekend, and tonight you're gonna go get some ice cream with me because I'm not letting you go home so you can mope over your paper for English class."

"But—"

"Nope." He's smiling, his adorable dimples poking through. "You're going, even if I have to kidnap you to make you go, Elliot. Now move it. I'm driving because I don't trust you to actually go there yourself."

"Damn. Pushy much?" I ask, returning a smile.

"I can be when I need to be. Now get moving." The palm of his hand lands on my shoulder, sending a chill through my entire body, and pushes me through the back-storage area of the store and out into the parking lot. The lights of his car flash as he presses the button on his key fob, and he opens the door for me. "In you go. And remember, I've done sports all four years, so don't even try to run off."

I roll my eyes and slide into the passenger seat. The smell of Gain vent freshener is like a smack in the face once he shuts the door and I'm stuck in the enclosed space. I tap at my thigh in amusement as I watch him attempt to action star slide his way across the hood of the car, ultimately ending in him just coming to a dead halt in the center. He twists his upper body around and flashes a smile in my direction, making my cheeks hot.

He grips the door handle and swings it open. He positions himself in his seat and says, "They make that look so easy in the movies. I guess it's safe to say I don't really have a future in the action movie industry."

"Yeah, you'd probably be right on that one."

The engine roars to life a moment later and he tosses his phone at me. "Pick some music for the drive."

"Any requests?" I ask.

"Just surprise me."

That's probably a pretty dangerous statement to make around me when it comes to music.

I go through a catalog of artists and music in my head trying to figure out the perfect song to play. Something tells me that my usual choices of Ariana, Britney, Selena or Gaga would definitely just scream gay, so it might be best to steer clear of them. Shawn Mendes could be a pretty decent choice. Straight people listen to him too, right? I input his name into the search bar on Spotify and start scrolling through some of his more recent songs.

Actually, on second thought, Shawn might not be the smartest decision. It may not be best to picture him while I'm hanging out with one of the school's poster boys. Even if Shawn's body looks like it was perfectly sculpted by the

Roman gods and given to the gays as a present, or the voice that comes from between those gorgeous lips is silky smooth and makes me want to do unimaginable things to him and —

No, Elliot! Stop! This is not appropriate!

I take the safest route and throw on some Post Malone.

"Okay, a little Posty. I can deal with that." He briefly glances over at me and smiles before pulling into the Dairy Queen parking lot and stopping at the speaker.

"Welcome to Dairy Queen, what can I get you today?"

"Hey, can I get a medium Reese's blizzard and — " he turns his head and whispers, " — what do you want? It's my treat."

"Uh, I'll just take a medium cookie dough."

"And I'll take a medium cookie dough blizzard too. That'll be it."

"Alright, please pull up to the second window and we'll have your total for you."

As he pulls forward, my phone starts buzzing again and I half expect to find a text from Aimee asking me how I'm doing, or a text from Hailey trying to blackmail me into doing something else for her. I slide it out of my pocket again and a Gmail notification lights up the screen.

To: cinderfella0204@gmail.com
From: milojuni1221@gmail.com
Subject: Re: name explanation
Cinderfella,

Yeah, I guess I can see your confusion with my screen name. I was kinda lost when I was trying to make up an email on the fly like that, so I just kinda threw some names together. And before you ask, no it is not my name. Well, not completely anyway. I guess you'll just have to figure out what it has to do with my name on your own time.

The Milo part came from one of my all-time favorite movies as a kid, Atlantis: The Lost Empire, and the Juni part came from Spy Kids, my other favorite childhood movie. I know both came out before either of us were actually born, or at least I assume, but they were pretty great movies. Hollywood doesn't make kids movies like that anymore which is actually kind of depressing.

But on another note, I cannot believe how tired I am, and it's not even 10 yet. Is this what it's like to start getting older? I should probably do some homework, but I can barely keep my eyes open while I'm writing this, so I think I might hit the sack soon.

I'll talk to you again soon though. I've missed our conversations.
— Milo

I guess I can assume my identity mission is pretty much back to square one. Although something tells me that Aimee may be a little more upset about this than I am.

"Here ya go."

I'm jolted back to reality by Cooper's voice and nearly drop my phone. "What?"

"Here's your blizzard," he says again, putting the cup in my outstretched hand. "A little jumpy?"

"No — sorry — I just kinda spaced out. Thanks."

"It's no problem." He pulls forward and parks in a spot facing the high school's lot across the street. "Any big weekend plans?"

"Probably just the usual, which generally consists of working and then going over to Aimee's house for a movie so I can avoid going home and dealing with Hailey and Tommy."

"I can for sure see why they might be difficult to live with. How have you done it all these years without slapping someone?"

"Believe me. It hasn't been without struggle," I say.

I've never actually told anyone but Aimee about what my family life was like growing up, mostly because pretty much everyone else in the school is either friends with Hailey and Tommy, or they know them. The last thing I need is for any sort of trash talk to get back to them. I would undoubtedly pay for it in the end in the form of blackmail by Hailey or some type of harassment or torture at the hands of Tommy and the rest of the team.

"I've never really talked about it, but Michael's actually the only dad figure I've ever had. My mom had me when she was still a senior in high school and my birth father had just started college, so he didn't really want anything to do with me or her."

"Oh, man . . . I'm sorry. That really sucks."

"It is what it is, I guess." I take a bite of my blizzard and chew on a piece of cookie dough for another moment or two. "And then my mom's dad told her that she could either get an abortion or get out, and so she moved in with Anna and had me a few months later. It sucked not really having the typical family growing up, but I wouldn't have had it any other way. Flash forward to the end of fifth grade, and I find out that she's been seeing the father of my biggest rival."

"Tommy's your biggest rival?" he asks.

"No, that would be Hailey. I actually didn't even have any contact with Tommy until they decided to tell us they were getting married and that we were all moving into a house together to be one big ole' happy family. Not that it was all completely bad. From what I remember we seemed to be relatively happy, despite Tommy becoming a bigger douche every day and me and Hailey competing over literally everything."

His deep brown eyes turn golden brown when someone's headlights reflect in the rearview mirror. I didn't expect for him to seem genuinely interested in what I have to say.

"What changed?" Cooper asks.

It's like someone's stuffed a hot poker down my throat. "It was right at the beginning of seventh grade. My mom just went in for a run of the mill checkup, which she hadn't been able to do for a few years because she'd been so busy running after me for so long. That's when they found it. They did a biopsy and discovered that it was a stage four breast cancer, they did everything they could, but it was too far gone already, so by the end of it their main priority was just making sure she was comfortable. Right before I finished seventh grade, she—" I can't stomach finishing the sentence and reliving it all over again. "It's been five years today."

"Elliot . . . I'm so sorry. I had no idea."

"I remember it like it was yesterday. Sometimes I still even have nightmares about it."

"You know that wasn't your fault though, right?" he asks.

"I mean, I know that now. But for the longest time I beat myself up for what happened. However, I don't know if Michael sees it that way."

"What do you mean?"

"Never mind," I say before taking another bite of cookie dough. "It's stupid."

Cooper hits pause on the Troye Sivan song playing in the background, another one of my own personal favorites, and lays his phone flat on the dash. The golden specs in his eyes are sparkling from flashes of headlights that pass by every now and then.

I don't know what it is with me and my strange obsession with guys with brown eyes, but they somehow give off earthy vibes, and, in extension, the promise of new growth. Suddenly I'm not so upset that Milo and Cooper aren't the same person. Even if that does mean he's more than likely straight.

"Elliot, I know I haven't known you for all that long, but I'd like to think of us as friends. Anything you have to say isn't stupid. It's important even if you don't think it is."

Would it be inappropriate to kiss this man right now?

The burning sensation in my throat has turned cold, sinking into the bottom of my stomach.

"What did you mean when you said you don't know if your step-dad feels the same way?"

His eyes meet mine, sending a wave through my body. My knees tremble.

"I guess I've just gotten the sense over the last five years that he blames me for what happened to my mom. Which would make sense because after that things were just never the same and now it's like I'm living in *Cinderella*, except I don't think this version will have quite the fairytale ending that everyone's used to."

"You don't know that," he says. The tone of his voice seems genuinely hopeful that things will start looking up for me sooner than later.

"Don't I though? I mean, I have very little saved up, my car is on its last leg, and the only school I was accepted to is ISU. I'm basically destined to be stuck here under Michael's thumb for the rest of my life."

"You might believe that, but I don't. You're a smart guy, so you'll figure it out."

"Thanks." I turn my attention toward a couple of kids hanging out in the high school's parking lot across the road and I can't help but imagine what it would feel like to kiss Cooper right now and to have my hands running through his hair and his skin brushing up against mine. Goosebumps are forming up and down my arms just from the thought of his lips against mine and from the subtle scent of his cologne that's wafting through the car. "Hey, Cooper . . ." It's just barely above a whisper.

"Yeah?"

"I—I should probably go home and get started on that homework now."

I've never been so relieved to see Tommy passed out on the couch as I am right now. I just don't know if I'd be able to handle him and his inevitable verbal abuse over how I'm not masculine enough to actually be a man and how big of a loser I am. And I can only assume that Hailey's upstairs chatting with her loyal followers about what they're going to do tomorrow to try and fit in, despite the fact that no one can actually stand them.

I make my way up the narrow wooden staircase, stopping only briefly to check out the photos of Mom and Michael on their wedding day. The day that the life I knew had officially been dug six feet under.

Up until the start of the year, my room had been sort of an oasis where I could escape all of the shit from the outside world. It was a getaway where no one else's opinion or thoughts about me or who I am mattered at all. But it feels more like a prison the closer I get to graduation now that I know I won't be going out into the real world with my best friend at my side every step of the way.

I collapse onto my blue and black comforter, my eyes watching the ceiling fan above me spinning around in circles. I slip my phone out from my pocket again and hit the reply button on Milo's email.

To: milojuni1221@gmail.com
From: cinderfella0204@gmail.com
Subject: Re: name explanation
Milo,

Now you're speaking my language. I was completely obsessed with those movies growing up. You can't really go wrong with a 2000s classic. I was so excited when my friend decided to let me use their Disney+ account so that I could binge-watch old movies and TV shows. Right now I'm rewatching Lizzie McGuire so that I can watch the movie again and I'm so excited because it's been so long since the last time I watched it. Please tell me you've seen it before. I'll be highly disappointed if you haven't. I just hope they finally get to do the reboot and it doesn't totally suck.

And I don't know if you should've actually told me that the two names hold a clue to what your real name is. I'm pretty good at solving mysteries if I do say so myself. Not that I'll be spending all my time trying to figure out who you are. I know you don't really want that.

I'm actually going to head to bed pretty soon myself, although I think I should probably do some homework first. I hope you sleep well.

Goodnight.
— Cinderfella

CHAPTER SIXTEEN

JUSTIN

Friday, April 3

Me and my partner Aimee decided to meet at her mom's coffee shop and bakery hybrid to work a little more on our theatre project.

"How have I never been here before?" I ask, walking through the door.

"I mean, it hasn't really been around all that long and not a lot of high school kids know about it. Everyone just goes to Starbucks instead."

"Oh, man. I'm sorry. That really sucks."

"It's not so bad. We have a pretty loyal crowd of regulars that keep us afloat."

"Well, you can't go wrong with that I guess."

We find an empty table in the corner by some outlets and start setting up our stuff.

"Can I get you kids some brain food or any coffee?" some woman asks with a smile.

"Hey, mom."

"Hi, sweetie. How was school?"

"It was really good. This is Justin, my partner for that theatre project that I was telling you about."

Her smiling face turns toward me. "It's really great to meet you, Justin."

"Likewise, Mrs. —"

"Please call me Diana. Can I get you kids anything? It's on the house."

"I'll just take my usual," Aimee says with a satisfied grin on her face before turning to look at me. "What about you?"

"Uh . . ." I stammer, looking at the chalkboard menu next to the counter. "Can I just get a medium vanilla iced coffee please."

"Alrighty. The Aimee special and one medium vanilla iced coffee coming right up," her mom says before heading back to the kitchen.

I pull a chair out from the table and slide my laptop from my bag. "So, where'd we leave off last time?"

"Well, considering we spent majority of the time trying to agree on what to do and getting shushed by the librarian, I don't think we actually made it very far."

"Oh yeah. Well, in our defense, that lady was pretty crabby. I did come up with an idea though. Well, sort of."

"Let's hear it."

"I think it would be a good idea to incorporate some our experiences with some of the stereotypes we've both faced as a Mexican man and an Asian woman."

"Yeah. I like that." Aimee's fingers start typing furiously away at her keyboard. "Although I will say that I haven't really had to deal with a whole lot of that yet. Obviously I've dealt with some, but I can imagine you've dealt with some stuff over the last few years with all that "build the wall" crap."

That's a bit of an understatement. I can remember a situation about two years ago very clearly. Me and a few of the guys from the team were out trying to find some new cleats and we wound up getting separated for some reason. Some bitchy middle-aged lady decided that I looked fishy just because I was talking in Spanish to my abuela on the phone.

She had the nerve to approach a sixteen year old and first, tell me that I was in America so I needed to speak American, as if that's a language, and then told me that if I was going to be talking like that then I needed to go back to whatever third world country I came from. Then she accused me of stealing the shoes that I had in my bag.

That's when I told her that number one, "American" isn't a language and that she obviously never paid much attention in school because it's actually North America, which is an entire continent that also includes Mexico. Second, I told her that technically speaking this country doesn't even have an official language. Then I told her that I was actually from here—not that it was actually even any of her business—and then proceeded to hold the receipt for my new cleats out in front of her.

The look on her face as I walked away was totally priceless and I would've given anything to get a picture of it.

"I guess it's been a little intense lately," I finally say.

Aimee's mom pops up again a moment later with my iced coffee, a frap, and a very large muffin. "Okay, so we have a vanilla iced coffee, a white chocolate Oreo frappe, and a chocolate chip walnut muffin."

"That is a lot of chocolate," I say as she sets everything down in front of us.

"What can I say, I have a bit of a sweet tooth," Aimee says.

"Can I get you kids anything else?"

I shove my straw into the lid of my cup and take a sip of heaven in a cup. "I'm all good here. It's delicious. Thank you so much."

"It's just as amazing as usual, Mom. We're all good here."

"Alright, just let me know if you guys need anything else. I'll be in the back."

I take another gulp of coffee and watch as Aimee's mom disappears behind a metallic swinging door.

Aimee's got her face practically shoved into her muffin as she's typing away at her laptop and I can't help but laugh a little bit. I can't quite figure out why Gabbi and the rest of the girls give her such problems. I mean, yeah, she's kind of — different — but that's not necessarily a bad thing. She's got originality and she's not trying to fit in with the rest of the girls at school just because she's afraid of what everyone else will think of her. She's one-hundred percent true to herself and it's a breath of fresh air.

She looks up and catches me staring. "What? I have chocolate on my face, don't I?"

"No, you're all good."

"Okay, cool." Aimee grabs a napkin from the middle of the table and wipes her mouth before turning her attention back to her laptop. "So, I almost feel like a good setting for this would be a store or something like that, or at least somewhere out in public."

"Yeah, I think that sounds good. I know I've had a few instances where people like automatically assumed I was stealing or something. I'm just not sure how we would fit Asian discrimination into it though."

"That's true. So maybe we should only majorly focus on one thing instead of both? I know you said you've been in a few situations. Would you be comfortable kind of diving into that?"

"Yeah, I have no issue with that. Whatever I can do to help, I'll do it." I run my fingertips along the smooth table top. We work in silence as I wait for enough courage to build up. Lord knows that if I don't do this now, I never will. "Hey, c—can I ask you a question?"

"It depends . . . was that the question?" She laughs and looks up at me.

"Oh—no—that wasn't it. I'm sorry if this sounds rude or anything, and I totally don't want to pry, but there are rumors going around—about you—are they true?"

Aimee tilts her head to the side; her eyes study my face. "There are lots of rumors going around about me, so you're gonna have to be a bit more specific. There are even rumors that I eat cats because of the whole Asian thing. I think that might be my favorite one."

"Oh—sorry—I mean the one about . . . you know." Why is it so difficult for me to get it out? "There's a rumor going around that you're into both guys and girls. Is—is that true?"

She leans in a bit closer and leans her chin against the top of her laptop. "Who do you think started the rumors, honey?"

"Why would you do that, though? Weren't you worried about what everyone would think about it?" I ask.

"Not really," she says bluntly. "In the end it all came down to what I thought of myself and whether or not I was happy. And I have some of the greatest friends I could ever ask for that are accepting of me in every way. It didn't really matter much what everyone else thought of me because those aren't the people that are gonna have my back when it really counts."

I guess I never really thought of it that way. I can't say for sure whether or not the people in my life would be totally cool with it, but I don't think they'd ever really make me feel bad about it.

I just can't gauge how my family would react. We've never really talked about sexuality. Other than in church, we've never really had to.

"And your mom is okay with it?" I ask.

"Of course. Both of my parents are totally cool with it. They just want me to be happy. They went straight out and bought a pride flag to display as soon as I came out to them."

"That's really great."

She's still staring at me, and I think she's half expecting me to continue on this conversation or make some sort of loud and proud declaration of support or something. I can't even imagine how fishy all of my questions look to someone that's actually out and proud.

"Is there anything you'd like to talk about?" she asks.

"What? No, I was just—we should probably get back to work."

CHAPTER SEVENTEEN

ELLIOT

Friday, April 3

"Hey, can you hand me that other bottle of cleaner? This one's empty," Anna says over her shoulder.

"Sure." I hit the shuffle button on Spotify again and set my phone down on the table before tossing her the second bottle of sanitizer. "I'm about done over here."

"Great. I'm about done too."

It was just the three musketeers closing up tonight, or at least it was until Cooper had to run off so he could get enough sleep for tomorrow's game. I enjoyed feeling a bit of familiarity with everything around here changing all at once. It's been nice not really having to focus on Aimee leaving and making a run for it to New York to start a new life without me.

No Cooper also means finally having the chance to talk to talk to Anna—alone—about everything. Or almost everything. Not too sure how she'd feel if I told her I was talking to some anonymous dude.

"Any big Friday night plans?" Anna asks as she sets the bottle of cleaner back under the counter.

"Well, apart from reading a bunch for history and English while more than likely trying to refrain from bitching out Tommy for his speaker vibrating against my wall all night, not really."

"You have all weekend to do that. You should go spend some more time with your friends. You're not gonna have a whole lot of time together when you're all busy with your own stuff in the fall."

"Aimee and Vanessa are both busy tonight, so I'm all on my lonesome for the evening."

Anna lifts her apron over her head and hangs it up on a hook bolted to the wall. "Ah, well I guess there's nothing wrong with a little bit of alone time every now and then. Not that I know how that is anymore."

"Yeah." I snake my arm behind Anna and flip the deli's main light switch off. It's now or never, I guess. There's no guarantee I'll have the guts to do it again any time soon. "Hey, can I talk to you for a second," I manage to force out.

She catches my eye. "Of course. What's going on?"

"I—" is all that comes out of my mouth before the fluttering in my stomach starts and my body starts to shake. Why is this so difficult? It wasn't this difficult coming out any other time. "S—sorry," I stutter. "I don't know why this is so difficult."

"You can tell me anything."

"I know . . . I know I can tell you anything. And that's what makes this so ridiculous. It's just that you've always been like a second mom to me, so it's just a little terrifying. I've been wanting to tell you for the longest time, but it was just never really the right time. I think I'm ready now, though." My fingers find a frayed string at the bottom of my polo and I exhale slowly. "I—I'm gay. That doesn't mean that I'm any different. I'm still the same old Elliot, so please just don't start treating me any different, okay?"

Anna wraps her arms around me and pulls me in for a hug, and now I'm crying, which is exactly what I swore I wouldn't do when I finally told her.

"Are you crying?" Anna asks, pulling away.

"No, I just got some sanitizer in my eye."

"You're such a terrible liar. You always have been."

I cock my head to the side. "Does that mean you knew?"

"Sweetie . . . you haven't exactly been low key about it." She laughs and wipes a tear falling down my cheek. "Your mom and I knew from the first moment you started putting on living room performances to Britney Spears. I am so unbelievably proud of you for finally having the strength to live your truth. I have been watching you struggle with this for so many years and I'm so happy you're finally at a place where you're figuring out who you are."

Here come the freaking tears again!

"Thank you," I manage to mutter.

"Of course. I'd never dream of treating you any differently, Elliot. You've always been my little bean and you always will be, no matter how old you get or who you love."

I open my mouth, but nothing comes out through the tears that are now pouring down my face and the lump that's taken residence in my throat.

"Have you told anyone else?"

"I've told Aimee and Vanessa, but other than that, no one else knows." I lean against the back of the glass casings and fold my arms up against my chest. "And I know I don't really need to say it, but I'd really rather no one else know right now. I just want to get through the rest of senior year without having to deal with comments from Hailey, Tommy, or anyone else."

"Your secret is completely safe with me. You can count on that. I just want you to be happy. That's all I've ever wanted for you."

"I know. And thank you so much for all the support you've always given me. You have no idea how much I appreciate that."

"So, since you're now being totally open with me, does that mean we get to girl talk about boys now?"

"Uh, I'm not sure if I'm totally there just yet," I say, heading through the swinging door and finding my locker.

"Does that mean there's no special guy in your life then?"

Do I actually respond to that one? And at this point can I actually say that there is?

"As of this moment, I can't say I'm seeing anyone," I say.

Technically not a lie. I'm not seeing Milo, just talking to him.

"Okay, well just know that if you ever do start seeing anyone, you can always talk to me about it and I'd be more than happy to give you any tidbits of wisdom. God only knows I've learned enough lessons to last a lifetime."

She's not wrong about that. I can't even count the number of times that Anna was over at our house because she got her heart broken again.

"I promise that if I get a boyfriend, I will let you know."

"Thank you. That is all I ask."

CHAPTER EIGHTEEN

JUSTIN

Monday, April 6

I've been back on campus a couple of times for tutoring sessions with Brooke, which thankfully has only been for calculus as of late. I think I have my A for advanced bio secured for the rest of the semester. Calculus is a different story though. I'd be kind of screwed if it wasn't for her.

Part of me has been sort of hoping to run into that guy Kevin around campus again during these study sessions. Not necessarily because I want to date him or anything, although he's definitely not a bad looking guy, but I'm realizing that I don't have anyone with experience to talk to about the things that I've been dealing with. It would be nice to not feel like I'm totally alone. I do have Cinderfella, but he's just as lost as I am with everything that's going on here.

"Come on, Justin. We've gone over these graphs multiple times, so I know that you know them."

"I don't know. Is it letter D?"

"Excellent! And can you tell me why it's D?" Brooke asks, sounding almost as annoyed as I am that it's taking this long.

"Honestly? Not really."

"It's option D because f of x was shifted three units to the right. To shift the closed interval to the right, you need to add three units to the endpoints of a and b of the interval."

"There's no damn point," I say, throwing my pen down on the table and leaning back in my chair. "I'm never gonna get any of this shit."

"You don't know that. You're a lot smarter than you give yourself credit for, Justin. You just need to be patient with it. Some brains click better with this stuff than others, but that doesn't mean you'll never get it."

"Have you been present during any of these tutoring sessions? Because we've been doing this stuff for months and none of it is sticking with me yet. Can we just be finished for the night? Please?"

"Just one more question, and then we can both be on our way, okay?" Her eyes are studying my facial expressions and she's watching my every move. "Is everything going okay? You seem a little distracted tonight."

My eyes trail along a scratch that's been etched into the wooden table top. "Everything's fine. Let's just get this over with."

"Are you sure?"

We're both silent for a moment. If she still suspects anything's going on inside my head, she's definitely not letting on about it.

"Okay, if you say so." She shuffles through the pile of papers in front of her. "Last question for the night, and it's a relatively easy one. A horizontal asymptote may intersect the graph of the function, true or false?"

"It's true," I blurt out.

"See, now that wasn't so hard, was it?"

"I guess not." I close up my textbook and slide it back into my back pack. "Are we good here?"

"Yeah. I guess we are. Justin, are you sure you're okay? You haven't really seemed like yourself lately."

No, I'm not okay. Is that what you want to hear?

I'm not okay in any way, shape, or form despite the fact that I have a pretty great family, I'm pretty well liked at school so I've never had any issues socially, a gorgeous girl that's totally obsessed with me, and I got into a really great school that's going to guarantee me a bright future. Despite all of that, I'm definitely not okay and I hate myself for that. I *hate* that all I can manage to do these days is complain about everything that's being handed to me.

"Everything's fine," I finally manage to say. "It's just a little stress."

Brooke and I nab up our bags and throw them over our shoulders before we head down the hall past the help desk toward the exit. "That's definitely understandable, but you can't let yourself get too stressed out. It's not good for you. You should find some time to relax."

I can't help but laugh as we're walking through the deserted parking lot. "Yeah, just let me know if you see any openings for that between this class, bio, Easter with my family, my theatre project, prom, graduation, my graduation party, and freshman orientation."

And I've managed to stress myself out again just mentioning all of the shit I have to do over the next month. How'd I even get myself to this point?

Brooke digs through her bag and pulls out her keys. "That sounds pretty rough, but I totally understand you have your responsibilities. Promise me that you'll find some time to unwind though. I don't want you getting burnt out."

I slip my key fob out of my pocket before turning to look at her again. Leaning against the driver's side door I say, "I promise I will *try* to find some time to unwind, but only because you asked me so nicely."

"Good! And I expect a full report on that relaxation time when we meet again next week."

"Got it," I reply before hopping into the driver's seat. "See ya next week."

"See ya!"

I slip the key into place and pull my phone out of my pocket. I swipe through the dozens of old notifications waiting for me, most of which are either from group Snapchats that I never asked to be a part of, or they're texts from Danny talking about killing the rest of the season again. It's all so condensed that I almost don't even notice the new email waiting for me from almost two hours ago.

To: milojuni1221@gmail.com
From: cinderfella0204@gmail.com
Subject: the scariest and most surreal moment of my life
Dear Milo,

Oh my gosh. I did it. I mean I actually did it!

And in hindsight of writing that opening line, I now realize that you have absolutely no idea what I'm talking about right now. At the risk of giving away too much information about my identity, which I know you don't want, I'll make it brief.

There's someone that's been kind of like a second mom to me my entire life that I've kept in the dark about a good chunk of who I am. And I've hated that every day of my life. I've hated that I haven't been able to go to her for any real sort of advice and that I've had to lie to one of the only people that I know has had my back through whatever and will continue to be there for me. So, I finally did it. I finally told her everything. Well, not everything because I don't know how she'd feel about me talking to a total stranger that I met online. She's cool, but I don't know if she's THAT cool.

It felt so surreal to open up to her and to be able to say those words to someone that's been around for the entirety of my existence. Don't get me wrong though, it was also scary as hell. I was pretty sure that my heart was going to explode out of my chest, but it didn't. Everything was fine. I was fine and I survived one of the scariest things I've ever done.

I don't think I'm ready to be out and proud and go to Chicago Pride or anything like that just yet, but it finally feels like I'm starting to make some sort of progress with the whole gay thing. I'm starting to feel like I could eventually one day become more confident with who I am and where I'm going in this life.

I know you have your own stuff going on, but I guess I just needed to get that off my chest.

Hope your Monday went well!

— Cinderfella

Wow. At least one of us seems to have some guts.

A set of knuckles against my window almost sends me flying through the roof of the car and I drop my phone onto the floor. Rolling down my window I shout, "Holy shit, Brooke. You can't just do that to a person in the middle of the night! Damn!"

Her eyebrows are furrowed. "Sorry. I didn't mean to scare you like that."

"It's fine. I guess I'm just a little bit on edge lately. What's up? I thought you'd be gone by now."

"You don't happen to have a pair of jumper cables, do you? My battery died."

"Again? What you need is to invest in a new battery," I say.

"Yeah, let me just do that with my twenty hours a week at Starbucks that has to pay for my shoebox of an apartment while I TA and tutor on the side for work experience."

Now I really do feel like a spoiled little brat.

"I don't have any. I'm sorry."

"Shit," she grunts.

"Do you have anyone that can come out and give you a jump?"

"My roommate said she could, but she won't be back in town for another like three hours, so I guess I'm walking home for now and I'll have to come back with her later tonight."

"Don't do that," I say. "It's late, so I'll give you a ride home."

"You sure?"

"It's way too late for you to be walking across campus by yourself. It's definitely no Decatur, but I'd still be careful late at night around here." I pat the passenger side seat and unlock the door as she makes her way around and plops down in the seat next to me.

Cinderfella's last email runs through my head the entire drive back to Brooke's apartment. I can't even imagine how amazing and empowering it must feel to be able to finally be open and honest with someone that's been with you from the start. I just don't know if I'm ready for that. Not yet anyway. I'm not sure how everyone's going to react to it, and I don't know if I could handle rejection from everyone that I know.

I pull into the little parking lot beside Brooke's complex and find an empty spot before putting the car into park. "Well, here we are."

"Thank you so much for the ride. Let me know when you get home so I know you got back in town safely."

"Will do."

"I'll see you next week then." Brooke grabs hold of her bag and lifts it into her lap before reaching for the door handle.

There's like some sort of rush of adrenaline running through my body right now, and the words are *begging* to be spoken. I've already taken on the identity of Simon Spier by talking anonymously with some guy in my school, and maybe—just maybe—he was on to something when he figured out it would be easier to open up to someone that you haven't known your entire life.

"Hey, Brooke—" I mutter.

I must look as bad as I think I do, because her face is white with terror. "Hey, are you okay? It looks like you've seen a ghost or something."

"I'm fine. It's just I—I'm—gay." It all comes out like word vomit and I can't look anywhere but the dashboard in the fear that I'll accidentally make eye contact with someone, whether that be inside or outside of the car.

"Oh."

Oh? Is that really all she's going to say to me right now?

"Wow . . . can't really say I ever expected that response," I say.

"I'm sorry. Was there a certain way you wanted me to respond? Because we can rewind this if you want to." She's smiling at me, which is making it really difficult to be annoyed with her and anything she has to say.

"Yeah . . . I mean no. I don't really know what's going on here anymore."

Brooke twists her body around and rests her hand on my arm. "Look, I know it's a scary situation and that it feels like you'll never get things figured out, but you will eventually.

And I feel honored that you felt comfortable enough to tell me. I do have to ask though, have you told anyone else?"

"You're joking right? Have you even *met* my family? I can't even tell them that I don't want to go to Stanford and be the hot shot doctor they want me to be. Do you think they'd really react positively to their son being abnormal?"

"Okay, a couple of things. Number one, you're not abnormal, so don't let anyone tell you that you are. Number two, I think they'll react better than you think they will. I've seen how they are with you and they love you so much. Especially your sister."

"I mean, I know they love me. It's just really scary when I know everyone has all these expectations for me. But I don't want what they want."

Her blonde hair is the only thing fully visible in the darkness. "Then what do you want?" She's studying me again.

"I just—" I pause for a moment and stare up at a flickering street lamp. "I just want the opportunity to be my own person and to figure out who I am and who I want to be. The thought of going away to Stanford and starting on the track to becoming a doctor just makes me physically sick. And then after I finish, I'm expected to come back here and start my own office and marry and have kids. That's never been what I wanted."

"That portrait of me," Brooke says in a matter of fact tone. "It's your art that drives you, isn't it?"

"You caught me. The day I got my acceptance letter to Stanford, I also got an acceptance letter to NYU's Studio Art program, so that's just the icing on top of the cake."

"Hey, that's awesome as hell!"

My fingers run along the outer curves of the steering wheel and I bring my attention back to Brooke. "You'd think so, right?"

"Is it not what you wanted after all?"

"I'm not saying that. I mean, it's great to know that I was able to get into the program, but it makes it that much worse knowing that I'll never be able to pursue that part of me."

The only part of Brooke's face I can actually see in the darkness is the white of her eyes, but I can feel the terrifying glare she's giving off. "Says who?" she asks. "Is that something coming from you?"

"Not exactly, but my parents only ever talked about me becoming a doctor when I was a kid. There's never been any sort of room for anything else. I don't even know how they'll react to their only son being anything other than totally heterosexual."

"But you also don't know that," Brooke says. "You owe it to yourself to explore other parts of yourself, even if it is terrifying. I remember when my brother came out. He was scared shitless, but it was like watching him throw a one-thousand-pound weight off his shoulders."

I can't say I expected that. It's not that I assumed me, Cinderfella, and that other gay kid (I think it's Sam or something like that) were the only gay guys to ever grow up in Lakeview. I guess I just never really stopped to think about it.

"Wait, your brother's gay? The one that wrote the book?"

"Yeah," she says. "I just figured you knew that already. The book is an LGBT love story. It was all over the article written about him in the paper."

"I can't say I caught that part."

Brooke's hand reaches for the handle again. She pauses for a moment and turns her head in my direction one last time. "I understand that this entire situation isn't ideal, and I can't even begin to really understand the sexuality part. But what I can say is that you don't want to follow in my footsteps when it comes to career choices. I'm almost twenty-eight and I'm just now going to school for the degree that I actually want. I spent so much time trying to do whatever it was that I thought I was supposed to be doing that I wasted so much time in a career I never wanted. I think you should talk to my brother. It might help."

"I'll think about it." The words are barely audible when they slip out of my mouth.

"Good." She pushes the door open and jumps out before poking her head through the door. "I'll see you next week, and I expect an update on the college decisions. Oh, and some new artwork."

That was probably one of the most terrifying moments in my life, but I've never felt freer.

Not five minutes after I get home, my phone starts blowing up with texts from Brooke.

Brooke: If I tell you something, will you promise not to get super angry?

That's probably not the best way to start a conversation with someone who spilled their guts to you not even an hour earlier.

Me: That depends. Does it involve me?
Brooke: Yes and no.

The three little dots pop up at the bottom of my screen.

Brooke: I may have told my brother that I knew someone from home that's going through a bit of a hard time with their sexuality and that maybe they could use someone to talk to that's gone through the same thing.

I don't even know how to reply to that.

Brooke: I know I should've asked you first, but I promise that I never said your name or told him anything about you. As of now, you are still completely anonymous to him, and it's your choice whether or not you want to talk to him.

Me: I get where you're coming from. And I can't get mad at you for trying to help me understand all of this. I don't know for sure if I'm really ready to reach out to someone about all of it just yet, but I will gladly take his email or whatever, and if I get the courage, I promise I'll talk to him.

She wastes no time in sending a reply with a link attached.

Brooke: Perfect! I've learned from experience that the guy rarely ever checks his email, so an Insta DM is probs your best bet. Keep me filled in!

I lean back in my desk chair and stare at the screen of my phone before finally getting the guts to click on the link embedded in her text, which takes me straight to the app.

Noah Carlisle, current author and former editor at Hale Publishing House. His entire profile is like some sort of shrine dedicated to the past year or two of his life in New York, and apparently a temporary life in Los Angeles. The sense of freedom and empowerment he must feel is practically dripping off the page, and I can't help but feel a pang of jealousy that I may never have that kind of life. The kind of life where I can live and work with my best friends in the world and attend events and just have fun living life and learning how to be okay with just pleasing myself.

My scrolling stops as a photo from 2019 Pride catches my eye. There he is, decked out in rainbow from head to toe, unapologetically himself.

Just once I want to know what that's like.

Before I even realize I'm doing it, I scroll back to the top of the page and tap on the messaging option.

Hi, so you don't really know me, but I know a little bit about you. Your sister is my tutor, and she also just so happens to be the first person that I ever felt comfortable enough with to open up to about who I really am.

Although, I guess if I'm being real, I don't really even know who I am. I don't know if I ever will. I guess at this point I'm just super confused and I don't know what I'm doing. As I'm sure you remember, being anything other than straight here isn't really the norm, so there's not a whole lot of people to talk to about it.

Brooke wanted me to at least reach out to you and say hi, so I thought I would go ahead and do it, although I'm not really sure what I expect to get out of sending this message to you.

I'm just kind of one big ball of confusion here.

Send.

CHAPTER NINETEEN

ELLIOT

Friday, April 10

I have never made so much fried chicken in my entire life. I don't think I'll ever be able to get the stench out of my nostrils, and I'm pretty sure there's not enough tea tree oil shampoo in the world that can get the oil out of my hair.

Despite the fact that I should be focused on the eight o'clock rush and I'm covered in flour and feel totally disgusting, all I can actually think about are the butterflies that have been fluttering around in the bottom of my stomach for the last two days. After Milo shot me an email the other night telling me that he'd finally told someone the truth about himself, I haven't been able to focus on much else. It's not that he's shouting his now undefined sexuality from the rooftops and said that he wanted to meet me as soon as possible because he's in love with me—although a boy can dream—but it's a start and it just means we might finally be getting closer to that point.

I peek over my shoulder at the clock on the back wall. It's 8:23 and the mini rush is finally starting to slow down, which means I can finally slow down on the frying rate. Cooper's in the process of slicing up a couple pounds of ham and turkey for Mrs. Bell, who was my second-grade teacher and hands down the sweetest woman I've ever met, while Debby is busy dishing out fried chicken and mashed potatoes and gravy by the pound for the now nearly vacant line of customers. It was for sure a slower learning curve for her, but she's gotten the hang of everything finally.

Although this job has definitely made me dislike working for the public, not to mention the smell of fried foods, I do have to admit that it wasn't a terrible first job to have. It has its days where it totally sucks, a big chunk of which involves the Sunday after church crowd, but it's been great knowing that I have a pretty decent support system back here. I don't see myself getting that anywhere else.

Anna comes bursting through the doors leading to our lockers and the back stockroom, nearly toppling into Debby as she hands out the last box of food from the rush. "Oh shoot, I'm so sorry. Are you okay?"

"I'm fine," Debby replies. "Are you alright though?"

"Yeah, I just got a call from the babysitter and Ethan got sick, so now I have to leave and go pick them up. Elliot, I'm gonna need you to take over for Debby so she can go home, and then I'm gonna need you and Cooper to close up for the night."

"I can stay and help them."

"You're already over twenty minutes passed the end of your shift. Go home to your kids and enjoy your day off tomorrow."

"Yeah," Cooper says, approaching from behind. "Elliot and I have this. You two go take care of your kids and we'll get everything closed up."

"Thank you guys so much," Anna says, hugging the both of us. "I promise I'll make it up to you."

"With your homemade banana bread?" I ask.

"If that's what you want, then you've got it."

Anna's banana bread is a pretty sweet reward, but I would've done it for free with no questions asked. She's done so much for me over the years that I'll never be able to repay her in a hundred lifetimes. I also haven't flown solo with Cooper in a while, which is a reward in and of itself.

The rest of the night actually went pretty smoothly, which usually happens any time Cooper and I work together. When we work together it's like—I don't know—it's like magic or something. When we're working together, it's almost as if we can read each other's minds and everything we do has a perfect flow to it. I can open my mouth to start asking him if he can hand me something, and he knows what it is I'm going to ask before I even ask it.

And I know that the last thing I need to do is become yet another statistic where the gay guy starts crushing on his male friend, and then gets heartbroken when things get weird, but something about this feels different. I don't think Cooper would ever intentionally make me feel that way or put me in that type of situation. It could be my bad habit of trying to see the best in everything and everyone, but I genuinely believe that he's not like that.

I made the decision to throw on a clean t-shirt I had in my locker after we finished the last of the clean-up. There's no way in hell I'm getting flour all over my seats again. My car smelled like the deli for a month last time I did that, and I just can't put myself through that kind of torture again.

"Any big plans tonight?" Cooper asks as he shuts the door of his locker again.

"On a Wednesday night? Definitely not. The only plans I have tonight are a shower and crawling into bed to watch Netflix with a snack before I pass out."

"As fun as that sounds, how about you come and get some food with me before all of that happens? My parents went out for their anniversary, so I'm on my own for dinner and I'd rather have some company."

How could I say no to that?

I mindlessly nibble on my bottom lip. "Fine, but under one condition. You have to pay since I wasn't planning on spending money on food tonight."

"I think I can work with that condition, but since you have a condition, I have one of my own. Since I'm paying, you have to drive."

I hold my hand out in front of me. "Deal."

"Deal," he echoes, grasping my hand.

The feel of his skin against mine sends a shockwave through me and the little hairs on the back of my neck stick straight up. It takes every muscle I have to hide the fact that my entire body is subtly vibrating.

I let go and lead him out of the store and into the parking lot, where the first sign of the impeding summer humidity hits me in the face like a ton of bricks. "Geesh, if it feels like this already, I dread June."

Really, Elliot? You're going to talk about the weather out of all the possible topics?

"Yeah," Cooper says. "I don't know how much longer I can handle this state and all its indecisiveness."

I unlock the driver's side door and lean over the seats to pull up on the latch of the passenger's side. "Do you know what you want?"

"Huh?" he asks.

"For dinner, I mean. Do you know what you want?"

"Oh." He chuckles and pushes his wavy locks from his face. "Well, I definitely don't want any chicken any time soon, so Dairy Queen is for sure out of the question. How about we share one of those little deep dishes from Mach? I'm kinda feeling pizza."

"I think I could go for that," I say, shifting into drive. "Sorry I don't have an aux cord, but feel free to browse through some of the radio stations."

Cooper flips through some of the channels for a solid minute before finally landing on a Halsey song. "I'll deny it if you ever tell anyone, but Halsey is my girl. Seeing her is definitely on my bucket list."

"Really? I didn't really peg you for a Halsey fan. I pictured you as more of the Post Malone, Travis Scott, Drake or whomever else fan."

"You don't really keep up on the trends, do you?" he asks, his eyes staring a hole into the side of my head.

"What gave it away?"

"Hey, that's not a bad thing. If I'm being honest, I only listen to all of it because it almost feels like I'm supposed to in order to keep up with all of my friends. If you checked all of my playlists, you'd definitely find a lot of Imagine Dragons, the 1975, and Broods."

I pull into a parking space in front of Mach 21 and cut off the engine. "Interesting. I can't say I ever knew you were so into the more alternative stuff."

"There's a lot about me you don't know." Cooper's arm brushes lightly against mine, and he's got the most adorable, yet somehow slightly mischievous, grin plastered on his face.

"Well, run in and grab the pizza and a couple bottles of water and then maybe you can fill me in on some of the stuff I don't know about you yet."

"Sounds like a plan," he says.

I'm not sure what I'm more surprised by. The fact that Cooper admitted to having a fear of dolls after watching *The Conjuring* for the first time at his grandma's house and then staying up all night convinced that her porcelain doll collection was going to come to life and kill him, or that he has a secret obsession with musicals. He's definitely much different than I expected him to be, which unfortunately just makes me want him that much more.

We're sitting in the employee parking lot at the store again and jamming out to the *Dear Evan Hanson* soundtrack, which is something that I can never seem to get Aimee to do with me no matter how much I beg her to. She's got her own interests, which I can respect, but that doesn't mean I have to like it. At least now I have someone to nerd out with.

"I should probably get home before my mom totally flips out."

"Same actually," I say. "Michael's never been as lenient with me staying out passed curfew as he has been with Tommy."

"That's really rough."

"Yeah . . . but it hasn't been too bad this year, I guess. Tommy's off doing only God knows what, Hailey's been driving herself crazy over the show and prom and all that, and Michael's barely been home since he bought a couple of other store locations, which is totally fine by me."

Cooper swipes his phone off the dashboard and opens Snapchat before shoving it into my hand. "Well, if you ever want some company, just let me know."

"Will do," I say as I input my username into the search bar and tap add. "There you go."

"Sweet. I guess I should probably get going."

"Yeah."

We sit in silence for another moment as I wait for him to push the door open and step out into the world, every passing second making it more difficult for me not to blurt out the g word and tell him how great I think he is and how much I just want to hold onto him and never let him go. That would be ridiculous and totally uncalled for though, right? That kind of thing only happens in the movies, and this isn't a movie. This is my life.

"Hey, Elliot," he finally says.

"Yeah?" I mutter.

"I—I may have sort of overheard your conversation with Anna the other night."

"You're gonna have to be a little more specific than—"

Oh shit!

The conversation with Anna from the other night. The one in which I divulged my deepest secret and finally told her I'm gay. I didn't know anyone else was around. If I had, I certainly never would've said anything.

This is it. My life is officially over.

It's one thing to have a secret thing for your hot coworker from the baseball team, but it's a totally different thing for him to know that there's even the slightest chance that you could ever have some sort of thing for him. Do I deny it and totally gaslight him to make him think he's crazy and totally imagined the entire conversation, or that he was dreaming? I've never been a very good liar though.

I open my mouth to deny everything, but all that comes out is air and the sound of me choking on my own words. My heart is racing furiously against my ribcage, and my hands are trembling in my lap.

Suddenly there's a hand against the back of my arm and I look up to find Cooper's eyes looking me up and down. He seems to be genuinely worried about me, and it somehow makes all of it that much worse.

"I—" I start to say.

Before I know it, Cooper's got his hands clutching my face and his lips are pressed against mine.

Is this really happening right now?

After an initial brief moment of shock, I find my groove and match his rhythm. My hands find his before slowly snaking their way up his arms. My fingers find the short tufts of curls on the back of his head as he pulls me closer, and the tip of his tongue softly grazes against my top lip.

I never imagined that his lips or the touch of his fingertips against my skin would be so soft and delicate. To be fair, though, I also never imagined that I'd be kissing Cooper Thompson in my car in the back parking lot of my evil stepfather's store. Today is just full of surprises.

Cooper's lips loosen their grip on mine and he slowly pulls back. I half expect him to have a dorky grin to go perfectly with the one I have, but all I see is the look of utter confusion and pain. He averts his glance in the direction of a large dirt pile on the opposite side of the parking lot.

That kiss was honestly one of the most amazing moments in my life. It felt like I was floating and like there was nothing and no one that could ruin it for me.

But maybe I was the only one that felt that way.

"I—I'm sorry," Cooper mutters under his breath.

"It's fine. I mean that was—wow—that was—"

"You can't tell anyone," Cooper says, still avoiding my eyes. "I'm just not ready for that. For any of it."

"Your secret is safe with me. You don't have to worry about that. And if you ever need someone to talk to, I'm here for you."

"I should go. I'll see you around." He wastes no time getting back into his car and speeding off down the road out of sight.

Not exactly how I pictured my first kiss.

The kiss replays in my head the entire way home. The softness of his lips against mine, the feel of his fingertips slowly caressing my cheeks. It was everything I'd hoped for and more. At least up until the part where he sped off into the night.

Now all I can think about is whether or not our friendship's been ruined and if he'll ever be able to look at me again.

CHAPTER TWENTY

JUSTIN

"Are we sure that this is a sufficient enough ending for it though?" The perfectionist attitude I was raised with is rearing its ugly head again.

"We've gone back and forth on this. It's a great ending. We don't need some huge finisher because we want the audience to come to their own sort of conclusion about things. It's fine," Aimee says, trying to pry the script from my anxiety driven hands.

My fingers finally loosen their grip on the stapled sheets of paper. "Okay, you're right. It's fine. We'll just leave it at that. We're totally gonna crush this."

Aimee's grinning and she looks rather pleased with herself. "We are, aren't we? I'll turn this in on Monday."

"Sounds like a plan." I start piling all my stuff back into my bag and look back up at her. "I'm glad you were my partner."

"We do work pretty well together, don't we?" Aimee grins again before taking a look down at the time on her phone. "I really have to go now, but I'll see you on Monday."

"I'll see you then."

Every time I finish a work session with Aimee on our theatre project, I leave wondering why the hell I never hung out with her before now. It's kind of sad that the project work had to end so soon, but I'm actually really proud of what we've created, and I couldn't have asked for a better partner. She's so much different than everyone else in school and doesn't pretend to be cooler than she is, which actually makes her the coolest person at LHS if you ask me.

I'm not saying that I don't love my friends like family, because I totally do, I'm just saying that I've started to realize that maybe I should've put myself out there a little bit more than I did. All the guys ever want to talk about is sports, girls, and video games, and all the girls ever want to do, specifically Gabbi, is flirt and tell me what I think I want to hear so I'll date them.

Not exactly the best company to keep around all the time.

Me, Danny, and a couple of the other guys from the team decided to get together and have a game night like old times, which I was pretty excited about until Hayden decided to bring Tommy Jenkins along. Again, not saying I hate the guy, but he's always left a bad taste in my mouth. Every time he says something, I want to punch the smug look right off his face. He makes his sister look like an angel, and that's saying something.

"Dude, I was at this stoplight party in BloNo last weekend that my buddy Brett got me into, and let me tell you, the amount of single college babes there was *insane*!" Tommy says in his bro voice.

I don't think he could be any more of a pretentious tool.

"Sweet," Liam says in between shooting zombies. "When we get to campus next year, you've got to hook me up with some of those parties, bro. Did you get any action after?"

"Aye, a gentleman doesn't hump and tell." Tommy sinks a knife into a zombie's head and glances at the rest of us before falling into a fit of laughter. "I guess it's a good thing I'm not a gentleman, huh? Hell yeah I got some action! But you know how the story goes. You sleep with her and then all of a sudden, she's all over you wanting some sort of commitment and to talk about feelings and shit. Had to let that one go."

That's definitely the smartest thing he's ever done. No way that poor girl needs to deal with him every day. Nothing would be worth the cost of that.

"Good riddance," Liam chimes in again. "Hey, have you decided where you'll be staying on campus yet?"

"I haven't yet, but anywhere has got to be better than my shit show of a house. If I have to hear Hailey rehearsing for some fucking musical one more time, I think my brain's gonna start bleeding."

That would imply that Tommy actually has a brain, so it's probably safe to say he doesn't need to worry about that.

"And don't even get my started on Faggiot. The dude's a loser."

And there it is. Yet another variation of the "F" word from the always so lovely Tommy Jenkins. I can only hope that one day he'll say that around the wrong person, and he'll get his ass handed to him on a silver platter. Each time I start to wonder why I'm still wasting my life away by continuing to hide in the closet in a world that's becoming more accepting each year, I'm reminded that people like him exist, and it forces me just a little bit deeper in.

"Dude," Danny says. "Not cool, no name calling in my house, okay? This is a chill space, and I don't need that disrupting the vibe we've got going here. Besides, don't you think that way of thinking may be just a little bit outdated. Even if your brother is—you know—what business of it is yours anyway? Shut the hell up, dude."

Did Danny Peters, my best friend in the entire world, finally just defend someone's sexuality against a douchebag bigot? I've always wondered his stance on it, but I was always too afraid to ask. The last thing I needed was to give myself away.

"Step-brother," Tommy adds.

"Well, whatever you want to refer to him as, it's not cool." Danny hits a few buttons on his ps4 controller and shuts off the game. "And on that note, I think it's time for all ya'll to leave."

"Come on, dude!" Hayden says. "Just one more game."

"No, dude. I'm exhausted and I want to go to bed. Some of us actually prefer going to bed at a decent hour the night before a game. You still good with passing out on the couch, Justin?"

"Yeah," I say, getting up from my spot on the floor.

"Sweet, then you can stay. The rest of you can get the hell out. You don't have to go home, but you sure as hell *can't* stay here."

I took Danny throwing out the rest of the guys as an opportunity to change into a t-shirt and a pair of shorts before finally crashing face first into the couch. My phone vibrates against my hand and an Instagram notification pops up on the screen.

One new private message from Noah Carlisle.

Hi, Justin. I'm so sorry I wasn't able to get back to you before now. The last few days have been insane with everything that's going on around here right now. I'm guessing my sister told you that I've been working on some stuff out in LA for the past couple of months, so I haven't been able to get to my phone a whole lot recently.

Anyway, I just wanted to say that I really appreciated getting your message and it's definitely bringing back a lot of high school memories, most of which have a lot confusion attached to them. And you're right, it's not an easy thing to deal with when you're living in a place like Lakeview. I can only hope that things are a least a little more accepting than when I was in high school. I actually didn't feel brave enough to come out to the world until I was almost 21, so you don't need to feel any pressure to come out before you're ready to.

And as far as knowing who you are, I don't think that any of us really know who we are. There are a few things that I'm still trying to figure out for myself, and I don't think that ever stops. Just let me know if there is anything you ever need to talk about, and I'll try to help with whatever I can.

"I swear I'm gonna have to make it a rule that nobody's allowed to bring Tommy around here. If I have to listen to him spout more of his mindless bullshit, I might actually deck him," Danny says before plopping down on the arm of the couch.

"Trust me, I get it." I push myself up and squeeze into the other corner of the couch before locking my phone and shoving it back into my pocket. "That was really cool what you said, by the way."

Danny slides off the arm and onto a cushion. "You're gonna have to give me a bit of a refresher."

"When you stuck up for Tommy's step-brother when he brought up the whole suspected gay thing," I say, my voice shaking.

"It was just the right thing to do. People can't just go around talking shit about other people behind their backs when they can't be here to defend themselves. Besides, it's no one else's business what his sexuality is."

My fingers glide over the edge of the couch's arm, and a knot forms in the pit of my stomach. "I just never really knew your opinion on it."

Danny reaches for the remote and starts flipping through whatever's on, which isn't a whole lot this time of night. "I guess it's never really come up before. But yeah, I don't have a problem with it. People should be free to love whoever they want."

"Well, that's good to know. Because I—" My words trail off and my heart's starting to race.

Is this actually happening right now? Am I about to do this?

"Huh?" he asks, still flipping through the channels.

"I—I'm gay," I finally blurt out. "So . . . yeah . . . that's it, that's what I wanted to say."

If Danny were any quieter, he'd probably be able to hear my pulse racing or the little butterflies doing somersaults in my stomach.

Maybe I shouldn't have told him. Maybe I would have been better off just keeping it all to myself like I have since I figured out I wasn't like everyone else. Maybe he's only okay with it if it's not something that directly affects him. Who knows if he's okay with his best friend of several years not being straight?

"And look, I totally get if you're not cool with that. I mean, I know that it's a lot to take in that your best friend in the entire world isn't exactly the person that you thought they were, so I get it if you don't want to hang around me or if you're uncomfortable with it. I can leave if you want me to."

Danny twists his body in my direction and crosses his legs. "Are you done?"

I just shake my head.

"Good, now maybe I can get a word in. I knew that you had some stuff going on, but I never in a million years thought that was what it was, so I *am* a little bit surprised. Look, man, I'm not gonna sit here and pretend like I know the right thing to say—because I don't—but what I do know is that you're still my best friend, no matter what gender you like. You've always been like my brother, and you always will. I hope you know that."

The all-too-familiar burning sensation is starting to run through my nose. My eyes bat at double their normal speed.

"I've got your back, Justin. And if anyone tries to mess with you, they have to deal with me first. Now bring it in."

Danny throws his arms around me and pulls me in tight. It's the most comforted I've felt in a really long time. The tears break through, rushing down my face and dripping onto the sleeve of his t-shirt.

CHAPTER TWENTY-ONE

ELLIOT

Tuesday, April 14

Cooper makes it really hard to be angry at him with that gorgeous head of wavy hair, long lashes, and those adorable dimples.

"Look, I know that I've been super weird since—you know—and I'm really sorry about that. It was just a lot to process."

I throw my political science book back into my locker and pull out my algebra book, which is tattered beyond repair and definitely on its last year of use.

Cooper leans against the locker next to mine. "Any chance you could forgive me and maybe give me a second chance?"

"I don't know. I know that this is all just super weird and confusing, but at the same time I've come to the realization of who I am, and I've accepted that part of me. It's just scary when I don't know from one day to the next if you're gonna get all weird and run off like that again," I finally say.

"I shouldn't have run off like that after I did what I did. The truth is that I really do like hanging out with you, it's just gonna take a bit for me to adjust."

I latch the door shut again before heading down to the other end of the senior hall for class. "Yeah, I guess I get that. I was actually in the same place not too long ago. It's really scary."

"Then do you think there's any chance I could get another chance to prove myself," he whispers as we walk side by side.

"I guess I'd be going against my own mantra if I didn't give you a second chance. Fine, but you only get one more shot at it."

"That's all I'll need," he says, smiling. We stop in the middle of the hall between both our classes and he looks back at me. "You work tonight?"

"I actually don't."

"Ah, well then maybe you can meet me later on tonight? I'm only on till eight."

"I think I can do that."

"Great, I shall see you tonight," Cooper says with a discreet wink before disappearing into Mr. Dalton's rom.

It felt like someone had turned on slo-mo mode for the rest of the day.

The only thing running through my mind all day was getting home so I could start picking out an outfit to wear tonight. I felt really bad that I was barely present during my last meeting with Vanessa for our project in Charlie's class, but every time I've seen Cooper outside of class, I've been covered in the smell of fried chicken and I've had a flour stain somewhere on my clothes. I'm determined to finally look like a normal human being around him for one of our hangout sessions.

My eyes keep darting back and forth between the little clock at the bottom of my laptop screen, and a webpage all about possible ways to take out extra loans so that I can stay in the dorm for a year, because even though I'm getting quite a bit in scholarships, it's still not enough to cover how crazy dorm expenses are. If I'm going to be forced to go to ISU after all, then I'm sure as hell getting out of here for a year, even if it kills me. Maybe by the time I'm done there I'll have my shit figured out enough to get my own place somehow. Anywhere has to be better than here, where I'm wedged into the tiny room between Tommy, who blasts his speakers against my wall while he's playing video games all night, and Hailey, who's busy blaring show tunes or rehearsing every night.

It's 7:49 pm when I hear a chime coming from below a pile of papers stacked up in front of me.

Anna: Are you busy tonight?

Me: I mean, sort of. Why?

Anna: I know you said you weren't gonna go to prom, but I think you should. I found this suit that was in really good shape that looked to be about your size, so I bought it.

How did I really not see this coming?

I start typing again.

Me: You really didn't have to do that.

Anna: I know I didn't HAVE to, but I wanted to. Just please do it for me. You can come over tomorrow and try it on and I can make any necessary alterations on it.

Me: Fine, I'll stop by tomorrow and try it on.

Anna: Thank you! That's all I ask. I have to go. I'm trying to put these little rugrats to bed!

I set my phone down on the desk and lean back in my chair. I know that Anna means well, but she has to understand that I'm more than capable of doing that sort of stuff on my own if I really want to. She has bills to pay and two kids to take care of and I don't. Every time she spends money on me, I just wind up feeling shitty and like I'll never be able to repay her for everything she does.

On the other hand, though, it might be kind of fun to go to prom now that I've got someone around. Not that I'm assuming Cooper will go with me since it is a school function, but it's also masquerade themed, so who knows what the night has in store for everyone. I just hope by some miracle that I do get to go with him, because he's pretty great.

But so is Milo. Or at least from what I *know* he is.

I find myself scrolling through old emails after his name pops into my head. Is it wrong to have these feelings for Cooper when there's obviously some sort of deep emotional connection with Milo? At least I think there's an emotional connection. Lately things have been a little quiet between the two of us. There's been the occasional catch-up email where we talk about the little trivial things in life due to the fact that we can't actually open up about our true identities, which is virtually the only thing keeping us from having any type of real relationship going, but it's mostly been surface level over the last couple of weeks.

Maybe we've taken things as far as they could ever possibly go. Saying goodbye could be the best thing for the both of us if things with Cooper are ever going to work out.

There's a light tapping on the door before it swings open and Hailey storms in, guns blazing and resting bitch face on.

"What the hell?" I blurt out before my brain has the chance to filter my words.

"What? At least I actually knocked this time."

I click the lock button on my phone and lay it back down. "What could you *possibly* want from me this time?"

"My research paper," she says flatly. "Did you finish looking over it yet?"

"Oh yeah." I sift through the pile of papers and pull out her research paper about genetic engineering of embryos for her dual credit English course. "It was fine. Minimal edits."

"Duh, I wrote it." She flips through the pages, no doubt to check my handy work. "Alright—well—thanks or whatever."

"Yeah," I mumble before standing up. "If you're always so sure that your work was sufficient the first time, why do you ask me to look over it for you?"

"And why do you ask so many questions?" She combs through the rest of the paper looking for any corrections and looks back up at me. "Well, if you must know, I've just been super busy with the show coming up next weekend and getting ready for prom and graduation and all that. I just haven't had the time."

"You could literally have anyone else do it though. So why me of all people?" I ask.

Hailey runs her fingers through her hair and tugs at the bottom of her top before heading back out into the hall, her eyes avoiding mine. "This better get me an A."

"Or what?"

She walks out, completely ignoring the rest of the conversation. I can't help but laugh as I settle into my chair again. Hailey may act all tough, but deep down she's all bark and no bite, which is leaving her threats emptier by the day.

My phone chimes and vibrates against the desk again.

Cooper: Hey, I actually got out on time. Are you ready?

Me: Yeah, where do you want to meet?

Cooper: Not sure if you'd be interested but I actually have the house to myself tonight. Would you be interested in coming out for a little bit? I could use the company.

I have to wipe the sweat from my palms onto my jeans.

Me: I mean, I guess I can for a little while.

The three little dots pop up briefly before disappearing again.

Cooper: If you're not comfortable with that, you don't have to. I just thought we could have a fire in the back yard since it's not too hot out.

Me: No, I'll come. I want to. I think I remember where you live.

Cooper: Sounds good, I'll see you soon.

It's already almost 8:30 by the time I get to Cooper's house. I got lost and had to ask him to send me his address after all, which I feel doesn't bode all too well for me in the long run, but we'll see.

Cooper basically lives out in the middle of nowhere, just like half of this damn town, so that means he has virtually no neighbors to get angry and file noise complaints, which he seems to be taking advantage of. He's already in the backyard with a fire blazing and the volume of his bluetooth speaker maxed out.

"Welcome to Chateau Thompson," he shouts excitedly upon seeing me.

"Wow, this definitely looks different than the last time I was here, granted that was like sixth grade."

He turns the volume down from his phone. "Well, my mom's gained a love for Pinterest over the last year, so she's decided to do a little bit of remodeling back here. I personally think she's gone a little heavy on the twinkle lights, but that's whatever."

"It looks nice. Like something out of a movie or something."

Cooper just looks at me for a moment before that famous smile of his pops up and he brushes his hand against mine. "Hi."

"Hi," I echo, now smiling back at him.

My stomach's in the middle of hosting a gymnastics meet and I'm not sure whether to kiss him, hug him, or let him make the first move after how things ended the last time we hung out. We just stand there for a moment staring at each other in silence before he motions for me to take a seat next to the fire.

He plops down in the chair next to me and grabs a bottle of water from a little ice bucket between us. "Do you want anything to drink?"

"I'm okay." My eyes are drawn to the dancing flames in front of us, and I can't help but wonder if any of this is real or if this is just some cruel dream that my mind cooked up for me. "So, how'd you manage to get the place to yourself all night?"

"Well, I told my parents that I had a really cute guy coming over and they needed to vacate for a while." Cooper throws his head back and lets out a laugh. "But in all seriousness, my dad's out of town on business this week and my mom is spending the evening with my grandma so she can take her to the doctor tomorrow for her post-op checkup."

"Oh yeah, I heard about that. Is she doing any better?"

"Yeah, they think they managed to get all of the cancer cells out, but they'll know for sure tomorrow if they got it all."

"That's really great." I turn my head back toward Cooper, and his eyes are glistening in the light from the fire.

"I like you, Elliot. Like a lot."

His teeth gently graze against his bottom lip, knocking the breath out of me and sending my head into a frenzy of thoughts I know I definitely should *not* be having. His hand reaches for my cheek, and his skin against mine is unlike anything I've ever felt. It's like I've lived my entire life floating through space, looking for something to hold on to, and now I've found it. Being with him — touching him — is the one thing tethering me to this world.

"What does that mean, though?" I ask. "For us."

"I don't know. I guess it just means that we'll figure it out as we go, if that's okay with you?" His hand slides from my cheek to the back of my head and his fingers run through my hair as he pulls me close. Our lips meet, and it's even more electrifying than the first time. The contact between us breaks and his eyes study every curvature of my face. "I just want to be with you tonight for as long as I can in this moment. No pressure to go further than we already have, is that okay?"

I can only manage a head nod before I pull him back in for another kiss.

CHAPTER TWENTY-TWO

JUSTIN

Saturday, April 18

I'm finally going to do it. I'm going to tell my sister everything.

My original plan was to sit down with both Steph and my parents and just get it all out in one quick confession, but then I figured that maybe it would be best to get the shock factor out of the way with Steph so that way I have her in my corner for when Mom and Dad figure it out. I feel like Mom might be okay with it, but Dad may be a different story. He was raised in a much different way than any of the rest of us.

I managed to convince them last night to let me drive up to Chicago to see Steph this weekend just by putting on the "little brother misses his big sister" face, and then convinced Steph to let me come up just by flat out telling me I needed to get away from Mom and Dad for the weekend. It was honestly way too easy to con both of them into letting me get what I wanted, although what I told Steph was a little bit less of a stretch.

Steph spent a good chunk of the afternoon showing me around campus and dragging me along to all of our favorite places in the city that we used to go to together when we spent summers up here with our grandparents. It got me feeling all nostalgic and triggered a few memories that I forgot I even had, like the fact that the two of us used to be so close before she became so focused on her future career in law and I started hyper focusing on keeping such a large part of my identity hidden from everyone around me.

I miss the time in my life before I ever had to worry about that. I miss the guy I was before, and I don't know if I'll ever be able to truly get back to him.

It's seven o'clock and Steph and her roommate decided to cook me a huge celebratory welcome dinner in her apartment, consisting of homemade pizzas that I really hope taste a lot better than they look. I've just never had the heart to tell Steph that she can't cook to save her life.

"Are you guys sure you don't just want to *order* pizza instead," I say, looking down at one of their failed attempts sitting on the counter.

"It's fine," Steph says as she rummages through a drawer for the pizza cutter. "It's just a little extra crispy. That's all."

"Extra crispy?" Bethany, her roommate, asks. "That's just a phrase people use to replace the word burned, because it sounds nicer."

"It's going to be *fine*." There's a knock on the front door just as Steph pulls out the pizza cutter. "That's probably Nick. You're gonna love him."

"Is that like your boyfriend or something?" I ask.

Both Bethany and Steph erupt into laughter.

"He's most definitely not my boyfriend," she replies. "The door's open, Nick! Come on in!"

There's a subtle click, and the door swings open and I quickly realize what was so funny. Nick walks in wearing a pair a skin tight black jeans, a mesh short sleeve shirt, and a pair of black boots. The curls at the top of his head have been bleached and he does his makeup better than most girls I've seen. It's all topped off with a single silver hoop in his nose.

Not exactly my type, but he's not bad looking either.

Nick catches a glimpse of the pizza and says, "Honey, what the hell is that?"

"It's the pizza I made for dinner," Steph says. She sinks the pizza cutter into the crust and it all cracks apart in one large chunk. "See, it's just . . . a little crispy."

"I know you're not about to serve that on a plate, because the only place that belongs is the dumpster outside, sweetheart."

I let out a snicker before I can stop myself.

Nick turns to me and looks me up and down. "Something funny? What's the matter, have you never seen a black gay man in makeup before?"

"I—I didn't—" is all that comes out of my mouth.

"I'm just messing with you," he says. "It was a joke, so don't take it so hard."

"Come on, you're gonna scare the kid to death," Bethany says with a smile.

"Sorry, I probably should've warned you about this one over here," Stephanie says to me. "Nick, this is my little brother Justin. Justin this is Nick from down the hall."

"Uh . . . hi," I stammer.

"Oh, so you're the other famous Herrera child I've heard so much about. It's great to finally put a face to the name." He smiles before turning back to Steph. "You remember that super cute guy I was telling you about?"

"The one from your design class?"

"That would be the one. Well, his fraternity is throwing a party and I could really use me a wing woman tonight to help me secure a date."

"Dude, do you not see that I have my little brother here? I can't just ditch him to go to some party with you," Steph says before throwing the destroyed pizza into the trash.

"He can come too! More people equals more fun, right? I'm sure he wouldn't mind tagging along."

"Yeah," Bethany says. "Be that cool older sister that brings him to his first frat party."

Stephanie's eyes find me and linger for a moment. "What do you say?"

"I say it sounds like fun. And someone has to be around to make sure you don't get drunk off your ass. It might as well be someone who can't actually drink," I say.

"See? It'll be fun," Nick says as he starts wiggling his hips around.

"Ugh! Fine! We can go, but only for a couple of hours, and then I have to get back here. And no pictures, because if my parents find out I brought him to a frat party, they're going to kill me."

College has really changed Steph. I remember back in my freshman year when Mom and Dad decided to let her have a little party for her birthday with some friends under the condition that I get to join. They tried to get her to drink a bottle of tequila they managed to smuggle into the house in their bag, and she just wouldn't do it. That's definitely not a problem anymore. I've never seen someone kick back so many shots and vodka lemonades. I can't say anything though. I've been throwing back as much jungle juice as I possibly can before someone figures out I'm only 18, but it hasn't really affected me much yet.

I'm standing across the room with Nick and watching Steph and Bethany tear it up on the dance floor with a couple of random dudes. "Is she always like this?"

"I guess so. She doesn't get like this a lot, but she does enjoy having some fun every now and again."

"It's just kinda weird seeing her like this."

"Seeing her like what?" Nick asks before taking another sip of whatever's in his cup.

"It's weird just seeing her so—I don't know—care free. Like she's finally figured out how to be her own person and have balance. We didn't really have that growing up." It might be the juice talking, but my lips are suddenly feeling a bit looser. "Was it difficult? Coming to terms with who you really are in a community that isn't exactly historically known for being accepting of it, I mean."

Nick's hand lowers and he sets his drink down on the mantle of the fireplace. He plants his eyes on me and stares in silence for a moment. "I mean, I guess it was kind of difficult. But I figured out that I actually made it so much worse in my head than it actually was. Having a really supportive brother and sister helped me a lot."

"That's great to hear," I say. "For you, I mean. I'm glad it worked out."

"Everything works out the way it's supposed to in the end and you—I mean we—eventually find the people that are going to accept us for who we are."

I could do it. I could just shout it to from the rooftop, and the only person that would give a shit is Steph, but she may actually be too drunk to care right now.

"Justin! Get your ass over there and dance with us," Steph says before draping her arms over my shoulders.

"I think I'm gonna pass. It's just fun watching you dance around like an idiot."

"You're no fun," she says. "Just another question, why did they decide it would be a good idea to start spinning the room?"

"Girl, that's just you," Nick says. "I think you might've had one too many tequila shots tonight."

"Oh, I guess that would also explain why I can't remember anything from before an hour ago."

"You're looking a little flushed too. Maybe we should go sit down. How's that sound?" I ask, grabbing onto her arm.

Suddenly her expression goes totally blank and she breaks free from my grasp before heading off down the hall in the direction of the bathroom.

"And there's my cue," Nick says.

"No, I've got this one. You just go mingle or whatever it is you're supposed to do at these things," I say before following a trail of pink glitter to the restroom.

If this is what frat parties are universally like, I'm not too sure that I could actually see myself being at one and enjoying it. It's fun to let loose every once in a while, but this level is completely insane. I can't count the number of people I've already seen run upstairs to either hook up or pass out in someone's bed.

"Steph?" I holler as I beat my knuckles against the bathroom door. "Stephanie, are you in there?" My call is met with a subtle groan and another round of gagging sounds that I became all too familiar with that time Steph got food poisoning when we were visiting Abuelita and the rest of the family in Mexico last summer. Steph's sitting on the floor with her back against the bathtub when I push the door open. "Hey, you alright in here?"

"I'm just peachy. Never been better," she says as she pulls her hair up into a bun on top of her head.

I squat down next to her and slide up against the tub.

Steph leans her head against my shoulder and lets out a subtle sigh. "Some night, huh?"

"You can say that." I rest my head against hers and stare forward at the cabinet doors. "Thank you again."

"For bringing you to this shitty frat party and making you watch me throw up?"

I can't help but laugh. "No, just for letting me come up here. I really needed to get out of that town."

"I know what you mean. Every time I go back, I can't help but feel like I'm reverting back to the person that I used to be and like the person I'm trying to become dies a little bit more. Why do you think I don't like to come back and visit very often?"

"Is that really who we've become?" I ask. "Scared of showing Mom and Dad who we really are and who we want to be?"

All I can hear is the sound of my pulse beating furiously in my ears and my cheeks are radiating heat. If I ever had a chance, it would be now. "Hey, Steph . . ."

Her head is still against my shoulder and she's running her fingers along the edge of her shoe. "Yeah?"

"There's something that I need to tell you. I've been wanting to tell you for the longest time, but it's never been the right time to do it. And I don't want you to freak out, because no matter what I'm still going to be the same little brother that loves to annoy the hell out of you." I take a deep breath and try to figure out how to form my next words. "I—damn—I thought this would be easier after I told a few people. I'm just gonna say it already. I'm gay. And I guess while we're at it, I really don't want to go off to med school and I was accepted to the art program at NYU."

Steph sits up. Her eyes fixate on the side of my face.

"Are you—surprised?" I ask, still studying the pattern of the cabinet's wood grain.

"Yes—but also no—I'm not really sure." She looks passed me for a moment, her expression going blank. Her lips slowly form into a smile before she makes eye contact again. "You know, I remember you being completely obsessed with puzzles as a kid. Do you remember that?"

"I mean I guess so, but what does that have to do with this?"

"It's like all these years you've been trying to put together this puzzle and create this image. And I've been watching you struggle to put the pieces together these last few years. I think part of me just sort of knew that the pieces you've been trying to cram into different places weren't pieces meant for *your* final image. They were meant for someone else's." She wipes away the streaks of eyeliner running down her face. "I didn't exactly know why it wasn't fitting together, and I hated myself for never stepping up and being the person that I knew you needed. I'm sorry that I was never a very good sister."

"Don't beat yourself up like that, Steph. I didn't even fully understand why it wasn't working until recently. It was something that I've needed to figure out for myself."

"Now it all makes sense. And now you've found the pieces of the puzzle that you've been missing all this time. But it's up to you to decide whether or not you want to continue trying to put together pieces that weren't meant for you just to please Mom and Dad, or if you're gonna finally decide to start putting things together in your own way."

"I don't know if I can. I'm not like you."

She sniffles and rolls her eyes as she dabs away the remainder of her eye makeup. "That's a good one. If I'd had it my way, this isn't the life that I would've chosen for myself. Law school? That's what they wanted, not me."

"But you always seemed so sure about it."

"I was just too chicken and obedient to tell them otherwise. I don't want to sit back and let you make the same mistake, Justin. You're so talented and amazing and you deserve to have everything you've ever wanted and more. If anyone has the courage to stand up to them, it's you."

"If I tell them about me, then you need to come clean about how you're feeling too."

"I don't know," Steph pulls her knees up to her chest and rests her arms on them. "It's a lot and it's terrifying."

"It is, but maybe it'll be easier if we do it together."

The corner of her mouth twitches. "Just let me think about it and I'll let you know."

CHAPTER TWENTY-THREE

ELLIOT

All I could think about was that final bell of the day ringing so I could make a break for my car and get to work as fast as possible, which is the exact opposite of the way I usually want my day to go. Even Aimee knew something was up in study hall last period, and as much as I wanted to open up to her about everything that was going on with Cooper, it's just not my secret to tell.

Anna decided to stick me on serving duty today, which I'm ordinarily not a huge fan of, but Cooper got stuck on prep duty, so we've basically been right on top of each other the entire night.

"Are you staring at my ass?" I whisper to Cooper in between customers.

His eyebrow quivers and he's smirking. "Maybe I am. Maybe I'm not. Good luck proving it."

"You think you're some hot shit, don't you?"

"No, I know I'm for sure hot shit." A chuckle escapes from his mouth and his nose crinkles up a little. "So, do you want to hang out after work tonight?"

"Well, it is a school night . . ."

"That's what makes it more fun." His eyes flick from me to an elderly customer pushing her cart down an aisle. He's silent for a moment until she disappears. He leans closer. "What could I do that would make it worth your while?"

"I think I might have some ideas on that. I can hang out until ten, but then I really have to get home. Michael flipped out the last time I stayed out passed curfew and he threatened to take my phone away."

"Oh, so you're a bad boy that gets in trouble, huh?" he asks, smirking again.

"Oh my gosh. Just go get your work done so we can get out of here on time."

"Fine." Cooper grabs the broom and starts backing up. "Just let me know what you want to do."

I slide the cooler doors open to wrap up the rest of the food for the evening.

"Aye, Faggiot, what's a guy gotta do to get some food around here?"

Tommy's standing on the other side of the glass with a couple of his douchebag friends from the football team.

"What can I get you guys?" I ask.

"Just three of the four-piece chicken strip meals," he says.

I pop up three small boxes and start loading them with all the tenders we have left. "What sides can I get you?"

"Just throw in all those wedges. And leave out the fag flakes. I don't want to catch that shit."

I pause for a moment before starting to load what's left of the wedges into their boxes as fast as I can. The quicker they're gone, the quicker I can get the hell out of here and not have to think.

"Hey, so if you were to get with a guy, would you be the guy or the girl in that situation?" he asks before exploding into laughter with his dipshit friends.

"Dude, come on. That's enough," Cooper says. "Why don't you just get your food and get outta here. I'm sure you have better things to do than hang around and be a dick."

"Coop, I didn't realize you were a fag lover."

I can see Cooper's face out of the corner of my eye. He's pale white and he's got that look in his eye that I know all too well after years of dealing with Tommy. It's usually followed by fight or flight.

"What—I—I don't know what you're talking about. I'm not . . ." Cooper's words trail off as he starts picking at his fingernails.

"Well you must be. It's either that or you're one yourself, so which is it Cooper Booper?"

"I—"

The double doors fly open and Anna walks in, nostrils flaring and lips curled inward. "Is there a problem here?"

I hear the ferocity in her voice and forget to breathe for a moment.

"No problem here. We're just getting some food and then getting out of here," Tommy says with a smile. "Isn't that right, boys?"

Anna flicks her eyes in my direction and raises her brow before returning her attention to Tommy. "Really? Because to me it sounds like you're harassing my employees, and that's just not okay with me."

"Anna, it's fine. Just let it go," I finally say.

"No, it's not fine. I don't care who your dad is, Tommy. It doesn't give you the right to come in and here and disrespect my employee—your own family—so you just need to take your food and go." Anna closes up their boxes and sets them on top of the hot case.

"Fine, we'll go." Tommy grabs the boxes before stomping away like a toddler.

"I'm sorry you had to deal with that," Anna says. "You two can go and I'll finish up here."

"But I—"

"You heard what I said, Elliot. We're just about done here anyway, so just head on out and I'll talk to you later."

Before I can get out another word, Anna grabs the broom from Cooper's hands and walks away to finish up sweeping. Cooper zips passed me and disappears into the back.

I follow his trail and lean up against the lockers. "Look, I'm sorry you had to be involved in that back there."

He twists in his locker combo and yanks it open. "It's whatever."

"I could really use that hangout sesh now."

Cooper pulls his keys out and shuts the door again. "Actually, I forgot I have a thing I have to do tonight. Rain check?"

"Yeah . . . sure," I mutter.

He shoots me a half smile before turning and walking away, leaving me behind in the dust.

I knew it would only be a matter of time before it bit me in the ass. I just didn't think it would be so soon.

CHAPTER TWENTY-FOUR

JUSTIN

"Good game, man," Danny says.

"Yeah, you too."

He grabs his bag out of his locker and takes a seat next to me while I finish tying my shoe. "So, you really told Stephanie, huh?"

"Yes, sir."

"How'd that go?"

I put my foot back down on the floor and look up at him. "It wasn't too bad actually. I was a little buzzed and at a frat party though, so that made it a little easier, I guess."

"Wait, you went to a frat party?"

"It's a long story," I say. "But it was for sure a conversation we needed to have, and it brought up a lot of important stuff."

"Hey, that's a good thing though. I remember how close you two used to be, and I think it would do you both a lot of good to get back there. Who's next on your list? Maybe Gabbi?"

And that's where things get a little more complicated. Up until the last couple of months, I tried entertaining the idea that maybe I was bisexual and could possibly grow to one day fuel a relationship with Gabbi, which was why I've continued trying and playing into her flirting. "Dude, I don't know. I know that I need to say something eventually, but I don't know how she's gonna react after all this time."

"I know it's scary, but you just need to rip the bandage off. You don't necessarily have to tell her the whole thing, but you owe it to her to end things before they go any further. You know she can be — sensitive."

"I know, and I will eventually."

"Okay." Danny stands back up and throws his bag over his shoulder. "See you tomorrow."

"See ya."

I finish tying my other shoe before slipping my t-shirt over my head and grabbing my bag out of my locker. The door shuts with a quiet click, and it suddenly hits me that this part of my life is almost over. It was never my favorite part of my entire high school career, but it's still really weird to think about it coming to an end in just a month, like maybe I should have enjoyed these experiences sooner.

Muffled music starts echoing through the locker room as I round the corner in the direction of the exit doors. The gym is almost completely dark except for a few lights in the middle of the room, and I can just barely make out a dark-haired girl in a red dress standing in center circle. She's staring in my direction with her hands interlocked in front of her and a bluetooth speaker blasting Shawn Mendes' rendition of "Use Somebody" at her feet.

"Congrats on the win tonight," she projects over the music.

"Oh, thank you." I finish the trek to the middle of the gym and stop dead in front of Gabbi. "I thought you would've left with everyone else forever ago. What are you doing here?"

She turns down the music on her phone and looks up at me. Even in her heels, the top of her head barely makes it to the bridge of my nose.

"I know that things have been crazy with you making all the preparations for the move to Stanford in a few months and exams and graduation coming up and all that, so I guess I just kind of wanted to make sure you know that I'm here if you need me through any of it."

"Well thank you. I really appreciate that."

"And since you're so busy, I finally just decided I'd grow a pair and do this myself." She takes a deep breath and straightens her shoulders out. "I guess what I'm trying to ask is if you, Justin Nicholas Herrera, will be my date to prom."

I'm not sure what I'm more upset about right now. The fact that I don't know how the hell I'm going to get out of this, or that I now have to listen to Danny gloating because he told me I needed to figure out some way to let Gabbi down easy before something like this happens.

"You're awfully quiet over there," she says, her fingers playing with the curled ends of her hair. "I'm kind of going out on a limb over here."

There's only one right thing for me to do. I have to tell her the truth once and for all.

"I—" A knot forms in my throat and I suddenly develop dry mouth. "I—yeah, I'll go with you."

CHAPTER TWENTY-FIVE

ELLIOT

It's been three days since Tommy came into the store raging about fag flakes in his food, which in hindsight was pretty funny because now he's an equivalent to a Karen. At least it was funny in my head. I think Cooper took things a little different than I did.

He barely spoke to me in class on Tuesday, didn't even bother to show up to school yesterday, and then missed first period today. I tried talking to him between classes, but he vanished into thin air every time I tried to. Not to mention he called in yesterday too. Anna claimed he sounded in pretty bad shape, but there's definitely more to it.

We've surprisingly been pretty slow tonight, so Anna's got Debby taking care of the front and I've been helping her go through some of the inventory to make sure we have everything we need for opening tomorrow.

"Okay, we have plenty of bacon, so we definitely don't need to worry about that," I say.

"Perfect, what about those little breakfast potatoes?"

"I actually didn't see any of those."

"If you want to go check the other big freezer, I can finish up this list, and if there's none there, go get some from the actual cases and let Keely know up at the office," Anna says, taking the clipboard from my hands.

"I'm on it." I venture out into the back stockroom. My legs seize up and I stop dead in my tracks. "Cooper?"

He glances up at me for a second before returning his attention to the inside of his locker.

"Hey, I heard you've been sick. Are you feeling any better?"

"Yeah, loads better," he replies, his words are short and monotone.

"I'm glad to hear that. I've missed you these last couple of days."

I don't know whether or not I expected him to say he's missed me too, but I at least expected something other than silence and a blank stare.

"Would you maybe be interested in grabbing some food after I get off? It's opening night of Hailey's show, so everyone's gone."

"I can't," he says.

"Oh, that's cool. Maybe tomorrow night after your game then?"

He pulls a draw string bag over his shoulder and slams the door shut before ripping the sticker with his name off the front. "No, I mean I can't do this anymore."

"You can't do what anymore?"

"This. You and me. Any of it. I'm not—" he leans in closer and lowers his voice, " — gay. This was all just a huge mistake. And it's nothing against you personally, okay? I'm just not . . . like you."

"Oh. Well, I guess that doesn't really mean we can't hang out anymore, right?" I ask.

"It's probably best if we don't, actually. I can't have people thinking that I'm—you know—so it's best if we're not seen together anymore, I think."

"Oh."

There's a burning in my throat that's snaking its way into my chest and through the rest of my body. Every muscle feels like it's been infused with concrete and could be smashed into a thousand pieces at any moment. My feet are bolted in place as I watch him disappear from the building one last time.

The only car in the driveway is Michael's. Not exactly how I wanted to spend tonight.

There's an envelope addressed to me sticking out of the mailbox, and as I pull it out, I see that it's from the admissions office at New York University. It's much too small to be the answer I was hoping for.

Michael's half asleep on the couch, one hand clutching the remote and the other holding onto a beer can. "You got a letter."

"I got it," I say, holding up the envelope.

"You're applying to out-of-state schools now, huh?" he asks.

"Yep."

He chuckles and takes a swig from his beer can. "Good luck paying for that."

"Well, judging by the size, I'm guessing I didn't get in." I shrug my shoulders and start heading for the stairs.

"Oh, I need you to work on Saturday night by the way," Michael hollers over the sound of the TV.

"But that's prom night."

"Well, I'm sorry, but that's just the way things are. We're shorthanded right now and I need you to go in to help out."

"Fine . . . whatever." I clutch the NYU letter closer and run up the stairs to my room. I throw off my uniform and slip into a pair of shorts before leaning back against my pillows and ripping into the tiny envelope with the inevitable death sentence for my future. My fingers tug at the letter inside and unfold it. "Thank you for your application to our Undergraduate Film and Television program. After careful consideration, we regret to inform you that we are not able to extend an offer to you at this time for the Fall 2020 semester. However, we do encourage you apply again at a later time." I crumple up the letter and toss it across the room in the direction of the trash can next to my desk.

CHAPTER TWENTY-SIX

JUSTIN

Thursday, April 30

What the hell am I doing here?

I'm at a table in the campus Starbucks wedged between a Shakespearean study group and a group of gaggling girls — who started off the evening studying for an econ final and are now busy scrolling through Pinterest looking for summer vacation ideas — just hoping that I happen to stumble across Kevin again. So far no luck, but I'm not sure exactly what I imagined would come from this. It's a big campus and I've never been all that lucky with things like this.

Lately I've found myself venturing into the depths of gay Instagram during my off time, and I do have to say it's been quite interesting. It was a little bit of a shock initially with all of the half-naked guys, as well as the occasional fully visible fitness model's butt, but it's been pretty uplifting getting to see legit gay couples be themselves and not feel ashamed of it.

I faze back out of the conversation the girls are having about their dream trip to Mikonos and pull Insta up again. I swipe across the screen and pull up my messages with Noah. They've all been very brief conversations because of his schedule, but he's been telling me all about his life in New York with his best friends and just the overall craziness of his life this past year when he almost gave up and moved back here permanently. As insanely hectic as it's all sounded, it's still made me crave what could be.

I watch another group set up camp in the corner before drawing my eyes back to the screen and start typing out a reply.

Me: That sounds pretty crazy. I couldn't imagine having to go through all that. It sounds like you were able to get everything sorted out though. It gives me hope that maybe there's a chance for me to get out of her after all. Can I ask you a question though? And it's kind of personal, so I'm sorry if it's a little too personal. You're out and all that, so I'll assume you've had boyfriends or have dated guys at least by now. What's that like, exactly? Has it been any different than dating girls? Granted you dated girls in the past as like a cover up or whatever.

My finger hovers over the send button for a moment as I read over what I wrote. I hit send and lay my phone face up on the table. My hands grasp at my venti iced coffee just as the little "Seen" note pops up under my message. An entire novel appears a couple of minutes later.

Noah: Thanks, Justin. I appreciate it. It's definitely been a pretty crazy last year. The last six months especially. It seems like everything went into hyper drive when they told me I needed to come out here for all the production stuff. As for the dating. I've definitely done my own fair share and it hasn't always gone well, which I'm sure you'll learn some day. It's sort of a rite of passage for a gay guy to meet and fall for a couple of bad apples before they find the right one. The LGBT community isn't exactly the healthiest in that way, more than likely because we spend a lot of our teen

years watching all of our friends date and don't get the chance ourselves until later. By that point I think we're just trying to play catch up, to say the least. And yeah, I did date a couple of girls in high school as a way to cover up the gay. Lakeview hasn't exactly been known for its accepting attitude. There is definitely a difference between how it felt to be dating a girl and how it's felt dating guys. Once you do it, it just feels right, and you really understand how it feels to finally be free.

Me: Freedom? Wow, what's that like? I can't remember the last time I ever felt like I could truly just be myself. I hope that I get that chance again someday though. The other night this girl who's been a friend since elementary school decided that she wanted to ask me to prom, and I panicked and said yes. How could I not? She made this entire scene with it and I feel like I'm like expected to go with her and to start dating her.

Noah: That sounds like a pretty complicated situation. I wish I could provide some more insight and some advice on what you're dealing with, but I have to say that I've never had to deal with that before. My family was pretty understanding with the whole gay thing. But everyone's situation is different. You say that you feel like you're expected to go out with this girl. Do you feel like you might have any type of feelings for her apart from just being friends?

Me: Honestly? No, I don't. I've tried to, believe me, and she's a great girl. I just can't get myself to feel that way about her.

Noah: That's perfectly fine, Justin. I just thought I would ask because sexuality is one giant spectrum and things can get pretty confusing. Especially when you're in high school. I know plenty of guys that thought they were gay only to realize later that they're really just bisexual with a leaning toward guys. If you don't feel it with this girl, then you don't feel it. You'll know it's right when you finally meet the person that you know you belong with because it'll feel effortless and natural. What you really need to work on now is deciding whether or not you want to take the chance on going to prom with this girl, knowing that she has real feelings for you, and risk hurting both her and your friendship. I need to go run some errands before it gets too late here, but if you ever need anything, feel free to message me, okay? I'm here to help in whatever way I can.

I lay my phone down again before taking another sip from my cup. Trying to figure things out with Gabbi sounds a lot easier said than done, and there's no telling how she's going to react. She's great and all, but she can be quite the drama queen and I don't think I could ever be prepared for that.

CHAPTER TWENTY-SEVEN

ELLIOT

Friday, May 1

"You will never believe who texted me during study hall." Aimee still has her face buried in her phone and she's scrolling through her texts.

I'm picking through my books, trying to figure out which ones to bring home for work. "Who?"

"Tate!" she says.

"Tate? As in the guy who slept with his coworker and then proceeded to think he could get away with it until you dumped him?" I ask, shoving my history book into my bag.

"Yeah, that one. He sent me this super long text about wanting to meet and talk and potentially see if we could work anything out and asked for a second chance."

"And what did you say to him?" I ask.

I feel terrible for even saying it, but I'm only paying like half attention to everything she's saying. It's not that I don't care, because she's my best friend and I totally do, but there is so much other crap going on right now that I just can't get out of my head. Like the fact that Cooper literally hasn't spoken a word to me since he cleared out his locker on Wednesday, despite having two classes and a lunch period together, and Michael isn't budging on his "no senior prom for Elliot" rule and has even enlisted Tommy and Hailey to ensure that I really don't show up there when I'm supposed to be at work. Anna says she's got some top-secret plan to make sure I get to go, but Michael is crafty as hell, so I don't know how well that's gonna work out for me.

"I told him to go screw himself," Aimee grins. "My life has been *so* much better since he's been gone. Plus, I have my eye on someone else now."

Not even the cuteness of the possibility that Aimee and Vanessa might be a thing is enough to shift my old happy self back into drive. "Well that's good," I say. I have resting bitch face, and I can feel it.

She's giving me that look again, and it makes my skin crawl every time. "Okay, Mr. Mopey. What's wrong with you?"

"Nothing's wrong with me," I reply. "I guess I'm just having an off day. Is that not allowed?"

"No, it's allowed. What's not allowed is having that off day extend over multiple days, like it has all week. Is it prom or something?"

"No, it's not prom," I say.

"Because if it is, just get on one of those dating apps and find a date."

I shove an old notebook back into my locker and peer around the door. "Seriously? A date for prom by tomorrow?"

"Yeah! You're cute, it shouldn't be a problem for you to get some sexy arm candy to bring. I'll even help you set up a profile!"

I throw my bag over my shoulder and latch the door of my locker shut. There's nothing I'd like to do more than open up to her about all the crap that's been going on lately, it's just that sometimes it's hard to talk to her about stuff like this. First of all, I can't exactly tell her that I was sort of seeing someone without her getting pissed that I didn't tell her in the first place, and then she'll want to know who the secret guy was. Second, as much as she wants to understand all of it and be there for me, she'll never be able to see it from my point of view. It's not even just about not having anyone to bring with me. Society sees girls who like girls differently than a guy who likes other guys. When it's a girl, a lot of people find it erotic and hot. When it's a guy, it's just disgusting and wrong and unnatural. She'll never understand what it's like to be in my shoes.

There is one person who will though, and maybe—just maybe—he'll have some words of wisdom or whatever.

"Sounds tempting, but I'm good," I say.

"Fine, but it's your loss. You could get a guy in like five seconds flat if you really wanted to." She throws the strap of her bag over her shoulder. "So, wanna come over to my place and binge-watch Netflix all night?"

"Uh, sounds like fun. There's something I have to do first though, so meet you there later?"

"Sure, just let me know when you're on your way. Love you!"

I watch Aimee disappear down the senior hall and around the corner before taking my leave in the opposite direction. As I move forward, the hall seems longer than it's ever been before. It gets a bit more difficult to breathe with every step until I stop in front of the familiar wooden door and I'm practically wheezing. My heart's pumping rapidly and I'm trying to avoid the urge to forget about the whole thing and make a run for my car, never looking back. My lungs suck in a deep breathe, and I pull the door open.

Charlie looks up from his intense marking session. "Elliot, this is a surprise."

"Oh, I--I'm sorry. I didn't realize you were busy. I can just come back another time."

"That's okay. I'm just going over the last of the projects," he smiles.

"Oh . . . okay."

I slide into one of the desks and stare dead ahead at the white board in front of me. Charlie leans forward over his desk and watches me for a moment.

"Did you have a question about the assigned scene work?" he asks.

"No. I actually wanted to talk to you, if you don't mind. I don't really have anyone else that I can talk to and I just feel like my head's gonna explode if I don't."

Way to go, Elliot. Now he probably thinks you've gotten yourself into some sort of trouble or something.

Charlie lays his red grading pen down and slides out of his roller chair. He circles around to the other side of his desk and leans against it. He hasn't taken his eyes off me since I opened my mouth. "You can talk to me about anything. This is a totally safe and inclusive space."

There he goes with that inclusive space stuff. I know all the teachers mean well when they say it and they really mean it, Charlie more so than some of the others I think, but I don't think they realize just how lame they sound when they say it.

"I know I can." I run my fingers over the cool desk top. "This year, especially this semester, has been pretty tough for me."

"Well, you *are* getting ready to graduate, so that's to be expected. The transition can be tough for some people."

"Exactly. But it's not just the transition into life after high school that's been an issue. It's just been everything really," I say.

"Okay, can you clarify on that? Really get to the root of what it is."

That sort of response has always been Charlie's specialty. He has a way of getting things out of people, even when they don't know what it is that's bothering them.

"It's not really something that I tell a lot of people, mostly because I know people will start treating me differently." I mindlessly drum out a beat with my fingers, habitually trying to diffuse yet another uncomfortable situation I've put myself in. "I'm gay, and that's something that has become much more prevalent in my life in the last few months."

"And you thought I might have some advice," he adds.

"Kinda," I say.

"I'm honored that you felt comfortable enough to be open with me about it. I know that it can be difficult to be honest about this with people." He crosses his arms and looks down at me. "One thing that you need to keep in mind is that this is something you need to come to terms with in your own time. I know that's the most clichéd answer, but it's also very, very true. Has it been on your mind a lot because you think you're ready to be public about it?"

"I don't really know. I guess I sort of am. Like, I'm tired of constantly having to worry about someone figuring it out and I'm tired of hiding, but at the same time I don't know if my family would be all that cool with it."

"I always advocate for being true to yourself, but if you're in a situation where you feel like coming out could be detrimental to your safety, I would say that you should wait until you're out of that situation. It's important to be happy and to be yourself, but at the same time, you also need to make sure you're safe should you choose to do so," he says. "Do you have a support system at all?"

"I do," I say. "They're extremely cool with it."

"Good. That's crucial to have."

"And I do have one more question. It might be a little personal though."

He uncrosses his arms and scoots himself further up on the desk.

"Do you have any advice for someone who's in a situation where they were seeing someone else in secret, but then the other party involved decided that they didn't want to take a chance on being outed so they disappeared and stopped all communication."

"That depends. There was no violence of any sort involved in this situation, was there?" He's getting a bit more serious now and his brow is quivering.

"No, definitely not. There was no violence of any sort involved. Just kind of a general question really," I say.

"Okay, then I would say that the person who disappeared is obviously very nervous and has a lot of their own stuff to deal with that they feel they need to deal with alone. And I know it sucks having to do it, but sometimes space is the best thing you can give them, no matter how you feel about them. Just figure out a way to let them know your door is always open if they need to talk about anything. That's really all you can do unfortunately."

I stand up again and grab my bag off the floor.

"Any other tidbits of advice you need?" he asks.

"No, I'm all good. Thank you, Charlie. I really appreciate you listening."

"My door is open any time. Just let me know if you need anything and remember what I said. Do it on your own timeline and be safe about it."

CHAPTER TWENTY-EIGHT

JUSTIN

I hit the reply button at the bottom of the page and start typing back.

> To: cinderfella0204@gmail.com
> From: milojuni1221@gmail.com
> Subject: Re: the death of my future
> *Dear Cinderfella,*
>
> *Wow, that's really tough. I'm sorry you didn't get in, but they said you could apply again at a later time. That's a good sign, right? You could always go to ISU, and then transfer. I know that probably makes it a bit more complicated, but it's still one possible option for you to take advantage of. Crazier things have happened, so don't give up on your future just yet.*
>
> *It's been a while since we last talked, and I'm really sorry about that. Things have been pretty crazy around here lately, which I know is my excuse a lot of the time, but it is what it is, I guess.*
>
> *How've you been lately other than getting the letter?*
> *— Milo*

> To: milojuni1221@gmail.com
> From: cinderfella0204@gmail.com
> Subject: Re: the death of my future
> *Dear Milo,*
>
> *Don't be sorry. It's as much on my part as it is yours.*
>
> *As for me, things around here have been really strange lately. At the risk of too much information, I thought I met someone, which I*

know is totally crazy, but I really thought I did. I should've known that it wouldn't have turned out the way that I wanted it to and that I'd wind up broken in a million little stupid pieces by the end of it.

Was I stupid for trying to make it work when part of me knew that it probably wouldn't? Am I a total fool?

— Cinderfella

That hit closer to home than I think he'll ever understand. I think that's precisely what's happening with Gabbi right now. I'm trying to make it work because I've always felt like that was what was expected of me, but things are different now. By some miracle, I've managed to come out to almost everyone in my life that's important to me, so why am I still trying to keep up this straight, all-American boy façade when it's not who I am?

It never has been, and it never will be me.

To: cinderfella0204@gmail.com
From: milojuni1221@gmail.com
Subject: Re: the death of my future
Cinderfella,

You're not stupid. I definitely get what it's like trying to force something that you know is never going to work because you think that's what you're supposed to be doing. We're almost brain-washed into thinking that by this point in our lives, we should have experienced some form of romantic relationship, and then we're made to feel weird if we haven't. That results in us trying our hardest to find that, even if it means we're putting our own happiness at risk.

But you know what? Enough is enough. Everyone deserves to find something great with someone that's going to love and appreciate every part of them, even us.

Which is why I'm ready.

I'm ready to finally shed these stupid fake identities and I want to meet you. The real you. And since I've taken some of your advice and started watching some of those romantic movies that you're always going on about, I want to continue that by doing it this weekend at prom. It's a masquerade theme, so it'll be perfect. We can reveal our identities together and take things from there.

— Milo

For the first time there's no hesitation in pressing send.

For the first time there's no doubt in the back of my mind telling me that this entire thing is a mistake. Everyone else gets to discover who they are at this time in their life, and damn it, I do too! Even if that means finally having to be honest with Gabbi.

I slide my phone off my desk and open the texts between the two of us.

Me: Hey, can you meet me in an hour? I really need to talk to you about something.

It's just after seven and I'm sitting on the hood of my car with Gabbi at the edge of the school's parking lot watching the sky transition into different shades of orange and pink. It's the perfect moment of peace I need before I spill my guts and life as I know it ends.

"So, what did you want to talk about?"

"We're just gonna go straight into it, huh?" I ask before letting out a chuckle. I lean back with my hands against the hood and look back up at the sky. "I just want you to know that I enjoy spending time with you."

"Oh boy, that's never a good way to start a conversation."

"Ugh, I know, and I'm sorry. What I'm trying to say is that I really do respect that you had enough guts to ask me to prom but—"

"But you don't want to go with me, do you?" she asks.

I tilt my head and take in the scent of Gabbi's perfume wafting in my direction. "It's not that I don't want to go with you, Gabs. It's just that I think it might mean something different for you than it does for me."

Gabbi stares into the void for a moment before sliding off the hood of my car and starts pacing back and forth. "I must look like a total idiot right now." She stops in front of me, her eyes like daggers. "It's someone else, isn't it?"

"What? No—I mean—sort of, but that's not what this is about."

"You know what, just forget it. Just forget about all of it. I can't believe I ever thought that I could ever have a chance. I have tried so hard to get you to notice me and to get you to realize that I am actually a pretty amazing person. I'm never going to be good enough for you, am I?"

"Don't say that. That's not what I'm saying at all."

"Then what are you saying?" She starts pacing again and then throws her hands up into the air. "Actually, don't answer that because I really don't want to hear it! You would be lucky to have a girl like me because I am amazing! Just have a nice life!"

"I'm gay!" It spills out like word vomit, and it's probably the easiest coming out confession I've ever made. "I'm gay, okay? And I'm sorry."

Gabbi looks like I've just punched her in the stomach and knocked out every ounce of oxygen she had left. "You're—" She leans against the hood and she drops her head. "Wow."

"I'm really, really sorry. This isn't how I wanted you to find out." I tap my fingers along the hood and nibble on the inside of my cheek.

Gabbi's looking past the grass field now and watching the cars as they speed up and down the highway. This was probably the last thing she expected to happen the day before her senior prom, but it had to happen sooner or later. I just wish I'd had the guts to do it before now.

"Are you okay?"

She slides off the hood again and pulls her keys out of her bag. "I just need some time."

"Yeah, take all the time you need."

She tugs at the door handle and pulls it open. "And you're sure that you're . . . you know?"

"That would be a yes."

She takes one last look before jumping into the driver's seat and pulls out of the parking lot, leaving me alone with the orange and pink sky.

I pull my phone out and do the next logical thing I can think of.

Me: Well, Noah, I did it. I was finally honest with myself about that girl I was telling you about. After I admitted to myself what I was doing, I decided to be honest with her, and it went about as well as can be expected. At least she knows now though. I am now out to all of the friends that I actually talk to and also to my sister. Next on the list is my parents, but I'm not sure that's something I can actually do. Truth be told, I'm pretty terrified, but it's not because I'm scared for my safety or anything. I know my parents love me and they'd never like hurt me or anything. I'm just scared of disappointing them. That's what I've always been afraid of and I think I always will be. What was that entire process

like for you? Do you have any tidbits of wisdom that could help me through all of this?

CHAPTER TWENTY-NINE

ELLIOT

Saturday, May 2

"So, we talked and decided that we're going together tonight," Aimee says.

"I mean, I thought we were going together tonight anyway," I reply.

"No, I mean *we're* going *together*."

It takes a moment before it finally clicks.

"Oh! When did that happen?"

"A couple nights ago," Vanessa chimes in. "We just finally decided that we're gonna try to make things work."

"You'd know that if you were around a little bit more," Aimee says.

"Yeah. I'm really sorry about that," I say. "But I'm excited for you guys."

Aimee grips Vanessa's hand and smiles. "It'll be tough with me being away in New York for sure, but we really think that this could be worth it."

"I'm happy for you guys and I'm sure everything is gonna work out just fine for the two of you."

"Aww, thanks, El," Aimee says, wrapping her arms around me. "But we really don't want you feeling like a third wheel or something tonight."

I slide off the kitchen stool and lean against the counter across from Aimee and Vanessa.

Things between the three of us have been distant to say the least. It's not that I haven't wanted to talk to them and tell them about every detail of what I've been going through these last couple of weeks. A lot of it just hasn't been my story to tell. Even though Cooper and I didn't work out in the end, I'd still never betray his trust by telling his deepest secret, even if he is claiming now that he doesn't have a secret to tell. I wouldn't want him to do that to me. And to now tell them that I'm finally meeting my mystery guy after all this time?

It's a lot to process even for me.

"What's going on in that head of yours, El?" Aimee asks.

"I actually won't be a third wheel tonight."

"Okay . . . and? You can't just say something like that and then skate on past it without any details."

"It's Milo, or whatever his real name is. We started having a conversation last night, and then one thing led to another, and we decided that it's finally time for us to meet. Tonight. At the dance."

"Oh my gosh!" Vanessa says. "That's so *romantic*!"

My gaze switches from Vanessa to Aimee. "What do you think about all of this?"

"Do you want my honest opinion?"

I just raise my eyebrow and try to mimic the look she gives me all the time.

"Look, I'm not gonna sit here and pretend that I'm perfectly fine with the guy that's been screwing around with my best friend's feelings for the last several months. All I'm gonna say is that if you're happy then I'm happy."

"Things are different now. I can feel it. But thank you for being happy for me anyway."

"You're welcome. Just know though that if he fudges up, I'm going to have a few choice words for him, regardless of who he is," Aimee replies.

"I wouldn't have it any other way."

A knock from the front door echoes through the entryway and into the kitchen.

"And that would be Anna with my altered suit."

"Alright, well you get that and we're gonna head downstairs and start putting on our faces for tonight," Aimee says as she drags Vanessa toward the basement stairs.

I chug what's left in my water glass and set it in the sink before making my way down the hall to the front door, where Anna's toting a garment bag in one hand and a pair of shoes in the other. Her eyes are shining in the sunlight and she's got the biggest smile on her face.

I swear I've never seen her this excited about anything.

I lead her into the living room, where she sets down the shoes and unzips the bag, revealing a classic black and white suit, reminiscent of something I swear I've seen Michael Bublé wear on stage on more than one occasion. "It's great," I say. "But you really didn't have to do this."

"Nonsense. I wanted to do this for you. I still have another ten years before I get to do this with one of my boys, and I know your mom would want me to make sure you enjoyed your senior prom and showed up looking like a total bad ass."

Throughout all of this, it never occurred to me just how different things might've been had my mom been around to help me through all of it. I might've had the courage to come out sooner than I did, and I might've learned how to be who I really am without fear of judgement from everyone else around me.

Hell, I might not be stuck living with Michael anymore if things had worked out differently.

"I'm sorry. I didn't mean to bring any emotions up like that," Anna says.

"No, it's okay. I enjoy talking about her. We don't really talk about her back at the house. It's almost like she never actually existed now, so I know she'd be happy that you're still trying to keep her memory alive. And I am too. Thank you for everything you do."

Anna lays the suit over the arm of the couch before wrapping her arms around me and pulling me in close. "You know I'd do anything for you. You're my little Elli Bear, and you always will be."

"I love you."

"I love you too." She pulls away and wipes away the tears running down my cheeks, just as she's always done. "Now enough tears. You have a big night ahead of you."

"Sorry, I didn't mean to get all emotional. I'm still not sure how I'm gonna get away with going tonight. I've got Michael breathing down my neck and he wouldn't let me get out of work tonight."

"Just let me take care of that one, okay? Michael's going to be at the new location tonight and he won't be back in town until after the dance. I am going to make sure you get to enjoy your senior prom."

"But—" I stutter.

"Nope. Don't even start with me. You're going and that's that. Now go try your suit on, I want pictures before you go."

"Fine. I'll be right back."

I've never understood why people feel the need to rent a limo for an event like prom.

Like you're literally spending hundreds of dollars to have a total stranger drop you off at a shitty location that the school could actually afford where you still have to follow basic school guidelines for behavior. On top of that, if you're a girl, you've probably already spent another few hundred on finding the perfect dress, finding the right makeup, and then potentially hiring someone to do your hair and nails.

It just seems like a waste to me.

It's already almost eight and we're just now making it to the dance because someone who will remain nameless — Aimee — wasted too much time dropping it low while we were all getting ready, so now we're all late. If you ask her though, it's called being "fashionably late" and "anyone cool does it".

One thing is for sure. I'm really going to miss that girl when she's gone.

I step out from the driver's seat wearing my suit and clutching the silver metallic mask that Anna bought for me. The passenger door swings open, and Vanessa steps out onto the pavement. As she slips on her faux diamond encrusted mask that goes perfectly with the black and white embroidered flower pattern at the torso of her dress, the solid black, longer back half of the bottom is blowing slightly in the wind.

"You look beautiful," I say.

"Aw, thank you! And you look pretty dashing yourself," she says with a smile.

"Why thank you," I reply with a fake tip of a hat. I put the cold metallic mask to my face and tie it at the back of my head. "Aimee, come on! We're already behind."

She sticks her arm out of the window of the backseat and motions for me to come over.

"Seriously?"

"Aren't you going to open the door? It's the gentleman thing to do."

I lean my hands against the door. "I thought you were above all the knight in shining armor stuff as — and this is a loose translation of your own words — a strong and proud bisexual Asian woman who doesn't conform to societal norms."

"You know, I don't know if I remember actually saying that one," Aimee says.

"Oh, you definitely said it. More than once, I might add. I'm sure that Vanessa can attest to hearing it a couple of times."

"Hey, don't drag me into this," Vanessa laughs.

"Okay, but even if I did say it, every girl deserves to feel like a princess at least *once* in her life."

I tug at the handle of her door and pull it open. She sticks out one of her legs before stopping to position her mask onto her face, and then steps out with the aid of Vanessa.

"Damn, if I'm not the luckiest girl in the world," Vanessa says with her mouth half open.

She really is gorgeous. She always has been.

Aimee's dress is this rich purple ombre color that subtly gets lighter as it reaches the flowing bottom until it's finally just pure white. Her sleeves hug her shoulders and the top is fit snuggly to her torso. There's also quite a bit of cleavage going on, which I'm sure Vanessa is thrilled about. The mask is, of course, over the top and purple to match the dress with the addition of glitter, rhinestones, and fake, painted on eyelashes. It wouldn't be an Aimee outfit if it wasn't a little crazy.

"You look stunning," I say.

"I do look pretty great, don't I? Okay, I'm gonna need a selfie before we get in there while we still have a little natural light." She reaches into her clutch and pulls out her phone. "Say prom 2020!"

The three of us bunch together in Aimee's front facing camera, which almost immediately triggers my need to ugly cry over the fact that the next big event like this that we're all at together will be mine and Aimee's graduation followed by her leaving me behind to start a new life a couple of months later.

Stay strong, Elliot. You still have some time.

Aimee tucks her phone back into its home and throws the chain strap of her bag over her shoulder. She drapes her arms around mine and Vanessa's shoulders and starts pushing us in the direction of the building.

Looking around, I see all of the douchebags that have tortured me since the first day of sixth grade when everyone started separating off into their own little cliques, and I was left with the weirdos that no one else wanted to hang out with. I never in a million years thought that one of those weirdos would wind up becoming my favorite person in the world.

Hell, I never thought I'd willingly spend an entire evening with the people that tortured me, but here I am, and I couldn't be more excited about it.

We pull the doors to the main building open and are immediately met by a gust of cool air conditioning that sends a chill down my spine and my entire body breaks out in goose bumps.

"Oh, thank God, there's AC. All of this would not be pretty drenched in sweat, and this mask only hides so much," Aimee says.

"I think you look great no matter how sweaty you get," Vanessa says, locking arms with Aimee.

"Aren't you just the sweetest."

"You two are nauseatingly cute," I say.

"You know you love it," Aimee replies before whacking me in the arm. "Speaking of which, where's this dream guy of yours?"

"He said he'd meet me out on the deck by the pool at 8:30 and he'd be wearing a crimson and black suit and a gold mask."

"Wow, this is really happening, huh?" Vanessa asks. "Are you nervous?"

"I'd say that's an understatement."

"Hey, you're gonna do great. Let's just get in there and have some fun. You've been waiting for this for months, and if he's not totally nuts about you in person, then obviously he doesn't deserve to have you."

"Thanks."

"And if he does anything stupid, I will not hesitate to slap a bitch, no matter who he is," Aimee adds.

"Yeah. I'm aware of all of this already. I just need you to make sure you're keeping your eye on Hailey and Tommy and making sure they don't get too close to me. I really don't need them ratting me out to Step Monster."

Vanessa sets her hand on my shoulder and squeezes. "You don't have to worry about a thing. I promise we'll keep an eye on them."

"I will make sure you have an amazing night." Aimee's eyes light up the second she hears the opening line to Lizzo's "Juice", and she drags us both inside. "You have to dance with us before you go!"

"Come on, you know I can't dance," I protest.

"I won't deny that, but it's your senior prom! This is the last chance we're gonna get to make fools out of ourselves like this, and the best part is that with these masks nobody knows who the hell we are anyway!"

"Yeah, just have some fun with us before you run off and leave us here," Vanessa adds.

The one thing that I've learned over the last few years is that there's basically no point in arguing with Aimee about anything, because she usually gets what she wants in the end, which can be either good or bad. On one hand, there's a lot of times when I'm not able to get what I want out of a situation because she's just so damn persuasive. On the other hand, I've been able to explore things outside of my comfort zone thanks to her trying to push me to do things that I wouldn't ordinarily do.

Aimee and Vanessa talked me into one song, which turned into another song. And another. And then two more, which isn't surprising when I'm shoved into a room with the two of them. They tend to bring out my more upbeat and outgoing side.

It's 8:25 when I glance down at my phone. My stomach is turning and I'm actually kind of scared that I might throw up on someone. My pulse is angry and there's a parade of bees rushing through my brain. I wipe a layer of sweat from my forehead and hope that I don't look as drenched as I feel. I catch Aimee's gaze and give her a quick, half-baked smile before taking in a deep breath and crossing the room to the back exit leading out to the deck, which has been decorated in string lights just like the inside of the building.

I pass by a couple making out against the railing in the shadows at the back end of the deck and make my way to the front end overlooking the pool. In the distance, I can just barely make out groups and couples strolling around the grounds and just laughing and having fun. I lean against the railing and peek out at a few leaves floating along the top of the water.

I peer down at my phone screen again. It's 8:38 and I'm starting to feel like a bit of an idiot. Sure, he gave me a description of his outfit, but that doesn't mean he'll actually show. Or worse, he might not even be who he says he is.

"What the hell am I doing?" I say to myself. "This was just a stupid idea."

I push myself upright again and take one last look out at the grounds.

"Cinderfella?"

The name completely throws me off guard and sucks all the air from my lungs. I take a moment to steady myself before I turn around. There he is in his crimson and black suit with a golden mask, just like he said he would be.

He's got gorgeous brown eyes and the most amazing wavy brown hair I've ever seen. I wish I could say that I know who it is on sight, but there are probably a dozen guys in my graduating class that fit the tall, dark, and handsome description.

Only I could be so lucky.

"You're him, aren't you?" he asks.

At this point I'm too shocked that he actually showed up to even think, let alone speak coherently.

"And you have no idea what I'm talking about, so I'm just gonna go now."

"No," I almost shout. "It me—I mean I'm me—I'm Cinderfella." I pause for a moment and avoid his gaze.

We stand in silence for a moment, staring at each other in complete disbelief that this is actually happening right now.

"Hi," he says, breaking the awkward silence.

I have to catch my breath. "Hi."

"Do you want to go for a walk or something?"

"Yeah, that sounds nice."

We head past the couple that's still going at it and walk side by side down the staircase and toward the winding path around the grounds. Every now and then, I glance at him to see if he might be doing the same. If he is, then he's not making it noticeable. The glowing lights of the grounds illuminate against his golden mask and gorgeous brown eyes.

"It looked like the guy was about to swallow her face," he says.

"Huh?"

"Uh, that couple back there that was—never mind." He swallows a laugh before running his hand through his hair. "Okay, this is kinda awkward, right? Is it just me?"

It's like a thousand-pound weight's just been thrown off my chest. "Oh, I'm so relieved I'm not the only one."

He lets out another laugh, this time a little louder and a lot less uncomfortable sounding.

"I really like your laugh," I say. "It's cute."

"Oh, thank you."

"No problem. I'll be real, I wasn't too sure that you were actually gonna show up here tonight."

We trail back around to the pool and find a couple of empty chairs.

"If we're being real, I didn't know if I'd show up or not. I've kinda been freaking out about it nonstop since I brought it up."

"No worries, I get it," I reply. "I also had this irrational fear that you weren't actually who you said you were and that you were some sort of old creeper."

"Ah damn, you caught me!"

Post Malone blasts from inside the building when someone opens the door and another huge group runs back inside. My eyes wander down the rest of his body, studying every visible curve of his face and hands, just trying to figure out who he might actually be. The corners of his mouth are curved up into a smile, and the water from the pool is reflecting off his face.

The tension in my shoulders relaxes a bit and I slump a little further into the chair. "For the longest time, I was scared to meet you because I was afraid that it wouldn't measure up to the image I had in my head."

"You were afraid that I wouldn't measure up?" he asks, his smile dimming a little.

"No, I was scared that I wouldn't measure up to *your* idea of *me*. Like maybe you'd take one look at me or figure out who I am, and then you'd just run as fast as you can in the other direction."

"Well, I haven't figured out who you are just yet and the night is still young."

I suppress a nervous laugh.

"I'm kidding. I'm sure you're a total catch." He scoots a bit closer. "So, do I get to learn your name now or what?"

"I think it might be more fun for you to try to guess it first."

"Oh, I'm definitely not falling for that one! I'll guess the wrong name and then you're gonna get either annoyed or disappointed that I didn't get it right the first time."

"I promise I won't get annoyed over it."

"Okay . . . fine . . . since you asked so nicely, I guess I'll just come out and say it. It's like ripping off a bandage, right?" I say.

"Exactly, just like ripping off a bandage."

My phone vibrates against my leg. "Hold on." I slide it from my pocket and pull up my texts.

Aimee: Code pink!

Me: What? What is that even supposed to mean?

Aimee: It's a code pink, dude. It's Hailey. We had eyes on her, and then she disappeared. I think she left!

Me: No! No! This cannot be happening right now! Please tell me this isn't actually happening right now!

I shoot my gaze back to Milo, who looks extremely confused.

"Is everything okay?" he asks.

I have one of two choices here. I could either stay and not worry about the fact that Hailey very well might be on her way back home, which is where I should be right now, and risk being grounded until the end of the summer when I finally move out. Or I could blow my chance to finally figure out who my mystery guy is and live to see another day.

"Everything's fine," I say. "But I hate to say that I really have to go."

"What? But what about—"

"I know. And I'm so, so sorry about all of this. But I promise I'll make it up to you and we can pick this up another day, okay?"

I run back toward the deck, typing as I go.

Me: I'm on my way back out to the car and heading home now. Thanks for the for warning.

I pull into my spot at the front of the house and sprint up the sidewalk and up the porch steps. The driveway is still completely empty, so the good news is that even if Hailey did decide to make a run back home, I beat her here, so I just might make it through the night alive.

I smash through the front door and make a beeline up the stairs, nearly tripping and falling face first into the final step. I throw off my jacket as I hit the landing and whip open the door of my room, and I'm finally home fr —

"Hailey . . . you're here . . . in my room." My jacket falls to the floor and I loosen my tie. "So, how was prom?"

Hailey crosses her legs and readjusts the bottom of her dress. "You know, I noticed this girl that was practically on my ass all night—I mean how could I not, she had this big and poufy purple dress and this extremely glittery mask—and then I wondered who else has a sense of style like that. That's when I remembered your freaky little friend with the fashion obsession and realized that the guy that was with her could only be one person, because let's be real here, I don't see her hanging out with anyone else."

"Please don't say anything. I just can't deal with any of that right now. I have so much shit going on, and you don't even know the half of it."

She raises her brow and just stares at me for a moment. "Fine."

"Wait . . . what now?"

"Fine, I won't rat you out to my dad."

"For real?" I ask.

"Of course, my silence is gonna cost you somewhat."

"Of course it is. What do you want from me now? Do I have to throw on a wig and take your finals for you? Or are we going a little bit more cliché here, so I have to do your laundry for a month?"

Hailey uncrosses her legs and hops off my mattress before strolling across the room to the door. "Help me prepare for my audition for the musical this summer."

I tilt my head to the side and squint. "Seriously? That's it?"

"That's it," she echoes.

"There's gotta be some sort of catch to this, right?"

"Nope, no catch. Just help me audition and then your secret dies between the two of us. Dad will never know a thing."

I fold my arms against my chest and look her up and down, just waiting for her to start busting up laughing at my expense. "And no tricks?"

"No tricks. Honestly, I'm really not all that bad."

I stretch my hand out in front of me. "Okay, deal."

"Deal," Hailey says with a smile, completely ignoring my outstretched hand. She steps back out into the hall and disappears behind her bedroom door.

I untuck my shirt and collapse into bed after prying my phone from my pants pocket.

Me: I made it home. Hailey beat me here.

Aimee: You've got to be kidding me! I swear if she says anything at all I'm gonna make her life a LIVING HELL. And you can count on that.

Me: She was actually really cool about it.

Aimee: You're joking, right?

Me: Actually no. She said that she'll keep my secret as long as I help her with her audition for the musical this

summer. I'm not sure if I trust her, but I guess I'll just go with it for now.

Aimee: Alright, but just be careful and let me know if she does anything shady.

Me: I will. Just have fun with Vanessa tonight and don't worry about me. Love you.

Aimee: Love you too!

I position myself upright on my pillow and kick my shoes off as I settle in between the blankets. It's still so insane to believe that we were together tonight, even if it was only for a little while. It just felt so . . . right. Like we were meant to meet at the moment we did.

I just wish things could've gone a little different.

I pull up my emails again and start typing.

To: milojuni1221@gmail.com
From: cinderfella0204@gmail.com
Subject: Sorry about tonight
Dear Milo,

Tonight was so amazing. I really enjoyed getting to talk to you, even if I didn't get the chance to learn who you are. I'm so sorry that I had to run off before the real climax of the evening. Do you think maybe we could arrange a time later this week to finally meet? For real this time?

— Cinderfella

To: cinderfella0204@gmail.com
From: milojuni1221@gmail.com
Subject: Re: Sorry about tonight

Dear Cinderfella,

I really enjoyed getting to meet you too, even though I guess we didn't ACTUALLY meet. I would like to get the chance to finally learn who you are and for you to know who I am. But tonight really got me thinking that I'm sort of glad we didn't get to reveal our identities just yet. I think that before I do this, I need to tell my parents first. If they know, then I think things would just be a lot easier. I hope you understand.

— Milo

To: milojuni1221@gmail.com
From: cinderfella0204@gmail.com
Subject: Re: Sorry about tonight

Dear Milo,

I for sure get wanting to tell your parents first, so no worries here. I'm just happy you're willing to finally tell them and let yourself be free.

Keep me updated on how things go. I can't wait to meet you.

— Cinderfella

CHAPTER THIRTY

JUSTIN

Tonight's the night. I'm finally telling my parents. I have to if I ever want to be happy.

It's just after nine when I finally pull my car into the driveway, and Mom and Dad are already home. I just hope they're in a good mood from watching their son's team win yet another game. The front door opens with a squeal and I step into the house. A rush of nerves takes over my body and my arms start to tremble under the weight of my gym bag. The sound of the shower running is echoing through the house, and the T.V. is blaring from the living room. My gym bag slides off my shoulder and I set it down beside the staircase.

"Hey, Mom. I'm home."

"I thought you would've gone out to celebrate with the team."

"I thought about it, but I was kinda tired," I say, taking a seat next to her on the couch. "What are you watching?"

"Some true crime documentary on Netflix."

"Oh cool." I stare ahead at the screen for a moment, but any noise coming from the documentary sounds like the parents from Charlie Brown. "Did Dad just get in the shower?"

"I think just a couple of minutes before you got here. Did you need take a shower?"

"No, I took one at school, so I'm good," I say.

I had originally planned to just come out to both of them at the same time, but maybe it would be easier to just deal with them one at a time since I don't know how either of them are going to react to it. My mom was raised in a very religious and devout Catholic household, and I know that my grandparents were raised with very small-town ideals, which were passed down to my mom. They've never appeared to be "anti-gay" per se, but we've also never talked about it before.

And then there's my dad, who was born and, for the most part, raised in Mexico, which isn't exactly known to be the most accepting place for the LGBTQ community. He's never really talked about his feelings toward gay people before, so I'm not sure if he changed his own moral compass from his more conservative upbringing or not. I'm travelling down this road totally blind, and it's terrifying.

It needs to be done sooner rather than later though.

"Mom, can I talk to you for a sec?"

She lowers the volume on the T.V. until it's just barely audible above the sound of the running shower. "Of course, sweetheart. What do you need to talk about?"

I take a deep breath in through my nose and exhale slowly. I thought that this entire conversation would get easier every time I did it, but it seems to only be getting more difficult. I really should've just grown a pair and came out to everyone all at once. It would've been so much easier in the long run. "Okay . . . I don't really know how I'm gonna say this right now."

"You know that you can tell me anything, honey. Is this about school?"

"I mean, that's part of it but—"

"I know that you're nervous about moving away from home and starting your new life at Stanford, but everything is going to work out and you're going to be so happy once you get settled in and get to experience so many new things. You'll see."

"That's the thing, Mom. I don't know that I actually want to go to Stanford and go to med school."

Her eyes are drilling into the side of my head and I'm so glad that I'm not a mind reader right about now.

"That's just your nerves, honey. Once you get to campus, everything is going to pass. You'll meet new friends and you'll be relaxed. You just have to give it time."

I settle further into the corner of the couch and turn my body so that she's in my line of vision. "There's also a little more to it than that." I tuck my hands into my lap and take another deep breath. "I have been putting this conversation off for so long, but I just can't do it anymore. I have to come clean and tell you if there's ever going to be any chance at all of me being happy. I'm gay."

Mom's gaze falls from my face to the floor and the color of her face lightens by at least two shades. The shower is still running in the background and it's the only thing I can hear other than the sound of the drumming in my ears. She's still staring at the floor and both her hands are clutching at her blanket.

"Mom?"

"No."

The one-word answer is like a punch to the gut.

"What?" I ask.

"We're not discussing this. You're just confused right now."

"No, I'm not. I'm not confused about any of this. This is who I am, and for the first time I'm feeling more like myself than I ever have before. I need you to accept me for who I am. Please, Mom."

She rips the blanket off her lap and stands up. She strolls along the floor before stopping at the bottom of the stairs. "You're my child, and I still love you, but I just can't talk about this right now. And please don't bring this up to your father. He's having a hard enough time at work as it is, and he doesn't need this on top of it."

I stay planted in place on the couch and avert my eyes back to the true crime gibberish, just waiting for her to disappear upstairs. My blood is boiling and the flood gates open as I rip my phone from my pocket and start a new email.

To: cinderfella0204@gmail.com
From: milojuni1221@gmail.com
Subject: i tried
Dear Cinderfella,
Well, I did it. Sort of.

I decided it might be a little easier to tell my parents separately, so I told my mom first because I figured she might react a little better than my dad would. I couldn't have been more wrong about that because it didn't go well at all.

I don't know why I even continue trying to just be myself. It's a total waste of time and I am going to continue being disappointed by it. It feels like my entire world crashed down right in front of me in less than ten minutes. I know that you were really excited for us to finally be able to work on having something real, but if I don't have approval from my family, I just don't think it's going to happen. You deserve someone that you can actually be with and who can be with you for real. I'm going to be forced into the cookie cutter life with a wife and kids after all.

I'm sorry, but you deserve better than what I could ever give you.

Please forgive me, but I think this may be the end for us.

I can't keep doing this. It isn't healthy for either of us.

— Goodbye, Milo

CHAPTER THIRTY-ONE

ELLIOT

It's been a week since I last had any contact with Milo, and I'm feeling more lost than ever. I tried sending him a reply, but there's never any answer, meaning one of two things. Number one, he's just ignoring anything I say to him, or number two, he's blocked me all together and I'm just wasting my time by sending anything else.

Aimee seems to feel bad about the entire situation, but I feel like deep down she's relieved that it's finally ended. I low key feel like she's gotten pretty annoyed from me talking about him for the last week.

Today is Aimee's birthday, which means her, Vanessa, and I will be spending the evening at her place watching movies and just hanging out. And then tomorrow it's off to Six Flags Great America for our senior class trip. I'm excited to just not have to think about anything other than having fun with my best friend for the weekend.

It's just before seven when I walk into the coffee shop to grab something to drink. If I'm gonna be up all night, I'm for sure gonna need some caffeine. Sleep hasn't been my best friend since everything went down, and I'm not sure if it'll ever go back to normal.

"Hey, how's it going?" Belinda, the server on duty asks. "If you're looking for Aimee, she's not here."

"I know, I'm just coming to get some sustenance for her birthday celebration tonight."

"That was a large vanilla iced coffee and a chocolate chip muffin, right?" she asks.

"That's the one."

"Perfect, I'll get that going for you right now."

Belinda swipes my card and hands it back before returning to the back to start on my order. I turn and face the few tables that occupy the space, immediately noticing a familiar face. "Oh, hey," I say. "It's Justin, right?"

His eyes peer over the screen of his laptop. "Yep. And you're—Elliot—Tommy's step-brother, right?"

I push myself away from the counter and hover over the chair opposite him. "That's me unfortunately. I'm actually really surprised to see you here. Not many kids from school know about it."

"That's what Aimee was telling me. She brought me here during one of our work sessions for the project, and I sort of fell in love with it."

"Yeah, this place kind of has that effect on people."

"Hey, Elliot," Belinda hollers from behind the kitchen door. "We're actually out of muffins, but I can make some more if you don't mind waiting like fifteen or twenty minutes for one."

"That's fine, I'll wait here."

"I'll have it done as soon as I can."

I reach for the back of the chair and inch it out from under the table. "You don't mind, do you? It's gonna be a few minutes."

"Of course not, be my guest," Justin replies.

I slide into the chair and start tapping my fingertips against the table. I've gone to school with Justin for years, but

I don't know if I've ever had an actual conversation with him before.

"Are you working on that self-reflection for Charlie's class?"

"Actually, I'm working on a questionnaire thing for roommate placement in the fall," he says.

"I still need to do that. I'm just hoping I don't get placed with some weirdo that has a secret collection of doll heads and likes to watch me sleep."

A smile slips through his seemingly stress-induced resting bitch face and a giggle pops out. "Fingers crossed for the both of us."

"For sure. So where did you wind up getting in? U of I, or did you get lucky enough to get in somewhere up north."

He looks at me again from behind his laptop screen and speaks in an almost monotone voice. "Stanford actually."

"Oh wow. That's pretty impressive, but you don't seem all too thrilled about that."

Justin looks up again and leans back in his chair. His eyes are wandering around the room and I can tell that I might've pressed an uncomfortable button.

"I'm sorry. I didn't mean to pry or anything," I say.

"You're fine. It's just a kind of complicated situation, I guess." He leans forward again and rests his arms on the table. "I'm not all too thrilled to be going if I'm being honest. My parents have always had this sort of idea for how they want my life to go, and I've never been in a position to have much say about that."

"Damn, that's tough. I'm sorry to hear you're having such a hard time with it. Have you tried talking to your family about it?"

"I did try, but we didn't get far enough into the discussion for me to explain myself before I was written off as just nervous about the whole thing. The fact of the matter is that I am ready to start a new life, just not the life they want," he says.

"Then you're just gonna go to Stanford and do what your family wanted you to do?"

"Yes? No? I don't know. It just seems a lot easier at this point to continue on with what they want me to do so I can avoid all the drama. But enough about me, where are you going for college? If at all, I mean. There's nothing wrong with deciding not to go to college."

Belinda pops back up front with my large iced coffee in hand and sets it down front of me. "Totally almost forgot about this."

"No problem," I say.

"We're looking at another ten minutes on the muffin. If you need me I'll be in the back, so just give me a holler."

"Thank you so much." I smile before jabbing my straw into the top of the lid before downing the first sip. "Damn, I needed that. But to answer your question, I am going to college. I got into ISU as expected, but it wasn't my first choice."

"There's nothing wrong with that. Sometimes you have to do what you have to do."

I'm not sure what I expected from Justin, but he's a lot different than I imagined he'd be. Apart from the occasional hi or having to work together briefly in a class, we never had much of a chance to really sit down and get to know each other over the past few years. He's smart and really sweet and just a super understanding person. I definitely wish that I'd gotten to know him just a little bit sooner.

The more I talk to him, though, the more my spider sense starts tingling. It just seems so . . . familiar?

Even more so than Cooper ever was. He's got a family that has these expectations for him, he has the same sense of humor, and a lot of the pieces of advice he gives sound a lot like something I would've gotten out of Milo. I just wish there was some way to know for sure. Even if he was Milo, I doubt I'd get a positive response for asking point blank.

"Alright, guys," Belinda hollers from behind the register. "It's closing time."

"Huh?" I ask. "You guys don't close until like ten though."

"Yeah, and it's now 10:15. I let you stay while I finished cleaning up, but I really do have to kick you guys out now."

"What?" I practically scream. "That means I totally missed Aimee's birthday pizza night and she is going to *kill* me!"

"She seems pretty understanding. Just tell her time got away from you," Justin says as he packs away his stuff. "I need to head home now though. It was really nice talking to you, Elliot. I'll see you on the bus tomorrow."

"Yeah, I'll see you tomorrow."

Justin and I head outside and to our separate cars. I slide into the driver's seat and pull my phone out of my pocket.

Aimee: The pizza just got here. –sent 7:08 pm

Aimee: Where are you? –sent 7:24 pm

Aimee: Are you on your way yet? –sent 7:47 pm

Aimee: We're all waiting here for you. We're gonna start eating without you. –sent 8:02 pm

Aimee: Seriously, dude. This isn't funny. Why aren't you answering? –sent 8:14 pm

Aimee: You're starting to really piss me off. Answer your damn texts! –sent 8:45 pm

Aimee: Just forget it. Vanessa's leaving now and the party's over. You better have a damn good excuse for why you bailed on us when we've been planning this for two weeks. –sent 9:58 pm

"Son of a bitch!" I scream at the top of my lungs. I look up from my phone and see Belinda standing at the front door and staring into my car. I poke my head through the window and smile at her. "Sorry, didn't mean to scare you or anything. Have a good night." I grin again before pulling my head back into the car.

Me: Aimee, I'm so sorry! I didn't mean to miss your birthday. I promise I have a good reason, so please just let me explain.

Read 10:21 pm.

I was up half the night trying to get Aimee to talk to me, but I gave up at like two this morning once I realized she wasn't going to say a word.

It's 6:57 am and I'm sitting in the school parking lot with the rest of the seniors waiting for takeoff and the opportunity to get the hell of out dodge for the day. There's a steady pattern of rain dripping against the top of my car and my Spotify playlist is playing in the background as I watch for Aimee to pull into the lot in her cute little bug.

I don't think there was ever a time in the last five years that Aimee and I ever went without talking for more than a few hours, so this entire situation is stressing me the hell out. And what if I've messed up so bad that she never talks to me again? I don't know if I can handle that!

I see a wave of movement from the corner of my eye. Hordes of seniors are running through the rain to the busses, and in the midst of them, Aimee in her bright pink and white converse walking calmly through the downfall with her umbrella.

The door to my car flies open and I practically float across the parking lot. "Aimee!"

She just shakes her head and continues walking.

"Look, I know you're pissed, but I promise I have a good reason for missing last night."

"What?" she screams at me, catching the attention of everyone around us. "Nothing to see here, people. Move it along." She zones in on me again. Her nostrils are flaring, and the little vein in her head is bulging. "What could've possibly been so important?"

"I was on my way there, but then I got caught up at your mom's shop when I ran into Justin."

"Okay? I'm waiting for the part where you had a good excuse."

"I'm getting to that," I say, scooching in a little closer. "We started talking and I totally lost track of time. Before I knew it, it was after ten and the conversation was so amazing. I think he might be Milo, Aimee."

She looks terrifyingly dead behind the eyes. "Are you kidding me right now?"

"No, really! I mean, I know it might be just a little far-fetched, but after last night they seem too similar for it to be a coincidence."

"You are unbelievable, Elliot. You know that, right?"

"Why the hell are you blowing up at me right now? I haven't done anything."

"Exactly! You haven't done anything except go on and on about this Milo dude for months! I put up with it because you're my best friend and I love you, but lately that's been all you've ever talked about and you're barely ever around these days."

"I'm sorry. I didn't realize."

"Of course not, you'd actually have to be around to realize that."

The muscles in her jaw are tensing up and her eyes are glossy and turning red.

"That's not fair, Aimee."

"I can't talk to you right now."

"So . . . are you saying that you like don't want to be friends with me anymore?"

"No, Elliot. That's not what I'm saying. I just need some time, so just give me some space for a little bit, okay?"

Aimee gives me one last glance before closing up her umbrella and stepping onto the bus.

CHAPTER THIRTY-TWO

JUSTIN

Friday, May 15

I'm tailing Gabbi in front of the Batman roller coaster.

"Gabs, it's been two weeks, are you ever gonna talk to me again?"

She spins around and her hair whacks me in the face. "What do you want me to say, Justin?"

"I don't know. I guess I'd just like to know that you forgive me or that you accept me or—or something like that."

"You realize that what you did was totally messed up, right? All the flirting and the making out and the making me feel like I had a chance was so messed up on so many levels."

"Okay, you're right. That was totally messed up and I'm sorry. I am so, so sorry that I hurt you. I never meant to go that far with things. It was my every intention to tell the truth about who I really am much sooner than I did. Could you possibly find it in your heart to ever forgive me?"

She shifts her weight from one leg to the other and tilts her head back. Her eyes are squinted from the sun that finally poked its head through the clouds. "I'd like to just forgive you and be able to put this all behind us, and I think eventually I will. I just need more time because it's a lot to process."

"I get it," I reply. "I totally do. But, could you also just maybe not tell anyone? I don't know if I'm ready for that to get out just yet."

"Don't sweat it. I may still be kinda pissed at you, but I'd never give away your secret like that." She wraps her arms around the back of my neck and pulls me in for a hug. "Just

go to Cali and figure your shit out, okay?" She loosens her grip
and steps back again. "And try to have a good rest of your day.
I have to go, Coop's waiting for me."

"Cooper? Is that a thing now?"

She fights a grin and tucks her hair behind her ears. "It's
new, but so far so good. At least I finally found a guy that's
not secretly gay."

"Well, good luck with that one. You deserve to find
someone."

"Thanks," Gabbi says, now smiling like a complete dork.
"I'll see you around."

"See you around," I reply, watching her walk away. I
backtrack on my steps and follow the trail of sweat stained
concrete back to Trolley Treats to join Danny for a quick bite
before it's back to getting on every stomach curdling ride we
can before it's time to go.

I'd be just as happy to cool off with some of the water
rides, but it looks like Danny has some sort of death wish.

"Did you do it?" Danny asks.

"I did, but it wasn't much use. She's still really pissed at
me."

He hands me the ice cream I ordered before I pushed it
into his hand to chase after Gabbi. "I guess that's to be
expected. She hasn't told anyone, has she?"

"Nah, she said she wouldn't do that. I guess now she's
talking to Coop though."

"That's good, isn't it? It means you're finally free to do
whatever and date whoever you want."

The tone of his voice is annoyingly optimistic.

"You'd think, wouldn't you? I think as long as my parents have a problem with it, I won't be doing any dating around. There's no way I could ever get away with that."

"Dude, you're eighteen and about to move across the country. Why can't you just tell your parents that you're gonna live your life however you want to live it?"

A laugh pops out before I can stop it, and I about shoot ice cream out of my nose. "You're joking, right? Unless you're actually from a Mexican family, you wouldn't understand that you just don't do that kind of thing. It's just now how things work. If your parents want you to do something, then you do it with no questions asked."

I happen to glance over Danny's shoulder and see that Elliot dude from last night sitting alone just a few tables over and eating nachos. He's slumped over his food and his face is smooshed up against his hand.

I scoop my ice cream bowl from the table and slide off the edge of the bench. "Hey, I'll be right back."

"Where ya going?"

"I just need to talk to someone really quick. Be right back." I stroll through the maze of families and high school kids and plop down on the bench across from Elliot, who practically falls off his from surprise. "Sorry! I didn't mean to scare you."

He grabs onto the edge of the table and wipes some chip crumbs from his shirt. "It's cool."

"Having any fun so far?" I ask.

"Totally."

"Are you sure about that? You seem pretty down over here. Where's Aimee?"

He pushes his boat of nachos to the side. "Yeah, I kinda messed up on that one. I didn't mean to spend three hours at the coffee shop last night. It was supposed to be a movie night for her birthday, and I missed it, so now she's pissed at me."

"That really sucks. But I know how that feels. I have a couple of people who are pretty pissed at me right now too— for different reasons of course—and I don't know if they're ever gonna get over it."

"That's a whole ass mood," he laughs. "But I'm sure things are gonna work out for you."

"And they'll work out for you too. You two have always seemed super close and it doesn't look like anything will ever get in the way of that."

"Thanks for that, but I really messed up this time."

I take another spoonful of ice cream before talking. "It might seem like that now, but just give it some time. She'll forgive you eventually. She might just need some time."

His sudden mood boost is made apparent by his straightened posture and the visibility of his adorable dimples. His bright blue eyes are glistening like tiny pools. It may be temporary, but for the first time in a while, the stress of all my own shit isn't as heavy.

"Thank you," he says, looking down at my bowl. "That looks really good. What kind did you get?"

"It's mint chip and cookies and cream. It's honestly the greatest ice cream combination ever. I'd describe as sort of a mint Oreo, but so much better." I take one last spoonful before pushing the bowl away.

"Aye, Justin!" Danny hollers from across the dining area. "I'm gonna head to the Batman, so just meet me there when you're done."

"And that would be my cue," I say, standing up again. "Just remember what I said. Give Aimee some time and you two will be tighter than ever."

I pick up my bowl off the table and toss it into a trashcan before following after Danny. I'm about halfway there when I hear a frenzy of footsteps behind me and a set of hands stop me in my place. The hand on my shoulder spins me around, and Elliot's standing in front of me, gasping for air.

"What the hell, dude?" I ask.

"You—you're," he says, still panting. "Shit I need to do more cardio."

"I don't understand a word you're saying to me right now."

He stands upright and takes his hands off my shoulders. "You're him."

"You're gonna have to be a little bit more specific than that, dude," I say.

"You're him. Mint chip and cookies and cream, like mint Oreo, but better." He steps closer. "You're him, Justin. You're Milo, aren't you?"

My body tenses up. Everything in my body is telling me to turn and run in the other direction, but it feels like someone's bolted both of my feet to the concrete trails. My breathing is shallow and I'm seeing spots, but I can't say for sure whether or not it's from the name or the rising temperature.

If he knows that name, that can only mean one thing, and I don't think I can handle this right now. There's nothing I'd love more than to just grab him and kiss him and shout over and over again that I finally found him, but there's another part of me that wants to run and crawl into a hole for the rest of my life. That part is so much stronger.

I can't do this. I can't be with him if I can't have the approval from my family.

It's all just too much.

"I—I don't know what you're talking about."

"Don't lie to me. I know it's you. I—it has to be you."

"You've got the wrong guy." The words feel razor sharp as they pass through my lips.

"No I don't," he replies. "I know it and so do you. You have a family that wants you to live a life you don't want. The sense of humor. The kind heart. All of it's the same. The ice cream was the final clue I needed to put it all together."

I step back a couple of inches. "I have no idea what you're talking about, dude. You have the wrong person here. I have to go, and please *don't* follow me." I back up a little more before running as far as my legs can carry me, which couldn't possibly be far enough right now.

CHAPTER THIRTY-THREE

ELLIOT
Friday, May 22

It's been a week since the senior trip. I know it's him. It has to be him. The pieces fit together too well for it to be a coincidence. And ordinarily I'd turn to Aimee to talk me off the proverbial ledge, but that whole situation is still a huge shit show and a major no go. I'm glad that she at least has Vanessa right now, but because of the new relationship thing, I don't really have Vanessa at my beck and call either.

On the bright side of things, I've officially finished finals, which means that graduation is now only two days away and I finally get an entire weekend off from work to prepare for a summer full of hard, manual labor at the store.

I'm laying across my bed and scrolling through TikTok—because what else do I have to do with my days now that I'm friendless and loveless—when there's a bang at my door, followed by Hailey bursting in uninvited as usual.

"Geesh!"

"What? I knocked first."

"What the hell do you want from me now?" I ask.

"I just need a guy's opinion really fast. I couldn't get ahold of anyone though, so I figured I'd just ask you."

"Ha ha. You're so funny."

She flips her hair and smiles at me. "I am pretty funny, huh? But for real. I'm going to a party out at Rachel's and I need like an honest opinion on this outfit. Is it too slutty or just the right amount of slutty?"

I look down at her skin tight, black and white floral crop top matched with a pair of short blue jean shorts and then back up at her.

"Well?" she asks.

"I mean, I guess I'd say it looks like the right amount?"

"Perfect!" She skips over to my closet door and starts fluffing her blonde hair in the mirror. "What's up with that look on your face? You look all depressed and shit, and I have to say that it's really dragging down my vibe right now."

It slips out before I can even filter myself. "If it's bumming you out so much, then why don't you just get the hell out of my room and stop bugging me? We both know you don't actually give two shits about how I'm feeling."

She spins around and looks at me while she continues to play with her hair. "You make me sound like such a horrible person."

"If the shoe fits, I guess."

My filter is most definitely broken at this point, and even if I was able to fix it, there's no way I'd be able to put this genie back in the bottle now that it's out there.

Hailey tiptoes across the wooden floor boards, the bottom of her shoes clacking below her, and slips slowly into my desk chair. She hasn't taken her eyes off me. "I mean . . . I don't like *hate* you or anything like that, if that's what you're thinking."

I push myself up and sit cross-legged on top of my bed. "Are you kidding me right now? You've hated me since the first time we met."

"I—I wouldn't say that. Hate is such a strong word here," Hailey says.

"You've done everything you can to make my life an absolute nightmare since we met, Hailey. You tease me and call me names and blackmail me for crying out loud. If that's not hate, then I don't know what is!"

"Okay, you're at a ten, which I can see is totally justified right now, but I'm gonna need you to bring it down to like a four. And I don't hate you, Elliot. I never have."

I slide closer to the edge of the mattress to see if she's having some type of seizure or something. "If someone is forcing you to say this, I'm gonna need you to blink twice for me."

"Don't be ridiculous," she says.

At this point, I can't really be too sure what's going on here. It's apparent that she's always hated me. Why else would she have made it her life's goal to make my life a total living hell? It was obvious that her dad and brother did enough of that already, and I didn't need her adding to it if that was the truth.

"Then what is it?" I ask.

She twirls the ends of her hair around her finger and doesn't say a word.

"Why have you done literally everything in your power to make sure that my life is horrible beyond repair? If it isn't because you hate me, I'd really like to know why."

She rolls her eyes and huffs.

"I'm waiting," I say.

"Oh my gosh, are you really about to make me say it right now?"

"Yeah, that's kind of the whole point of me waiting for an explanation."

She rolls her eyes again before rolling across the floor in the chair to get closer to my bed. "I've always been kinda jealous of you, you big idiot. There, are you happy now that I said it?"

I lean back and examine her face. Her eyes are avoiding mine and her hands are still messing with her hair. She bounces up to her feet and starts pacing around the room, the sound of her shoes fills the silence between the two of us.

"How could you ever possibly be jealous of me?" I ask.

"Because I just am. Back in grade school you were always like one of the smartest kids in class and you had an amazing mom and you had these really great friends. I was so angry with you about that, because that was what I wanted. And then when all of us moved in together, I saw how your mom was with you. She was always so supportive and so sweet, and she encouraged you in whatever it is you wanted to do. As we got older, I felt like I had all this pressure on me to be little miss perfect. My dad pretty much *forced* me into cheerleading and dance and the National Honor Society, and he expected nothing less than straight A's from me." Hailey stops pacing the floor and takes a seat at the edge of my bed. Her head is dangling over the floor and tears are rushing down her face.

"I'm so sorry," I say. "I had no idea."

She looks up at me and dabs at her face. "And through all of that, you got to continue being just you. There was no pressure for you to be someone that you didn't want to be. And I was jealous of that."

"All that time, I was jealous of you."

"Of me? Seriously?"

"Yeah. All these years, you had someone that believed you could continue to do better and improve yourself. You had that support system behind you pushing you to achieve great things. I'm just sorry that it had to be your dad and Tommy."

"That makes two of us." A smile breaks through the tears. "But they're really not all that bad. They're just a bit of an acquired taste."

"If I haven't acquired a taste for either of them yet, then I highly doubt I ever will."

"You probably have a point." She laughs again and wipes away more of the running tears. "But I just want to say I'm sorry for anything I ever said or did to you. I know the apology doesn't make up for how terrible I've been, but I want you to know that I really do mean it."

"Well thank you. I appreciate that."

She smiles, and for the first time, I think I can see a future where we might actually be friends.

"So, should we like hug now or something?" she asks, extending out her arms.

"Um—baby steps, I think—but I do appreciate the gesture."

"Agreed. Well, I should probably go fix my makeup before I head out. Can't have anyone thinking I have a heart after all, right?" She hops off the edge of the bed and treks across the room. "Hey, I know it's last minute, but do you want to like go to this party with me tonight? It's probably gonna be totally lame and it would be nice to have someone that doesn't totally suck ass."

"Uh, sure. Just give me like ten minutes to get ready."

"Cool, I'll meet you downstairs in ten."

"I'll see you then." I hop onto the floor. "Actually, as long as we're still in the sharing spirit, there is something that I want to say."

Hailey pokes her head back into the room. "Yeah?"

"I'm gay."

She takes one look at me and smiles. "I know. I'll see you downstairs in a few."

CHAPTER THIRTY-FOUR

JUSTIN

Tomorrow's the day that my entire high school career has been leading up to.

It's also the day my entire future is finally set in concrete, because once I walk across that stage and get my diploma, my next big step is moving across the country to begin the life Mom and Dad have always dreamed of for me.

I'm standing in the middle of my room staring at the cap and gown hanging from the back of the closet door when I hear a knock and see movement from the corner of my eye.

"Hey, Mom says dinner's almost ready," Steph says.

"Okay, I'll be down in a few."

Steph got back home for her summer break just a few days ago, and it didn't hit me until now just how grateful I am to finally have someone in the house who knows what I'm dealing with.

She inches further in and sees me staring at my cap and gown. She leans against the wall and says, "It's finally here, huh?"

"Yep."

"I still remember my graduation. I was so excited to finally get out of that school, but I didn't realize how terrified I was until after the high from the day was gone. Can I give you one piece of advice?"

"Sure," I say, plopping down onto my bed.

"Enjoy the day while you can. I didn't realize that day just how much my life was actually about to change and looking back on it I wish I would've taken my time to just enjoy everything that was going on."

"Thanks for the tip."

Steph makes herself comfortable next to me and ruffles my hair the way she always does when she's getting ready for a heart to heart talk.

"Something's going on, so talk. Is it because Mom didn't take it very well?"

"Yes and no," I say. "It's complicated."

"Then start talking. I have the entire summer, so I have nothing but time."

"I should've known you wouldn't just let it slide." I chuckle and turn my head slightly so she doesn't see me trying to fight off the tears. "It's just the way she looked at me when I told her. She looked at me like I was some kind of monster or something, and it about killed me. And now I'm scared to open up and be myself and there's this guy who's—"

"A guy? You've never mentioned a guy before."

"That's the complicated part. We started talking—and it was totally anonymous at the time—and we got kinda close and we were about to reveal our identities to each other and try to figure out how to make something work when the whole thing with Mom happened. And then I guess he figured out who I was by putting some pieces together and he came up to me and told me that he knew, which I totally freaked out over because I know that it would probably make Mom and Dad uncomfortable if I did try something with a guy. So I denied everything, ran off, and I haven't spoken to him since."

Her eyes are wandering around the room and she lets out a sigh before leaning back against my headboard. "That's pretty intense."

"You have no idea."

"I do have one question though. In that entire explanation, you went on and on about how all of this would make Mom and Dad feel, but not once did you actually talk about how *you* feel about all of this. Why is that?"

"I mean, I don't—I don't know."

"Okay, then how *do* you feel about all of it? How do you feel about this guy?"

I fall back onto my pillow next to Steph and stare up at the ceiling. Not once during any of the times I've come out to someone these past few weeks, has anyone ever actually asked me how I feel about everything that's going on. The truth is that I've been so dead set on pleasing everyone else that I never stopped to think about it.

"I don't know," I mutter. "I mean, Elliot is kind and he's funny and he's really smart. He's the kind of person that asks you how your day is, even if he's having a really bad day himself. He does anything he can to make sure you feel comfortable and like you're actually heard, and he has a way of making you feel like you matter. And then there's the whole college thing." I pull myself up and stare forward at the wall. "How did everything get so messed up?"

"I've been asking myself that same question for years," Steph replies, watching me as the gears turn in my head. "What's on your mind?"

"I have to tell them, don't I? Mom and Dad, I mean."

"That's entirely up to you. You should do whatever feels right." A ding from Steph's phone draws her attention to the screen. "Mom says dinner's ready. We should get down there."

"You know you're no help at all, right?"

She laughs before jumping up and ruffling my hair again. "What are older sisters for? Now come on; I'm starving."

I used to really enjoy our family dinners, but ever since I tried to come out to Mom, there's just been this awkward sort of tense feeling that I really hope Dad never asks about some day. It used to be filled with Mom and Dad's laughter as Steph and I would tell them all about our days, and then it turned into Steph telling epic tales of her adventures so far in college. Now it's just weird silences sprinkled in with mindless discussions about the weather and summer plans and cheap small talk. I'd seriously rather listen to Tommy Jenkins talking on a loop than go through another dinner like this one.

"So, do you know how you did on your finals yet, Stephanie?" Mom asks.

"Uh, not yet," she replies. "But any day now. They sent an email that they're still waiting on a couple of professors."

"Well, I'm sure you did amazing as always, Mija," Dad says.

Stephanie never takes her eyes off the piece of broccoli she's picking at with her fork. "Thanks, Papá."

"What about you, Mijo?" Dad asks me.

"Uh, yeah I got all A's."

"That's great! I knew you could do it. Keep this up, and you'll be following in your sister's footsteps before you know it!"

Oh, I think I'm much closer than anyone knows to being like Steph. I already hate the life I'm being forced into. Give it like a year, and I'm sure I'll be drunk and throwing up in random frat house toilets too because I can't handle my own reality anymore.

Steph's fork hits her plate with a loud ting, and she wipes her mouth with her napkin. Her eyes dart back and forth between the three of us.

"Everything okay, sweetie?" Mom asks.

"I can't do this anymore. This dinner is already awkward as hell, so I'm just gonna come out and say it. I don't want Justin to follow in my footsteps, okay? I don't want him to be just like me. I was trying to figure out a way to tell you guys this, but my grades this semester weren't so hot."

Dad sets his water glass down and his stare intensifies. "Do you mean you're failing?"

"No, Papá. I'm not failing. I'm just saying that there was so much pressure all semester to do perfect and I just couldn't live up to the girl you want me to be. I'll be doing my senior year because I've already come this far, but I'm not going to law school next year."

"Oh yes you are," Mom interjects. "You've made the plan and you're going to stick to it. This family sees things through, and we support each other."

"Oh really? We support each other? That's really rich, Mom."

"Mija! I know you may be stressed out and have cold feet, but you do *not* talk to your mother in that tone."

Steph brings her napkin up to her face and dabs away at the newly formed tears. "You're right, and I'm sorry that I got snappy. But I won't apologize for deciding that this isn't what I want to do."

I can feel the need to spill my guts boiling over, and I don't know if I can put a lid on this one. I can only take so much pressure before I finally pop like a balloon. "I have something I need to say too."

"Justin, honey, now isn't the time," Mom says. If her eyebrows were lifted any higher, they'd be part of her hairline. "Can't you see we're already dealing with something here?"

"But I—"

"Justin."

"Fine. I need to be excused." I throw my napkin down on my plate and push myself from under the table. I sneak behind Steph—who at this point is now full on crying and pleading for them to not make her go to law school next year—and set my sights on the escape route up to my room. Before I can even make it out of the dining room, my feet stop in their tracks. It's now or never. "No, not fine. I'm not going to continue living like this. I can't do this shit anymore. I'm done pretending like everything is just fine."

My eyes lock on Steph, a grin is threatening to break through her tears.

"Watch your language, Mijo."

"I'm sorry for swearing. I have tried to be your perfect kid—we both have—but not anymore. I understand that you want us to have a decent life and not have to struggle the way you two did, but we're not you. No disrespect, but the fact that you think you can force this idea of what our lives should be on us, without even asking us for that matter, isn't right and it's totally unfair."

I snake back around and take my seat across from Dad again. His gaze is blank, like he has no idea what's going on or where both of our outbursts are coming from.

"I don't want Stanford, Apá. I never have. I just went with it because I know that's what *you* wanted for me, and I know you didn't exactly have the greatest upbringing, so I wanted to make you happy. But I was doing it at the expense of my own happiness, and I just can't do it anymore. I got into the Studio Art program at NYU, and that's where I'm going in August. I'm not going to Stanford." I take in a deep breath and hold it there for a moment before slowly exhaling.

I think that's all the bravery I have in me for one day. There's no way I'd be able to stomach a negative reaction from Dad if I told him that his only son is gay, so that's probably something better left for another time.

My heart is beating rapidly against its cage in my chest and my head is reeling. It seemed like a bright idea when I was going through the confession in my head, but not so much now.

Mom hasn't blinked in almost an entire minute and her leg has been nervously bouncing for just as long. I know she just wants what she thinks is best for me, but I need to start doing what I *know* is best for me for the first time in my life.

"Please say something, Dad."

I feel a subtle squeeze of my hand, which does help a little with the rising nausea.

"I'm disappointed, Mijos," he says. "I'm disappointed in myself."

I reposition myself in my chair and tilt my head slightly.

"I remember coming to the states when I was just a little boy. Things weren't easy when I first came here. I barely spoke any English, but my father pushed me to learn so that I could better fit in with my peers. He always told me that I had to work ten times harder than everyone else if I wanted to prove that I deserved to be here. That didn't always work though, because I still had people that would make fun of me for my accent or because I was a teacher's pet. I finally told my parents that I didn't want the things that they wanted, and they wouldn't listen to me. I love my parents very much, but I never felt like I was able to be myself. That's when I vowed that I would never make my own children feel the way that I felt growing up."

In my eighteen years, there has never been a moment I saw my father cry, let alone show any kind of weakness. I can see his eyes welling up from the across the table, and there's a slight quiver of his bottom lip. He rests his hand on Mom's and their fingers intertwine.

"And now look. I've become my parents after all, and for that I'm truly sorry."

"What are you saying?" Steph asks.

"I want you to be happy — the both of you — and if that means creating a new plan that works for you, then you have my support every step of the way. I just want you to know that I love you no matter what. I want you to always feel like you can be who you really are, because your happiness is what's most important to me."

"I appreciate that. I appreciate all of you," I finally say.

"Can we promise each other something?" Steph asks. "Can we promise that from here on out we'll always be honest with each other about what we want?"

"I promise," Mom says.

"I promise, Mija." Dad repeats. He takes one last bite of porkchop and pushes his plate forward. "So, tell me all about this art program."

"What do you want to know?"

"Everything," he says. "I want to know everything so I can brag about my artist son."

CHAPTER THIRTY-FIVE

ELLIOT

Sunday, May 24

"So, how do you feel, Mr. Graduate?" Anna asks.

"Hot," I say, zipping down my gown and letting some air flow through. "But it feels pretty good. And very unreal."

"I bet." Anna pulls me in for a hug. "I'm so proud of you."

"Thank you. I just wish Mom was here to see that I finally did it."

"She knows, sweetie. And I know she's so proud of you right now." She loosens her grip and peers over my shoulder. "Aimee! Get over here so I can get a picture of you two in your gowns with your diplomas."

"That's really not necessary, Anna," I say.

It's too late though. She's already framing me and Aimee together for a photo, and I don't know if I can continue fake smiling like everything's fine and dandy. I wrap my arm around Aimee and rest it on the small of her back as we hold up our diplomas. The tension is practically radiating through my bones.

"Okay, and on the count of three, I want some big smiles! Ready?" Anna says, grinning from ear to ear. "1 — 2 —" She looks up from the screen of her phone and glares at us. "Those are the worst smiles I've ever seen. You can do way better than that. You guys have just graduated high school! That's something to celebrate!"

Aimee leans in toward me and whispers through her grin. "How is it she's more excited about this than we are?"

I can't help but laugh for the first time in over a week, and Anna takes the opportunity to snap a photo before either of us ruins it.

"There you go!" Anna slides her phone back into her purse and wraps her arms around the both of us. "I'm so proud of you two. You've both come so far."

"Thanks," I say, my voice monotone.

Anna backs up a few steps and looks up into my eyes. "Look, I know that things didn't work out the way you wanted them to with NYU and it really sucks. But just look on the bright side. You're finally free and you can move out of this town."

"With what money, though?" I ask, holding back the flood. "I mean, I have a savings account, but it's nowhere near enough for me to live on my own right now."

"Actually, that's not exactly true," she replies.

"What do you mean?"

Anna digs through her purse and pulls out an envelope. It no doubt has some cheesy card inside she picked up from the drugstore on the way here. She extends out her hand and I slide the envelope from her fingertips.

This was exactly the kind of handout I *didn't* want from Anna when she has her own problems to worry about.

"I *was* going to wait until tonight to give it to you, but I figure now is as good a time as any."

"Anna, I can't accept whatever's in this card."

"Just open it, Elliot."

I stare at Anna and Aimee before tearing the paper open and pulling out a card with "Congrats Grad" scrawled across the front. My heart drops down into the bottom of my stomach as I my eyes scan over the scribbled words inside. There's a burning in my throat and my vision is clouding.

My dearest Elliot,

If you're reading this instead of me telling you everything I want to say, then that means I'm gone and for that I'm terribly sorry. There's nothing I would love more than to see you walk across that stage and become the amazing man that you are destined to become. I want you to go out into the world and do the things that I was never able to do. I want you to make mistakes and find yourself and learn how to love yourself unconditionally, because you are so strong and capable of so much more than you think you are. I love you so much, Elliot, and I want you to have the life that you deserve to have. It's time for you to go out into the world and make it your own.

Love, Mom

My fingertips brush across the curvatures of her signature, feeling the imprint from the weight of her pen as she wrote it five years ago. The burning in my throat has intensified, threatening to destroy any bit of composure I have left in me.

I can feel the warmth of my tears rush down my cheek as there's a subtle squeeze of my hand and I'm brought back to reality.

"You okay, El?" Aimee asks, her voice wavering.

All I can do is look up at Anna. "H—" is all that escapes from between my lips.

"Your mom wanted to make sure you were taken care of in the event that something was to ever happen to her, so she took out life insurance for herself when you were just a little bean. That's just the kind of mom she was."

My face is drenched now, and it feels like someone's tied my esophagus into a little knot. "But, why now? Why not back then?"

"After she got sick, she told me that she didn't want anyone else knowing about it, because she wanted to make sure that this would be used only by you. She made me promise not to give it to you until the day you graduated high school."

Aimee's hand finds mine again and grips it tight. She uses her other hand to wipe the tears falling down my cheeks.

"See, even when your mom's not here, she's still here for you," Anna says. "I know it's not a whole lot, but it should be enough for you to get on your feet and help pay for at least half of your time at ISU."

"Th—thank you," I manage to get out. "Thank you for everything."

Anna wraps her arms around me again and pulls me in tight. "You're going to do so many amazing things." She loosens her grip and smiles up at me. "I'll see you both tonight for dinner. I really need to go pick the boys up from the babysitter."

"We'll see you tonight. Five o'clock, right?" I ask.

"Sounds good to me."

Aimee and I watch as Anna disappears into the hordes of families. Vanessa pops up out of nowhere and half hugs, half jumps the both of us.

"Watch the hair, babe." Aimee says, readjusting her updo.

"Sorry, I'm just so proud of the both of you!"

My eyes dart back and forth between the two of them. "So, does this mean that the two of you are talking to me again?"

"I don't know—are you done just totally abandoning us?" Aimee asks.

"Alright, I guess I kind of deserved that one. I'm sorry that I let myself get so obsessed with the whole Milo and Justin thing. That's done now, so you don't need to worry about it."

"What do you mean it's done?" Vanessa asks with her big puppy dog eyes.

"It was a whole thing and he just decided that he didn't want to talk anymore. And then I confronted him while we were at Six Flags and I—"

Aimee throws up her hand. "You did what now?"

"Yeah, I sort of went up to him and full on accused him of being Milo. But he denied it. All of it. I know he is though because it all just fits too well together for it to not be him."

"Well, maybe he's just not ready," Vanessa says.

"I don't know. Either way it goes, I realize that I deserve to be with someone that's gonna want to be with every part of me. Someone that won't have to hide behind a computer screen just to talk to me."

"Okay, hold on just a second! Have I not been telling you that for months now?" Aimee says.

"Okay, I don't need the attitude. I know that I was being stupid, and I should've listened to you sooner."

"Well as long as you finally get it, that's all that matters. I'm so sorry that I totally flipped out on you the day of the trip. I was out of line."

"It's fine," I say. "I know things have been really weird and tense. Let's never fight again though, okay?"

"Deal," Aimee says before pulling me in for another hug. "We did it. We actually graduated."

"I know, it's totally insane."

Suddenly it hits me what this means for us. It's our last summer before we both go off into our new lives as college students. This all just means we're one step closer to being apart for the first time since we've met.

"Everything's gonna change now, isn't it?" Vanessa asks.

My eyes dart back and forth between Aimee and Vanessa. As much as no one wants to admit, nothing is going to be the same ever again. "I think so." I focus in on Aimee again, who looks to be about five seconds away from bawling her eyes out. "How will I get through this without you?"

"No! No way we're doing this now," she replies, dabbing under her eyes. "There's no way I'm letting you ruin my makeup right now. Besides, we have our entire summer before anything's changing, so just cool it."

"Someone's a little touchy," I say, grinning like a complete moron through my tears.

Aimee's face is glowing up until the second she glances over my shoulder, and then it's replaced by the worst stink face I've ever seen. "Hey, I think someone wants to talk to you."

"That can't be good."

Michael's standing there with that usual smug look on his face. I was so excited by the prospect of finally getting the hell out of here that I didn't stop to realize that I actually have to survive a little longer under his roof until I can find a place to live. It'll be difficult considering every time I look at him or Tommy, I want to put my fist through a wall.

"Hey, what's up?" I ask.

"First, I just wanted to say good job on graduating. That's a big accomplishment."

"Uh, thank you."

"I also need you to come in and work tonight for Debby."

Ope, there it is! I knew it had to be something. It can never just be a compliment with this guy. Is a *you did great, kid, so congrats and have a good rest of your day* really too much to ask for?

"What? Can't you get someone else to do it? I have graduation stuff tonight."

"You're the only other person left to do it after Mr. Thompson quit," he replies.

"Fine," I say out of habit.

Michael just shakes his head and turns to walk away. I can only assume he's looking for Hailey and Tommy so he can give a real congratulations to something in his life that doesn't bring trouble to his existence.

"No!" I shout over the chattering and congratulatory squeals. Something just hit me, and now I'm riding on an adrenaline high that I hope stays long enough for me to get out everything I need to say. "I'm not doing it."

Michael turns back. His nostrils are flaring, and I've never seen him look more annoyed in the time I've known him. "What did you say?"

"I said *no*. I'm not coming in tonight, so maybe you should get off your lazy ass and put down the beer and do it yourself for once, you sad, miserable bastard."

Michael's less than a foot from my face now. "You listen here—"

"No, *you* listen." It's taking every muscle I have in my body to hide the fact that I'm shaking like crazy. "I am done with you and your family and that stupid ass sorry excuse for a store." I take in a deep breath to calm my nerves before the next words fall out of my mouth. "I have had it with the way you've treated me for the last five years. I know for a fact that you only tolerated me before that because of my mom. And as much as I know you want to blame me for what happened to her, it wasn't my fault. She was too busy trying to deal with your shit on top of being a parent to me. A real parent, unlike you! I am done taking your bullshit. And I'm moving out, because I can't do this anymore."

Michael's shoulders bounce up and down and he starts to laugh under his breath. "You're moving out, huh? Where are you gonna go? How are you gonna support yourself?"

"Do you really think I don't have my ways? I have been preparing for this moment for *years!*"

Aimee steps forward and intertwines her arm with mine. "He'll move in with me until he can find a place of his own. We'll be fine."

"Yeah, we will," I say with a smile. "Have a nice life, Michael. I'll be by tomorrow to pick up my stuff."

I link arms with both Aimee and Vanessa, and we disappear into the crowd.

Telling Anna about the way I told off Michael over dinner was completely exhilarating. She looked like a proud momma bear the entire time. Aimee's parents seemed more than happy to have me stay with them until I can get my own place, which I'm so fortunate for.

It wasn't my original intent, but I let Aimee talk me into going with her to Project Grad, the all-night party hosted by the school for all the graduating seniors.

It didn't help that she mentioned it right in front of Anna, who thought it was an excellent idea, so now I'm sitting in the school's parking lot with Aimee, preparing to walk inside one last time.

"We can still turn back now. It's not too late, you know," I say.

"We're not turning back, Elliot. Why do you want to skip out on this so bad?"

"Because I don't want to have a run in with Justin, okay? I didn't have much of a choice the last week of school, but every time I see him, it's like a slap in the face. I know it's him and as soon as he figured out it was me . . . he just didn't want anything to do with me."

"Look, I know it's difficult, and I can't even imagine what you're going through right now, but you need to understand that you deserve better," Aimee says. "You shouldn't let this derail your life. We're gonna go in there and we're gonna have some fun with all the inflatables and the games and we're gonna pig out on all the snacks, okay?"

"Okay, you're right. I'm sorry."

"Good, now let's go!"

Aimee practically pushes me out of my own car before hopping out and dragging me through the parking lot and up to the front of the building. There's a line of people leading into the front doors and a couple of checkpoints with teachers checking any bags for signs of alcohol.

"I still can't believe I let you talk me into this," I say.

"We're gonna have a good time, so stop complaining so much."

We finally make it past the checkpoint system and decide to head straight for the food tables to stock up on pizza, soda, and cookies before finding a table at the far end of the cafeteria.

"So, what do you want to do first?" Aimee asks.

"I say we hit up the photobooth before the inflatables because we're gonna be all red and sweaty."

"Good point. Photobooth it is."

I shove a slice of pizza into my face just as Hailey decides she wants to slide up to the table next to me.

"Howdy," Hailey says.

If Aimee's jawline was any more clenched, she'd probably crack all of her teeth. "What the hell do you want?"

"Whoa there, tense much?"

I finish chewing my slice and dab at my mouth with a napkin. "Aimee, it's cool. It's a whole thing and a story for a different time, but we're cool now."

Aimee purses her lips and looks Hailey up and down.

"I know you don't believe it right now, but I'm gonna prove it to you," Hailey says. "I'm sorry that I've been such a bitch."

"You have been. Don't mess this up, because you won't get another chance."

I don't think there's ever been a time that I've sat with both Aimee and Hailey together, let alone shared a meal with both of them. The only thing keeping me from wanting to tear out my hair is that Aimee is typing away at her phone, more than likely texting back and forth with Vanessa, and Hailey's busy taking selfies, all the while I'm busy watching Tommy and a couple of his buddies harassing Sam Green, the only out gay senior.

"Hey, I'll be right back," I say to Hailey and Aimee before jumping up and striding across the cafeteria. I'm for sure still riding from the rush of telling off Michael earlier. I just hope it ends as well as that did. I watch as Tommy and his boys follow Sam down an abandoned hallway. I'm trailing close behind them when there's the slight pressure of a hand against my shoulder and my body's yanked to a stop. "What the hell are you—" The words leave my brain as Justin's face comes into view.

"Hey, can we talk for a second? Please?"

His big brown eyes make me weak every time I see them.

"Wh—I—can this wait for a second?"

"It'll only take a minute. Elliot, I—I—"

A subtle grunt echoes from down the hall.

"I'm sorry, I can't do this right now. Sam's in trouble."

I break free from Justin's grip and dash down the hallway as fast as my legs will carry me. There's a second set of footsteps coming up fast behind me.

"Just leave me alone, guys," Sam says.

"You were just totally checking out my ass, weren't you?" Tommy says, almost grinning.

"Dude, no. Why would I do that?" Sam asks.

"Like I get that I'm pretty attractive, but I'm not a piece of meat, so just don't stare at me, dude. That's not cool."

I swear every time Tommy opens his mouth, another one of my brain cells dies. I'm surprised I'm not completely brain dead at this point.

"Again, I wasn't staring at your ass." Sam's got his arms crossed and he's trying to back away. "My eyes weren't even anywhere near you."

"Oh, then you must've been checking out one of my buddies then. You like what you see or something, you little faggot?"

Nope, that's the line and he's officially crossed it. I can't stand by and let all of this happen. Not again.

"Okay, Tommy. I'd say that's enough, don't you think?" I say. "Let's just all go and have some fun and just enjoy the last night we'll all ever be in this building together, okay?"

"Stay outta this, Faggiot. It's not your problem," he says.

"Aye! Dude!" Justin shouts, putting his arm against my chest and pushing me away from Tommy's view. "I think that's just about enough out of you for one day, so why don't you guys get the hell outta here and leave Sam alone."

"This isn't your problem either, Herrera. So just get the hell out of here while I deal with this faggot."

"Actually, it became my problem when you started dropping the F word, yet again. Why don't you just cool it and leave him the hell alone? Don't you think it's getting a little old?"

Tommy turns his attention from Sam back to Justin. He's got that smug look just like his father. They really are a carbon copy of each other. "Well, if you have a problem with it, that must mean *you* must be some kinda homo too then." He pokes a finger at Justin's chest.

I bite my tongue for a moment and play out all the ways this could end in my head, most of which involve Justin getting punched for one reason or another.

"Is that what it is? Are you a homo too, Justin?"

Justin's breaths are getting heavier and his chest is puffed out. There's a well-defined clench to his jaw and his nostrils are flaring. I think this is the first time I've ever seen him angry, and it's a bit terrifying.

"You know what, Tommy? You caught me." Justin finally yells, poking him in the chest right back. "Yes I am. I am a *massive* teenage closet case and I am sick and tired of you thinking you have the right to stand around and be a dick to everyone. News flash, dude. No one actually likes you in case you haven't noticed. You are a low life loser destined to be stuck in this town forever just like your father. So why don't you take your low-budget crew and get the hell out of here."

Tommy steps forward with his fists clenched "You want to say that again, gay boy?"

There's a hand on my shoulder and Aimee steps in. She gets in Tommy's face like the bad ass bitch she is and says, "Do *you* want to say that again?"

Hailey struts up beside her and gets in his face too. "Seriously, dude. Just go calm the hell down. You're not intimidating anyone here."

I never thought I'd see the day that Hailey would actually be defending me — or Justin Herrera for that matter — from Tommy and his barbaric ways of thinking.

Tommy backs away from the girls and for the first time actually looks scared. I don't blame him though. I wouldn't want to severely piss off Aimee either and Hailey looks like she could handle herself well in a fight for someone who's so little.

He looks both me and Justin up and down before backing away and disappearing down the hall in the direction he came from.

I glance up at Justin, who's chest is still rising and falling rapidly. His eyes are glossy and his face is pale white.

"Justin . . . I—"

He looks over at me before hiding his face. "I'm sorry. I just—I can't." He bolts to the other end of the hall and disappears outside through the senior hall doors

"What was that all about?" Hailey asks.

"Don't even worry about it," I say. "It was nothing important."

Without even trying, Tommy managed to screw everything up for me once again. It feels like someone's taken my heart and decided to use it as one of the inflatables, and the only thing keeping the tears from flowing is the fact that I'm stuck in this damn school for the next several hours.

CHAPTER THIRTY-SIX

JUSTIN

Monday, December 21

I honestly never thought I'd be so grateful to be back in Bloomington, Illinois of all places. Don't get me wrong, New York has been absolutely amazing these past few months, but I never stopped to think how brutal the winters would be up there. At least here I have less of a chance of dying from exposure after only five minutes of being outside.

It's just after four o'clock when my train pulls up outside Uptown Station. One plane ride, two lay-overs, a train ride, and a thirty-minute delay later and I'm finally home. I'm just hoping Steph's actually here because the sooner I can get a shower, the better.

I follow the trail of passengers off the last step of the train as I button the bottom half of my coat and secure my hat on my head. The cold air thrashes against my face as I make my way through the freshly fallen thin layer of snow and into the building to find a bathroom. My bladder's been ready to explode for the last half hour and I *refuse* to use those nasty ass bathrooms.

Before heading back out into the lobby with a newly empty bladder, I do a double-take in the bathroom mirror. Removing my hat again, I smooth out the annoying cowlicks in my hair, which I've let grow quite a bit since moving out east back in early August. I also started letting my beard grow out, which thankfully keeps me from looking like a high school sophomore that's just touring campus, and I let some of the new friends I made give me a lesson in proper clothing. My roommate Ben calls it the obligatory New York makeover that almost every Mid-West kid gets when they finally get to leave home.

It's so crazy to think how much has changed just in the last five months since I've been away, and not just my physical appearance. I just feel different these days. Almost lighter somehow. There's something about being around like-minded people that's more freeing than I could've ever imagined it would be.

I slip my hat back on over my ears and head back out to the lobby to find Steph, who's nudged into a corner half asleep with a Starbucks cup and her wireless headphones.

She glances up at me as I approach, looking just as annoyed as I feel right now. "Well it's about damn time!"

"I know, I'm really sorry. The train got delayed and my phone died, and I think I lost my charger somewhere."

"Excuses." She shoves her headphones back into their case and slides it into her coat pocket before jumping up to her feet. "You ready to head home now?"

"Yes please! I need to wash this plane ride off me as soon as possible."

I readjust the duffle bag draped over my shoulder and follow Steph back out into the cold air. Thankfully the snow isn't coming down very fast yet, but with the way this state is I wouldn't leave anything to chance. I slide into the front passenger seat of Steph's car and toss my bag into the backseat, nearly smacking her in the face with it in the process. She scowls before starting the car up and cranking up the heat. I pull her emergency charger out of the glove department and plug my phone in.

"How's it feel to know you only have one semester left?" I ask.

"I'd be lying if I told you I didn't cry out of sheer happiness after I took my last final. I'm so ready to just be *done* so I can get on with my life already."

"Any plans for after you graduate now that you're not going to law school anymore?"

"Honestly? I don't have a damn clue what I'm doing, and I couldn't be more ecstatic about it." She turns the stereo volume up and *Evermore* plays softly from the speakers. "For the first time in my life, I don't have every little thing planned out for me, and I fully intend to revel in that for a little while."

I've never seen Steph look this carefree or genuinely happy in my entire life. It's great to finally see her doing her own thing.

"What about you? Anything big planned for the rest of the school year?" she asks.

"Actually, I do. You know how I got offered that design internship at Hale Publishing over the summer?"

"Yeah."

"Well, they offered it again and I decided to take it. I start after I get back into the city in a couple weeks."

"That's really great, Justin. I'm glad you're finally doing something you enjoy."

"Thanks."

Steph turns the volume up a bit more and I slide my phone back out from the middle console. I'm greeted by an over-abundance of dings and vibrations as the power finally kicks back on. I swipe through school emails, group chats, a couple texts from Danny, and then the one I've been waiting to read.

The look in my eyes and the smile plastered across my face can't help but give me away.

Steph's eyes burn into the side of my head as I read through the rest of my texts. "I know that look."

"I don't know what you're talking about," I say, nibbling at my bottom lip and avoiding any eye contact.

"Oh, please. Don't even try to lie to me right now because you're not that good at it. I *know* that look. I know *all* of your looks because I get the same ones." She merges onto the highway and turns the music down a couple notches. "It's him, isn't it?"

"Maybe."

"Would you guys just stop with the back and forth and make it official already? You're starting to give me whiplash, dude," she laughs.

"It's only been a couple months, so give it time, would you? I've never done the whole "official" thing before, and it's stressful and I don't know what I'm doing.

My friend Hannah talked me into going to a Halloween party a couple of months back, despite me kicking and screaming and swearing up and down that I would *not* wear the Spider-Man costume she picked out for me. Of course, she got things her way after I got a couple shots in me, and it turned out to be one of the greatest nights of my life.

After everything went down with Elliot and Tommy on graduation night and I reacted to the situation by running away like a coward, I didn't think I'd ever get the courage to open up to anyone else ever again. I didn't think I deserved to be happy after I spent all that time playing with Elliot's emotions and then I just ran off like none of it ever mattered.

Things are different with Chase though. We got to talking that night after a friend of Hannah introduced us, and there was just this immediate connection. He's been helping me through so much of my own shit and helping me realize that up until that point there was a lot of internalized homophobia keeping me from being who I'm supposed to be.

I've learned that I'm allowed to rewrite the false narrative I spent so much time creating for myself and that I'm allowed to find love.

"Are you happy?" Steph asks.

"For the first time, I think I am."

"Then that's all you need to know. If he makes you happy and you make him happy, then maybe one of you should man up and tell the other."

"I know, you're right," I say. "I've been putting myself through the ringer long enough."

"Does that mean you're finally gonna tell dad?"

"That's a lot easier said than done."

"You told him about NYU, and he was totally fine with it. Maybe his views are a little different than you think."

"Yeah, but that's a hell of a lot different than telling him that his only son is gay when he was raised the way he was." I set my phone back down and stare straight ahead. The flurries have almost doubled in size in the last fifteen minutes and are hypnotic as they bead against the windshield. "I'll figure something out."

I've never seen Mom so excited to see me. I guess that's what happens when you move almost 900 miles away. I'm greeted by Willow, the little ball of golden fluff with the cutest bark I've ever heard. Mom and Dad blamed the new family addition on being empty-nesters.

It's weird being back in my room after all this time. Everything's exactly the same as the way I left it, but at the same time everything's completely different now. *I'm* different now. There's a certain lightness to the atmosphere that wasn't here before. It's only been a few months, but this life feels like it's light years behind me now.

I toss my dirty clothes into the basket by the closet before slipping on a fresh pair of briefs and throwing on my new skinny jeans and a black and white striped sweater. I slide down into the desk chair I spent many nights smashing out papers in and peek through the window as the snow continues falling to the now totally covered ground in large chunks. My attention's drawn to the file tray sitting on the top tier of the desk and my fingers grasp at the letter that changed my life forever.

"Dear Justin, Congratulations! It is with great pleasure that I offer you admission to the Stanford University Class of 2024." A chuckle is just barely audible as the vibrations tickle at my throat.

"That feels like such a long time ago now," I hear from behind me.

I lay the letter flat on the desk top and swivel around in my chair. "Hey, Mom. Is Dad back yet?"

"Not yet; he's on his way back though. Do you think you could run by the grocery store and pick up a bag of red potatoes? I promised your sister I would make them, and I completely forgot to pick up more."

"Yeah, I can do that. It's no problem," I say.

Mom smiles before settling herself at the corner of my bed, still staring at me.

"What's up?" I ask.

She nods in the direction of the letter face down on the desk. "You've certainly come a long way since then."

"Yeah, I guess so. I'm still the same guy though."

"Except you're really not. You've changed, and that's not a bad thing. I've watched you grow into this confident and happy young man these last few months, and I couldn't be prouder of who you're becoming."

"Mom, I—"

"Just let me finish," she says.

I just nod my head and lean further back into the chair.

She takes a deep breath and her stare intensifies. "A few months ago, you told me something that was deeply personal, and I reacted poorly. Actually, I reacted worse than poorly. That night, I failed as a parent and there is no excuse for my behavior. I thought that I was protecting you because I was scared of how others might treat you, but the truth is that I became one of those people I wanted to protect you from as soon as I discounted who you really are."

There's a knot the size of Texas settling in my stomach and twisting up my insides that not even the deep breathing exercises I've been working on are helping. My vision's getting hazy as I struggle to see through the building tears.

"Are you happy?" she asks. "Are you happy with that boy I've been seeing on your social media?"

I pause for a moment.

When the hell did my mother start using social media?

"I—I don't know what you mean," I say.

"You've never been a great liar, Justin," she says with a grin. "Your face lights up in all the pictures you have together, and I've never seen it like that before. Does he make you happy?"

All I can do is nod as I fight back the water works.

"That's all I could ever ask for as a parent. I'm so sorry if I ever made you feel like who you really are and what you want isn't important. I love you so much and I just want what's best for you, and that means letting you be who you were born to be."

"I—I don't know what to—thank you." I break the restraints holding back my tears and throw my arms around her.

"Of course. If you're happy then I'm happy, sweetheart."

She pulls back and I take the free spot next to her as I wipe my tear stained cheeks.

"There is one other thing I need to tell you," she says. "I told your dad."

I open my mouth to speak but nothing comes out.

"I wanted to tell him to give him time to sit with it so that when you finally did get the courage to tell him, it would be an easier discussion for you to have."

"And how did he take it?" I ask.

"He was a little surprised at first, but he took it really well. He just wants you to be happy in life and for you to have the freedom to make your own choices."

"I need to have a talk with him tonight, don't I?"

"It doesn't have to be tonight, but I think it's time you had a discussion with him about it so you can move on with your life once and for all. In the meantime, get your butt to the store and get those potatoes."

CHAPTER THIRTY-SEVEN

ELLIOT

Monday, December 21

"It took you long enough!" Aimee shouts as she throws her arms around me.

"You try apartment hunting in the snow with Hailey and see if you can still be early to something, okay?" I say, kicking the snow off my shoes before I walk inside.

"That's on you for agreeing to live with her next fall, so I don't even want to hear it."

I slide my coat off and hang it up in the entryway closet before sliding my shoes off and setting them by the door. There's another knock and Aimee practically breaks the door as she whips it open and Vanessa leaps into her arms.

"You're home!" Vanessa squeals. "I've missed you so much! And oh my gosh, you cut your hair?"

"I did it this morning," Aimee replies, running her fingers through the bits of hair resting at her shoulders. "Do you like it? Or is it too short?"

"It looks so good. You're just as beautiful as ever, babe."

"Aw, thank you."

Vanessa pulls Aimee in for another hug, this time planting a kiss at the top of her head.

"What am I? Chopped liver?" I ask.

"Oh! I'm so sorry, I didn't see you!" Vanessa loosens her grip on Aimee and squeezes me, practically tackling me to the floor in the process.

"I wonder why," I laugh.

"Oh shut up, you know I love you." She pulls back and smiles at me. "Where's Coop? Is he still coming?"

"He wasn't able to make it, but he'll try to make it for tomorrow's movies."

Life's been strange the last few months, if that's even the right way to describe it.

Aimee's parents let me stay with them for the summer until I was able to move into the freshman dorms. It started off just being the three amigos all day every day, but then one day I got a text from Cooper apologizing and wanting a chance to prove himself. My first reaction was obviously to tell him to go screw himself, but I couldn't get my talk with Charlie out of my head. I finally agreed to have lunch only to find out he worked up enough guts to come out to his parents. They weren't happy about it and basically disowned the guy, so he's been living with his older sister in Bloomington ever since.

Despite his parents being ignorant shit heads, I've never seen him look so free.

My one condition to giving Cooper a second chance was that we try to rebuild a friendship from the ground up. There was nothing if I didn't learn to trust him again. I don't know if things will ever turn into anything than what we have now, but it's different than it was the first time. There's no secrecy or sneaking around.

We're able to be our 100% selves for the first time.

"Well that's a bummer. But I guess that means more snacks for us!" Aimee grabs Vanessa by the hand and leads us into the kitchen, where her mom has obviously been hard at work getting ready for our Christmas movie marathon.

"That's a lot of food!" Vanessa says.

"Yeah, it's kind of our tradition. We make a bunch of snacks for our movie nights and then whatever's left we box up and give away as treats on Christmas day," Aimee explains, grabbing a piece of peppermint bark. "Seriously the best Christmas desserts in town."

"You're just saying that because I'm your mom and you have to."

"Oh totally," Aimee laughs. "But for real, this is the place to be if you ever want to be put into a sugar coma."

"And everything's just about done here," her mom says, digging through a cabinet. "I just need to top the Oreo truffles with the chocolate sauce and let it freeze for about twenty minutes. Except I think we're all out of the sauce. Do you think you guys could keep an eye on the chicken parmesan so it doesn't burn while I run to the store and grab another bottle?"

"Hey, I can go get it if you want so you don't have to go out," I say.

"Are you sure?"

"Totally. I wanna say hi to Anna anyway."

She reaches into the fridge and pulls out a tin with little candy canes printed all over it. "Would you take this to Anna then? I told her I'd give it to her next time I see her."

"Will do." I reach over the counter to grab the treat box and swipe a piece of peppermint bark.

Everything in this store is the exact same way it was when I quit almost seven months ago. The same layout, the same customers, and the same annoying music blasting from the intercom speakers. I haven't been here since before graduation back in May and I haven't spoken to Michael since I flipped out on him after the ceremony.

Tommy hasn't said a word to me since the fight he almost got into with Justin.

Now there's a name I haven't said in a while. I tried sending him an email after that night to apologize for everything that went down, but after he didn't reply I knew things were finished for good. It was my fight and he didn't have to step in like that to save me, so I can't help but feel like it was partially my fault in some way. The last I heard he was on his way to New York to start his new life as an art student. After that I blocked him so I wouldn't be tempted to keep stalking him on Instagram. Some things are just better left alone and in the past where they belong.

The bottom of my chukka boots echo beneath me as I make my way to the deli at the back corner of the store. The closer I get, the more I can smell the all-too-familiar scents of fried chicken and potato wedges. None of it has been missed one bit.

There's a couple of new kids working tonight that I'm pretty sure I recognize as freshman from last year. That's just how the cycle goes; a couple of seniors leave so that two others can take their place and start the cycle all over again someday.

"Hey, Brittany, could you do me a favor and start on some more gravy for me?" Anna asks.

"Sure thing."

"Hey, don't work these kids too hard now," I say, grinning.

Anna stops for a moment before turning to face me and her eyes light up. She slips her apron off before making a break for the double doors separating the deli from the rest of the store. She pulls me in tight and says, "Why didn't you tell me you were coming by today?"

"I didn't know until a few minutes ago. Aimee's mom needs another bottle of chocolate sauce and she wanted me to give you this tin."

"Ooh," she says, grabbing it from my hands. "It's the peppermint fudge I ordered. This stuff is so good. So, did you get your final grades back yet?"

"Yeah, all A's this semester."

"See! I knew you could do it and you were freaking out over nothing. You've got to give yourself more credit."

"I know," I say, rolling my eyes. "I'll try harder at that."

"You better! And are you and Cooper still doing alright?"

"Things are pretty good." My face is getting hot.

"Does that mean he's your boyfriend?" Anna asks, poking at my arm and trying to be as annoying as humanly possible.

"No, that word hasn't happened yet. We're taking things slow."

"Dude, you've been taking things slow for months now. Hurry up and hit the fast-forward button already!"

There's a loud crash from the back of the deli, followed by a few choice words that I'm pretty sure the cashiers heard at the front of the store.

"I think that's your cue," I say.

"These kids are going to be the death of me, I swear. I have got to find a new job." She gives me one last hug before heading for the doors. "I'll see you on Christmas for dinner. Six o'clock sharp, and don't be late."

"I wouldn't dream of it." I stand in place as she disappears behind the doors and assesses the damage before high-tailing it to the other side of the store to find the baking aisle.

My phone vibrates against my outer thigh.

Aimee: Hey, you about done? We're setting up the movie now.

Me: Yeah, I had to stop and talk to Anna. Grabbing the chocolate now and then I'll be —

I glance up and my fingers stop moving. My heart is thumping in my throat, and my limbs are frozen in place, so even if there was enough brain function going on, I wouldn't be able to run anyway.

I almost don't recognize the guy walking toward me. His black t-shirt, cargo short, and converse wardrobe has been replaced by skinny jeans, form-fitting sweaters, and a pair of brown chelsea boots. His well-kept boy next door hair has grown a bit since I last saw him and now lays in messy, but cute, side-swept waves that perfectly compliment his new stubble beard.

We both stand in complete silence for a moment, unsure of what to say after the way things were left.

"Elliot . . . hi."

"H—hi. I didn't expect to see you here"

"Likewise," he replies.

"Well, you look really good," I say.

"Uh—yeah—you too. Did you lighten your hair?"

"Yeah, just something I thought I'd try it out."

"It suites you."

"Thanks," I reply.

"Yeah."

Someone just kill me now and put me out of this misery, please.

I shift my weight from one leg to the other and fold my arms up against my chest as Justin looks around and avoids having any eye contact with me.

"How've you been lately?" I ask. "I heard you went to NYU after all."

Justin brings his attention back to me, and my stomach lurches. The sound of a thousand tiny bees in my head is drowning out the music being cranked out from above us.

"Yeah I did. It's been really good. Did you ever get into the film program?"

"Unfortunately, no."

"I'm sorry to hear that. That really stinks, but there's always next year, right?" He just had to slip in that old optimistic outlook in there.

"I mean, I was pretty bummed at first, but I kinda like it now. I didn't get to pursue film, but I figured out I actually really like communications, so I think I might do something with that."

"Well at least you found something you like and you're happy," he replies.

I just shake my head.

"You are, right? Happy, I mean," he says, taking a step forward and shoving his hands into the pocket of his coat.

"Yeah, I'm most definitely happy."

"Good. That's really good to hear."

"What about you?" I ask. "Are you—you know—happy? With your life in New York?"

A smile tugs at his lips and his dimples poke through. For the first time I see this light in his eyes that wasn't there before. It reminds me of that look Cooper had when he told me he finally came out.

"Yeah, I'm happy. Happier than I've ever been actually."

"And do you have a—" I start to say. I lean against the cooler behind me and my cheeks go red. "No, you don't have to answer that. It's really none of my business."

"Do I have a what? A boyfriend?"

All I can do is awkwardly smile and stand there like a doofus while he stares at me.

"No? At least I don't think—it's kind of a weird situation, I guess. Do you have a—you know?"

"I guess it's kinda complicated. It's actually Cooper," I reply.

"Wait, Coop's—" Justin's mouth is gaping open and his eyes have just about doubled in size.

"I was just as surprised as you," I laugh. "It's a long story for a different time. We're not, not together, if that makes any sense. Like you said, it's a weird situation."

"That makes total sense. But I'm happy that you're happy."

"Yeah, you too." I look down at another text from Aimee. "I should probably get going, but it was really nice seeing you, Justin."

"I should head out too," he replies. "It was great to see you too."

I turn to walk away, but the urge to say something else stops me in my tracks. "I really am happy for you, Justin. You deserve to be happy."

"Thanks," he says, smiling again.

I turn again and head down the baking aisle to find that chocolate sauce.

"Elliot," he calls, stopping me again. "I don't know if you'd be interested or not, but would you like to meet up for a coffee like old times before I have to head back in a couple weeks? Maybe we can catch up?"

I have to fight my forming grin as I turn to face him again. "Uh . . . yeah. That would be really nice. We'll sort something out soon. I still have your email address."

"And I still have yours. So, I guess I'll talk to you later."

"I'll talk to you later." I grab the sauce off the shelf and look at him again. "By the way, you never did tell me what the "Juni" part in your email address meant."

"And here I thought you were an expert detective that would've figured it out." He laughs and slides his hands from his pockets. "It's my first and middle name. Justin Nicholas."

"That's clever. I definitely never would've figured that one out."

"I'm sure you would've. But I should really get back home. I'll see you around."

"See you around," I say as he smiles one last time and disappears around the corner.

I can remember there being a time that I would've run so fast after that man to make some sort of grand romantic gesture and finally just kiss him. A few months back there was nothing that I wanted more, but the truth is that I don't know how things in this lifetime are going to work out. I never have and I never will.

What I do know is that we were thrown into each other's lives for a reason, whether it was for both of us to learn some type of lesson to take into our first real relationships, or maybe the cosmos are trying tell us something much bigger is in store for us down the line. The way I see it is one of two things could happen here: Number one, this could be the beginning to a long and prosperous friendship that I carry with me for the rest of my days, or number two, this could be the beginning to some epic tale that not even I—the sappy hopeless romantic—am ready for.

The one thing I've learned through all this is to never say never.

ACKNOWLEDGEMENTS

There are so many people that had a hand in helping me bring this story to life. I could never possibly thank everyone enough.

To my amazing sister Renee, who's been my biggest cheerleader throughout the entire writing process, thank you for being the very first audience member and pushing me to keep going. And thank you for putting up with my long writing hours during our *Jane the Virgin* binge-watching sessions.

A huge thank you to my editor and dear friend Eleanor Stamer, who fell just as in love with this story as I did from the very first page. You got all the pop culture references that I was scared no one would get and made me feel like this was a story worth telling.

To Mom, thank you for being accepting of who I am, and for encouraging me to be the very best that I can be. I love you!

To my good friend Jordon Greene, thank you so much for putting up with my excessive questions and pleas for help. This wouldn't have been possible without your guidance.

I would also like to thank *you*, the amazing person who took the time to read this story. Without you, this story would just be lost in the void. Always remember that you are so much more than you give yourself credit for.

And last, but certainly not least, a huge thank you to my amazing cover artist who helped me bring the art to life. I know that I probably annoyed you with all of my questions and requests, but thank you so much for being so amazing at what you do.

*"... you're not abnormal,
so don't let anyone tell you that you are"*

About the Author

Alex Blades was born and raised in a small Central Illinois town, where he spent his teen years writing short stories and creating new worlds. He's a lover of cheesy romantic comedies, an avid coffee addict, and earned a BA in English from Illinois  State University. Alex strives to provide a more diverse view-point and help bridge the gap of representation in literature for those who need it.

His debut novel, *If I Fall*, is available on Amazon.

Visit Alex Online
www.alexbladesbooks.com